THE MODERN GIRL'S GUIDE TO MAGIC

TO MAGIC

THE CHARMING COVE SERIES

LINSEY HALL

CHAPTER
ONE

ARIA

THERE WERE many reasons that I should never use my magic. One of those reasons was the horrified bride now standing before me, with new magical jowls that made her look like Winston Churchill.

And it was all my fault.

My job was simple. As the salesgirl at Kensington Wedding Cakes, I had to bring the samples to the brides and answer their questions. But we were London's poshest bakery, which meant that our customers were the wealthiest and most difficult brides.

Anyway, back to the magic—which I knew I wasn't supposed to use. Humans didn't know about it, and we witches kept its existence quiet. But I *did* use magic—unintentionally!—which was how Bridezilla ended up with her very impressive jowls.

1

It had all started out well enough. I'd welcomed Clarissa Bentham-Wilkes, her maid of honor, and her wedding planner to the shop and settled them at their table. We had a lovely area for the cake tasting—a round table draped in white linen, with six ornate chairs that had been painted wedding white. It sat next to the counter where I worked, plating up samples and pouring champagne.

When the debacle had started, I'd been minding my own business at the counter, carefully arranging slices of red velvet next to Chantilly cream. I'd just added a spray of baby roses to the plate when the bride had loudly complained that the penis straws for the hen party were the wrong color.

"I said I wanted rose gold, Bella! Not baby pink." It was the acid in Clarissa's voice that really got my attention. She was so vicious that it made the hair rise on the back of my neck.

I chanced a look at the table and saw the resigned expression on the wedding planner's face, along with the faintest hint of worry.

Code Red!

I abandoned the cake and poured three glasses of champagne. I put them on a silver tray as the bride turned to the wedding planner.

"Mary, I'm rather peeved with you," she said to the wedding planner. "I've spoken to the animal handler, and he said that the doves cannot be dyed rose gold because apparently, you can't put dye on living animals. But *you* promised me rose gold doves."

"I didn't say that, Clarissa." The wedding planner's tone

was so level that I could have used it to hang a picture. "I said we could ask about the paint. I'm sorry it won't work out."

"You're *sorry*?" The bride's face turned red. "How is that going to get me rose gold doves?"

"Champagne!" I cried when I arrived at the table. "A toast to the bride!" I set the glasses down, carefully avoiding the scattered array of penis straws and a pile of lace that looked like it might be the veil. It was unusual for the customers to bring so much wedding paraphernalia to the store, but I certainly wasn't going to mention it. The wedding planner pulled some napkin fabric samples out of the way as I moved to set her glass in front of her.

The bride snatched the glass before it could land on the table. "I'll take that. She's working, after all."

If anyone needed a drink, it was the wedding planner. Up close, I could see the strain in her eyes and the shadows beneath them. We shared a quick look of camaraderie. We both knew what it was like to work the minefield of wedding planning for Britain's elite.

The bride took a sip of the wedding planner's champagne, then arched a brow at me. "Well? Aren't you supposed to bring us cake as well?"

"Of course." I pasted on my best smile, then turned and went back to the counter.

Her voice followed me, though it was clear she'd turned back to the wedding planner. "You're going to need to talk to the animal handler about the swans as well. While I was visiting to select the swans who would proceed me down the aisle, I stepped in swan poo! In my lavender Louboutins! That cannot be allowed to happen at the wedding."

"I'm not sure we'll be able to control that," the wedding planner said. "That's what swans do. Perhaps we could have a flower girl scatter rose petals instead?"

"That is *so* overdone. We just need the swans to be trained better."

Clarissa was in for a rude awakening if she thought anyone could train a swan not to poo wherever it pleased.

The barrage of criticism continued, along with threats to sack the wedding planner if she didn't sort out the issue with the swans. I'd lost enough jobs for screwing up that the litany gave me secondhand anxiety.

I really couldn't screw this job up, either. It was the sixth one I'd had since I moved to London—cleaner, waitress, and sex toy salesperson among them. I wished I could say I'd left those jobs willingly, but I hadn't.

Most of the time, I'd been fired for *unexplained disasters*. What my human bosses didn't know was that those disasters were the result of me being unable to control the magic that occasionally exploded out of me. Most humans didn't know magic existed, and I had to keep it that way.

My wonky powers were the reason I'd left Charming Cove, the seaside village in which I'd grown up on the Cornish coast. It was the most beautiful village in England, and there had been an entire magical community hidden on a picturesque street overlooking the sea. But with my iffy magic, I hadn't fit in. Eventually, it had been enough to drive me from the place I'd once called home.

I'd ended up at Kensington Wedding Cakes, where everything was about to go spectacularly to shit. When I carried the cake to Bridezilla's table, I saw that the wedding planner had tears in her eyes.

I *hated* bullies.

A steady breath calmed me only slightly, and I tried to push down the anger bubbling up inside me.

I set the platter down as carefully as I could, but I must have transferred some of that anger to the cake. As soon as the bride took a bite, she developed a set of jowls that would do a bulldog proud.

I gaped, horror-struck.

The wedding planner and maid of honor were speechless as well.

"What?" the bride demanded. "The cake wasn't that good. It certainly couldn't have knocked you speechless."

I knew for a fact that the cake was phenomenal, so I didn't take the insult personally. I also hadn't made it.

"Um, are you allergic to anything?" the wedding planner asked.

"Almonds, but I already told the baker. Why?"

"Well...." The wedding planner pulled a mirror from her purse and held it up so the bride could see her reflection.

Oh, no, oh, no, oh, no. This was *so* not good. I'd screwed up last week as well, though not nearly this badly. If my boss found out, I could be out of a job. I looked up at the clock. Myra was meant to be in at any moment.

I needed to fix this. But how?

She bride screeched, her enraged gaze on me. "You put almonds in the cake!"

"We really didn't!" I said, scrambling for a solution. "I guarantee it. Absolutely no almonds."

She pointed at her face. "Then explain this."

"Um..." Did almonds really give a person jowls? I supposed it looked like swelling. "How is your breathing? Are you itchy?"

"It's fine, thank God. But that's not the problem. The problem is how I look." She shoved back from the table, her breath heaving. "If there are no almonds in the cake, you must have been eating some and got them on your grubby little fingers and transferred it to the cake."

"I didn't, I promise. I don't even like almonds." I did, actually, but she didn't need to know that. I reached for the tray of cakes. "Let me take this out of your way." I pulled the tray away from the table but fumbled it in my haste. The entire thing flipped over, and red velvet cake splattered all over the white lace veil.

The bride screeched. "Careful! That veil is worth more than your life!"

Ouch. Also, maybe a bit of an exaggeration. "I'm so sorry!"

"Ooh, you..." She stomped towards me, her finger raised. "I am going to *ruin* you!" She stomped her right lavender Louboutin. "I will write a review so bad that your shop will never have another customer. Kensington Wedding Cakes will *suffer.*"

Of course, that was the moment that Myra walked in. Needless to say, I was out of a job fifteen minutes later. To make matters worse, I was also out of a home. I'd rented my little flat from Myra, and now that the job was kaput, so was the flat. She'd given me only two days to get out.

And because I was a genius, I'd ended up at the local pub.

The original plan had been to ask for a job, and I had. But the owner had wanted me to have a few beers with him first, to prove I knew my ales (which I did, of course). Unfortunately, I hadn't got the job, but I had got drunk.

Which was why I was now leaving the pub far too late at night. As I stepped out onto the pavement, cold, wet rain drops landed on my head.

"Seriously, world?" I tipped my head back and groaned, but that was the only whinging I let myself do.

I made my way to the little flat that would be my home for just two more nights. The entrance was through a narrow alley, but that was fine because the rent was cheap.

To my left, a small head popped out of a rubbish bin. The black and white face hissed at me, and I flipped him the bird. The badger had lived in the alley beneath my flat for the last few months, and he'd been a right wanker the whole time.

As I unlocked the flat, I gave the badger one last look. He'd raised a paw out of the bin and extended one little finger.

"Oh, piss off," I said as I stifled a laugh.

His head popped back down into the bin. He really ought to be living in the countryside—I'd never heard of badgers in the city—but he seemed content.

As I walked into my cozy little space, the smell of foliage calmed me. I might live in the middle of the city, but my flat didn't know it. Plants covered every surface, kept alive by the magic that surrounded me. My wonky power required an outlet, and since I didn't use it because it always blew up in my face, the plants had become that outlet. They thrived, and I had no idea what I'd do with them when I had to leave here.

"It's about time you got home," a crotchety female voice sounded from the darkened corner, and I whirled.

My grandmother sat in the chair, looking for all the world like a TV gran with her floral dress and neat white bun —as long as one ignored the martini glass in her hand.

Surprise flashed through me. I hadn't seen her in years, and my heart warmed. "What are you doing here?"

"Come to see my favorite granddaughter, of course." She rose and gave me a hug, wrapping her arms tight around me. The scent of lavender and baby powder wafted over me, and I breathed in deeply. She was everything about home that I missed.

"I'm your only granddaughter," I said against her hair. She was much shorter than me, though her presence was the size of a house.

She pulled back and smiled. "You would be my favorite even if I had a hundred."

I grinned. "Seriously, Gran." Cecilia was her proper name, but she went by Cici with other people. "Why are you here? You've never visited me before."

She sipped her martini. "Because you needed time, dear."

I still needed time, if the disaster at the bakery was any indication. The last thing I wanted to do was return home as the magical loser I'd been when I left. "My magic isn't any better."

"You haven't been practicing, so of course it's not."

"How do you know that?"

"That's what Boris reports."

"Boris?"

"The badger, dear."

Of course my grandmother had sent a spy. "If I still need time, why are you here?"

"Because *we* need *you*. The shop needs you. The whole *town* needs you. And if you don't come home, we'll lose everything."

CHAPTER
TWO

ARIA

THE WHOLE TOWN NEEDS YOU.

The words rushed through my head as I stared at my grandmother. "You can't be serious."

"As serious as an over-boiling cauldron."

"Gran, if the town needs saving, then I'm not your witch. You're out of luck unless you need a failed bakery assistant or sex toy salesperson who exploded a box of dildos and sent them flying down the street."

Gran raised a brow. "Flying dildos?"

"Like seagulls at the beach. Except they were pink, blue, and purple." I cringed at the memory. "Let's just say I was sacked."

Gran laughed. "You're proving my point. You're magic, darling!"

"Sure, a magical disaster." Witches could manifest their

desires by using the magic inherent in the ether, that ephemeral stuff that surrounded all of us. There was a limit to what a witch could do, of course, and some were more powerful than others. But me? Every time I tried to use my magic—or didn't try, like at the bakery—it went disastrously.

"A bit unpracticed, maybe. But not a disaster. Don't say things like that!"

"I spent my entire childhood practicing, just like every other witch. And unlike them, I still stink."

Gran turned in a circle, gesturing to all of the plants. "But just look at this! No way there isn't magic here."

I looked at my beloved plants. Pink ranunculus and purple violets and an explosion of yellow orchids by the tiny window. That window didn't stand a chance of letting in enough light for this bounty, and yet it still grew. "Of course there's magic here. But you know that plants like me. I'm not doing any magic intentionally to make them grow so well."

"That's why you're the one for this job. Added to that, you've been invited. *Specifically*. We need you for this."

I crossed my arms and leaned against the side of the ratty sofa. "Invited to what? And why now? Charming Cove has been fine without me for the last seven years. Eight, actually." Had I already turned twenty-six?

"It's not fine anymore. Lionel Sparrow has lost his damned mind and is planning to leave the Garden of Enchantment. He says he wants to retire."

I frowned. The Garden of Enchantment was a section of the woods near Charming Cove that contained the most potion and spell ingredients of any place in the UK. Massive old trees surrounded a wonderland of greenery and flowers that were used to make hundreds of different potions and spells—and that was before one started digging for minerals or asked some of the birds for their feathers. There was nowhere else like it in Britain—the world, probably. It was the most diverse garden by a mile, famed for the incredible quantity and rarity of its contents.

Lionel Sparrow had owned the garden for decades and sold Gran the vast majority of what she needed to make the potions and spells in the shop. Without him, she wouldn't have what she needed to stay open. And it wasn't just her store at risk. Our shop brought in patrons from all over the UK. They stayed in the B&Bs and ate in the pubs, shopped in the stores, and visited the tiny museums. We weren't much of a magical tourist town, but the visitors we had came primarily for our shop.

Our shop.

I lived in London now. There was nothing about Seaside Spells that was mine. I'd left it behind long ago and forfeited any claim I had to it.

"I still don't understand how I'm meant to help," I said.

"He has no heirs, if you'll recall. Lived alone his entire life with the garden as his family. Now, he's looking for someone to inherit."

"And you want me to go charm him?" I laughed a bit, the sound dry and surprised. I couldn't charm a cat into drinking cream—there was no way I could convince Lionel Sparrow that I deserved to inherit the garden. It was true that I'd spent a lot of time there as a child and we'd developed a strange friendship of sorts, but I hadn't seen him in years.

"Not quite," Gran said. "He'll be holding a competition to find the person who deserves to inherit the garden. You will be our champion."

This time, I really did laugh. I laughed so hard I had to sit on the couch. "You've lost your marbles, Gran."

"I've done no such thing." She glared at me. "You have a gift for plants, and you're the one who is going to win this for us."

"Why don't you do it?"

She scoffed. "I'm too old. He won't choose an heir his age."

"You'll live forever."

"Of course I will, but he doesn't know that." The confidence in her voice made me smile. She wasn't immortal, but I couldn't handle the idea of a world without her. Even if I hadn't been home in eight years, she was still my rock—especially after my grandad had died. I'd worshipped Erwin Mackey, Gran's husband of forty years and the best man I'd ever known. Both of my parents had died when I was young, and he'd been the father figure of my childhood. His death ten years ago had almost destroyed me.

"I know where your head is going, and you need to get out of there," Gran said. "He wouldn't want you to be sad over him."

I nodded, my throat tight. "Yeah, course."

"So you'll come home to help?"

"I can't control my magic. I'm useless to you."

"Useless!" she scoffed. "True, there's something a little strange about you. That's part of your charm. And it will be part of your strength, I'm sure of it."

"If someone else wins, won't they just sell the ingredients to us like Mr. Sparrow did?" I knew it was unlikely. We'd worked so hard to win that contract with him. Whoever won the grove would likely keep the plants for themselves. Someone clever could make a mint from the place.

"It's possible, but not probable, and you know it. For one, Serena Faraday is competing, and you know she'll hoard it all for her apothecary shop."

I grimaced. I really didn't like Serena—she'd been one of my worst bullies in school—and there was no way she'd sell to us. Gran was right.

"Still, Gran, I really don't think I've got what it takes."

"None of that now. It's time for you to come home and help the family." She gestured to the plants. "Anyway, what were you planning to do with all of this now that you're out on your arse?"

I sighed and looked around. She had a point. I didn't have anywhere to live, much less a way to save my plants. And I had basically no money, since Myra wasn't going to pay me for the last two weeks. I ran a fingertip over a frilly fern, feeling deep in my gut that my plants would like to live somewhere less crowded and with a little more natural light.

"Fine." I rose. "I'll come home. But no promises that I can save Seaside Spells."

"Just try your best, dear. I have faith it will work out." She smiled and tossed back the last of her martini. "Now, let's go."

Aria

TEN MINUTES LATER, after Gran had magicked my plants into a single old cardboard box and the rest of my possessions into another, we were headed towards her car.

I locked the flat for the last time with no sorrow.

"This way, dear." Gran gestured to the little yellow car at the far end of the alley.

I must have missed it when I'd come home from work, probably because I'd been distracted by Boris. As if he'd heard me thinking about him, his little head popped up from the rubbish bin, and he gave a toothy grin.

"Time to go home, Boris," Gran said. "Come along." She headed down the alley to the car, and Boris jumped out of the rubbish bin to follow. I grabbed the two boxes that were stacked neatly on the ground by the fire escape ladder and hurried after them.

We were on our way within minutes. Fortunately, it was so late at night that London traffic was light. My grandmother drove like a madwoman, of course, weaving through imaginary traffic as she barreled down the road.

My gaze snagged on a magazine sticking out from between the seat and center console. As the streetlights flashed by and illuminated the interior of the car, I noticed the telltale sparkle of the *Magic Mirror*, the most famous magical publication in England. It had been years since I'd seen one, so I pulled it out and looked at the cover.

A man's face stared out at me, so handsome that he might as well have been a movie star. Dark hair and a jaw that could cut glass complemented blazing blue eyes and a full mouth that looked far too soft for his face. *Magical Britain's Sexiest Bachelor* read the text under the image.

Of course it did.

Callan Hawthorne was the most powerful mage in Britain, as well as the wealthiest. He also looked like...*that*.

I scowled at the 2D version of him, hating how it brought up old, angry feelings. "Why the hell do you have this, Gran?"

"What?" She glanced at it. "You know I subscribe to the *Mirror*. Every self-respecting witch does."

"Yeah, but *this* edition? You should have binned it."

"I know you hate him, darling, but he's still the most powerful man in England."

"Not as powerful as you."

"True. He is a mere man, after all."

There was nothing *mere* about Callan Hawthorne, but I didn't say it.

"I like reading about his exploits," Gran said. "He's always dating some new supermodel or other. It's all very glamorous."

"Glamorous. Sure." But even I knew about all the women he dated. Even human news outlets featured him, and it was impossible to avoid the many stories about his endless rotation of girlfriends.

Gran shrugged. "Anyway, it's important to keep track of the competition, darling."

The competition. As if. In addition to being a terrifyingly powerful mage, Callan Hawthorne was a property magnate who owned half of the magical world. He'd come from nothing—from nowhere, as far as anyone could tell—and by the time he was twenty-five, he owned at least ten percent of the magical properties in Britain. He was a modern type of magical person, stepping out from the shadows and engaging with human businesses as well as their magical counterparts. Some people said he was all business these days, but I could almost see the power sparking in his eyes.

I shoved the magazine back between the seats. There was no way in hell I'd be thinking about him.

"I know you hate him for what he did, but it's been a long time," Gran said. "There's power in letting it go."

"*What he did?*" She said it like he'd done something minor. Something forgivable. "He built over Grandad's tower." We called the place Grandad's tower, but it had technically been a ruined fortress on the banks of the River Fortitude, a small, glittering stripe of water near our village. Grandad hadn't technically owned the tower—no one had, as far as I'd known—but it had been his spot. His special place. He'd taken me fishing there every summer, and hunting for wild mushrooms in the fall, and searching for the best snowflakes in the winter. When spring came, we went to see the wildflowers that grew around the fallen stone ramparts.

When Grandad had died, it had been the one place I'd been able to see his spirit. On calm days, if I were the only one there, he appeared as a collection of silver sparkles that smelled just like him. It was the most comforting place in the world.

Until Callan Hawthorne showed up.

He'd bought the land from someone—who, I had no

idea, because we all thought it was owned by the town—and converted the space into a café and late-night bar. It had turned out beautifully, of course, and the townspeople enjoyed it.

But I hated it. And I hated him. Ever since he'd built the place, my grandfather's spirit had disappeared. How could I not hate him?

"Rest, dear." She patted my leg. "I can feel your angst from over here, and it's giving me heartburn." She picked up the enormous Coke that was sat in the cupholder and took a long drink, then followed it with a big bite of a partially wrapped biscuit.

"Are you sure it's not your snack?"

"Psh. A woman needs sugar to survive. Now go to sleep. I'll have us home by dawn."

It was a good idea. Gran had always been a night owl, and I *was* exhausted. There was just something so comforting about being with my grandmother that I couldn't help but let my guard down and feel sleepy.

"If you're sure. But wake me if you want a break."

"Of course I'm sure."

I drifted off moments later, but wasn't able to leave the memory of Callan Hawthorne behind. My consciousness transitioned from the car to the past, to that sunny day when I'd been lying in the warm grass that filled the interior of the tower ruins. The sound of the river rushing by had been a soothing lullaby, but not as soothing as my grandfather's scent. He'd appeared when I had, that telltale collection of silver sparkles, and hovered nearby as I'd watched the clouds drift overhead.

When a noise had startled me upright, I'd found myself staring at the handsomest man I'd ever seen. Tall and broad, he had to be at least five years older than my seventeen. Maybe even older. A dark fisherman's jumper had stretched over his broad shoulders, and he'd stood with one leg propped on a rock, as if he were an explorer scouting out a new land. Strong forearms had been exposed by the blue wool of his jumper, and he'd hooked his big hands into his pockets.

I'd dragged my gaze away from his forearms, wishing I weren't so obsessed with them, because who the hell became obsessed with forearms, anyway?

The breeze had blown his dark hair back from a face that looked like it had been pulled from the pages of a romance novel: brilliant blue eyes, high cheekbones, a chiseled jaw, and lips so full that they were almost out of place. Scratch that—I'd no longer been obsessed with his arms, but rather with his mouth.

"Real people shouldn't look like you," I'd blurted.

"What was that?" A frown had creased his brow, and somehow, it had made him look even more attractive.

"Um, I asked where you came from. I thought I was alone." As heat had burned my cheeks, I'd hoped he bought it. With any luck, the breeze had carried my first idiotic sentence away from him.

"Just visiting." He'd hiked a thumb over his shoulder. "I parked out by the road, so you probably didn't hear me approach. But I can go if you want privacy."

I'd looked over to where the shadow of my grandad had hovered, but the silver sparkles were gone. Grandad had always had excellent timing. He'd probably heard my ridiculous statement and decided it was time to go.

"No, that's okay." I'd gestured to the ruined stone walls. "Look around. It's a great place."

"It is." He'd turned, inspecting it.

I'd jumped up, unable to help myself, and hurried towards him. He'd been standing right near a nook in the wall that had a secret message inscribed into the stone, and I'd suddenly been desperate to show him. I'd been desperate to show him all kinds of things, including my boobs.

Chill out, idiot. Start with historical sites first.

I'd felt his gaze on me as I went to the wall and pointed to the nook. "Check this out. There's a place where someone scratched a little picture of a ship. It's so weathered that it's got to be old."

I couldn't hear him, and I hadn't dared look to see if he was coming over. But when he'd arrived, his scent had washed over me in a wave that smelled like evergreen and spiced soap. He'd stood close enough that I swore I could feel his body heat, and a shiver had run down my spine.

"That's very cool." His voice had been a low murmur above me, and I'd looked up.

Holy crap, he was tall. I was the shortest girl in my year at school, but this guy was a giant.

He'd looked down at me, his gaze catching mine, and something had passed between us that made the air feel thick and heavy. I'd swallowed hard, then looked towards that castle wall that had a perfectly positioned window.

"Come see." I'd led him towards the window, pointing

out the view of the flowering pear tree that was framed by the ancient stone.

He'd leaned down to look, and I couldn't help but sniff him. Just a little bit—too much would be weird, right? I'd just wanted to see if he smelled as good as I thought he had.

And yes, he did. Heavenly.

We'd spent the next hour together, with me showing him all the best parts of the castle. It had been the most magical hour of my life—until the rain started.

Then it had got even better.

He'd crafted us a shelter using just his magic. He was a mage, apparently, though he'd said he didn't use his power much. We'd huddled beneath the sheet of tin as the rain pounded on it. He'd even offered me his jumper, and greedy witch that I was, I'd taken it. The scent of it had been enough to make my breath come faster in my lungs. The sight of him in a T-shirt hadn't helped, either. His broad shoulders had pulled at the fabric, which had tapered perfectly at his trim waist.

Had he had his shirt tailored? It was the only explanation.

But nah, he hadn't seemed like the type.

As the rain had softened, I'd realized how close together we were standing. Like, crazy close.

I'd looked up to see his brilliant blue gaze on my face. His full lips had been slightly parted, his cheeks barely flushed. For the faintest moment, it had looked like he might kiss me. I'd even pressed up on my tiptoes.

Then he'd closed his eyes. "Just out of curiosity, how old are you?"

"Seventeen, why?"

When he'd opened his eyes, there had been the faintest hint of regret there. "Another time, then. It was nice meeting you, though."

"What? I'm old enough."

"Of course you are. The problem is, I'm too old."

"Are you secretly a two-hundred-year-old vampire?"

He'd laughed, then shook his head. "Looks like the rain has stopped."

I'd looked out and realized he was right.

"It was nice to meet you, Aria."

With that, he was gone. He hadn't even stopped to get his jumper back. He'd just disappeared.

I didn't see him again until I learned that he'd bought the castle and planned to build a café and bar around it. The boring work that he hadn't wanted to talk about was actually him being a self-made billionaire. The youngest in the UK, in fact, and one who had an excellent eye for properties.

I'd hunted him down and demanded that he stop construction on the tower. *My* tower. Grandad's tower. I'd been the one to show him all the cool hidden features. Hell, I might have even sold him on the place.

And this was the thanks I'd received?

Actually, I wish I'd got a thanks. Instead, he'd laughed. When I'd demanded that he stop construction, he'd laughed. Not a big laugh—more of a small, surprised chuckle. But it was more than I could handle. I'd thrown a blast of enraged magic at him and stormed out.

It was the last time I'd seen him, and the last time I'd seen Grandad's spirit.

CHAPTER

THREE

ARIA

A RAY of sunlight woke me from my dreams. The bright beam seared through my eyelids, and I groaned as I rubbed my eyes. Blearily, I blinked them open to see that we were on a narrow lane cutting through the rolling green fields that bordered the sea near my hometown. I shoved away thoughts of Callan Hawthorne and focused on the view ahead.

"We're already there?" I asked, my voice rough.

Gran handed me her now warm Coke, and I took a sip, almost gagging at the sweet taste. "I don't know how you drink that stuff, considering that your cocktail of choice is a martini that's been shown a picture of vermouth."

Gran laughed. "I like the finer things, what can I say?" She nodded towards the sparkling sea that had just appeared over the horizon. We were on the cliffs high above the ocean, and the farther we drove, the more we would see of the sea that stretched out below. "Not long now."

Good. I needed a shower and a stretch.

As she turned left and drove towards the sea, I looked around. I'd forced myself to forget how beautiful this place was, I realized.

Boris padded up to the center console beside me, snuffling as he looked out the window. Up close, his fur looked soft, and he smelled sweeter than I'd have expected, given his most recent accommodation.

Finally. His voice drifted into my head. *London was a shithole.*

I gasped, looking at him. "What did you say?"

Gran laughed. "Talking to you now, is he?"

"How did you know he would? Is that why you sent him?" Witches couldn't speak to all animals—at least, not most of us. But occasionally, an animal would take a liking to us. They were essentially familiars, but I'd never had one.

"I thought he might," Gran said. "Though I'm not surprised he didn't speak to you in London."

Beside me, Boris shuddered. *Horrible place. Good rubbish, though. Pizza and chips almost every night.*

I thought of the people drunkenly stumbling down the street where I lived, popping into the chippies and pizza places after leaving the bars. At least there was one perk to living on a party street—for Boris, anyway.

"Nice to meet you, Boris," I said.

Of course it is.

I grinned and looked down at him, debating giving him a

little pet. Probably not a great idea until we'd got better acquainted.

Gran didn't slow as she passed Grandad's tower, and I was grateful. It was too far away to see much detail of the place, but it was impossible to miss the café and bar that had been cleverly built into it. I'd only visited The Keep Café once, and I hated to admit that Callan had done an admirable job constructing something that didn't distract from the historic stone structure.

It didn't matter in the long run, though, because the presence of so many people meant that Grandad's spirit wouldn't return.

"I know you hate it, dear." Gran pointed to the small buildings that now dotted the descending hillside ahead of us. "But we're almost home."

I looked away from the tower and towards the direction that my gran pointed. Ahead, the land dipped down to the ocean, and the roofs of Charming Cove appeared. The winding streets were bordered on either side by old two- and three-story buildings painted different pastel shades. Many of the buildings had a view of the small harbor and the sea beyond. The majority of the town was human, with only a select few of those knowing about the existence of the magical street on the western side.

As we drove towards the little village, it felt like I was leaving the grime of London behind. The sun shone brightly as we entered the first street and made our way past store-fronts and houses. People walked along the pavement with shopping bags and coffees, smiles on their faces as they took in the beautiful day. The non-magical people of Charming

Cove were aware that the weather was better here, with more sun and less rain than in the rest of Cornwall, but they had no idea it was because of the magic coming from Foxglove Lane. The entire place was so quaint that it almost hurt to look at it.

Gran drove down the steep road, nearly reaching the harbor before she turned right at Carole's Tea Shop at the corner of Foxglove Lane. The street was only visible to magical people, and I felt a little frisson of power race over my skin as Gran slowed the car to pass by the familiar shops that I hadn't seen in so long.

Foxglove Lane was located about twenty feet above sea level on a small cliff that overlooked the Atlantic. To the left was the cove and sandy beach that gave Charming Cove its name, but that was the human part of town. We were higher up on the cliff. Buildings bordered the inland side of Foxglove Lane, and the side of the street that overlooked the ocean had no buildings so that everyone could enjoy the view.

A path ran along the grass, which widened out every now and again to form small gardens. The townspeople adored their gardens, with themed groups in charge of each section. Gran's bridge group had their own section, while the school had a plot for vegetables, and the men's wild swimming club designed something different every summer.

Waves crashed on the rocks below, and I could hear them even through the glass. I strained to pick up more of the sound, and Gran rolled down the windows.

"How did you know?" I asked.

"You always did love the sea."

A bittersweet feeling rushed over me. I'd forgot what it was like to be around people who knew me. My transient lifestyle in London hadn't allowed me to make any real friends. Even if it had, it was hard to drop my guard around non-magical people.

"Thanks, Gran." I reached for her hand and squeezed it, still thrilled by the feeling of being near my grandmother.

I looked to the right, taking in the shops that had once been so familiar. Surprisingly, they still were. Why mess with perfection, right? Small and charming, they sat so close to each other that many of them shared walls. Seashells and glass fishing floats decorated the fronts of some, while others were characterized by diamond pane windows or large store-fronts that displayed the best the magical world had to offer.

Memories rushed over me as the buildings passed by. Margot's Tea & Cake Parlor had been my favorite place to go after school, along with my friend Tabitha. Tabitha had been the most fun a person could be.

Next to the tea shop was the bookstore, which sold everything from popular human fiction to spell books that put themselves back on the shelves when you were finished with them. A pub separated the bookstore from Codswol-lop's, the chippy next door. The benches in front had been *the* place for the popular boys of our school, but it wasn't full of such fond memories for me. When I'd been fourteen, I'd exploded a rubbish bin right in front of my crush, Will Rennet, and from there, my reputation as a magical dud had been solidified. I'd been embarrassed enough to want to sink into the pavement, but that hadn't been the worst of it. Those boys had made it their life's work to let me know how uncool I was. They needn't have bothered—I was well aware.

We passed the clothing shops owned by the trio of old sisters who had been pure terrors if you didn't put your clothes back on the rack, and the pub where I'd had my first pint. It was a charming place with a seaside theme, but it, too, was filled with memories.

We passed the grocers and two more pubs, along with an off-license for liquor and uniquely magical libations. We were nearly to the end of the street, where Seaside Spells was located, when my heart began to race.

As I caught sight of the quirky building with its four crooked chimneys, I couldn't help but eat it up with my eyes. The three-story building had been constructed of local stone over four hundred years ago, and I loved every weird detail, from the diamond pane windows on the first floor that glittered in the sun to the blue sign over the door that proclaimed it to be the "Finest Purveyor of Magical Potions & Spells in the United Kingdom." We'd won the award for twenty years running. But without our contract with Lionel Sparrow, we'd lose more than that designation. With no ingredients for our potions, we'd lose the entire shop.

And now I was supposed to save the place. *Me.* The failure.

I sighed as Gran pulled around back to park the car. "Gran, you really must be smoking something if you think I'm the one who can fix this mess."

"No, darling. I'm not smoking anything. Not yet, at least. And I'm sure you're the one." She patted my leg. "Now come inside. We've got work to do."

Callan

Through the plane window, I could see the rolling hills and fields of Cornwall. They created a patchwork quilt of verdant green that extended all the way to the brilliant blue sea, and something in my soul warmed at the sight.

I rubbed a weary hand through my hair as the plane began its descent. It had been a long week of negotiations in Oslo, and they'd left me feeling even more burnt out on the business. I loved what I did—acquiring properties and renovating them into something spectacular had been a passion of mine since my father had taken me on jobs with him as a kid. After he'd died, I'd taken the family business and turned it into something bigger. I'd lost him young, and his lessons had driven me, shaping who I would become and what I would do. It had been almost a compulsion, and I'd been pushed by his ghost for so long that I was starting to wonder if I was still doing what I wanted to do, or doing it just because it was what I'd always done.

The plane landed with a bump, roaring down the runway at the small airport near the sea. It had been hidden by magic, a worthy expense. As much travel as I did abroad, I didn't want to have to deal with human customs and immigration authorities. I might live my life like a human for the most part, but following all of their rules was too tedious.

As the vehicle came to a complete stop, the flight attendant appeared from the front of the plane. He held my coat over his arm. "Your car should be waiting just outside."

"Thank you, Trevor." I stood and took the items, then strode to the small door.

Noah, the other flight attendant, pushed it open, and I descended to the ground. Immediately, the fresh green scent of Cornwall swept over me, carried by a cool breeze. I closed my eyes and drew in a deep breath, enjoying the warmth from the sun sparkling overhead. This close to Charming Cove, it was usually sunny.

"Glad to be back, sir?" The sound of my driver's voice broke through my concentration, and I opened my eyes to see him standing next to the dark green Range Rover that acted as my vehicle whilst in Cornwall.

"Always, Garrett."

He gestured to the car. "Well, she's ready and waiting for you."

I didn't correct him that the car was an *it* and not a *she.* Old Garrett was too good-natured for that kind of rebuke. Instead, I smiled and took the keys from him. "You've got a ride home?"

"I do indeed. Trevor up there is always so accommodating." He pointed to Trevor, who stood at the top of the stairs, watching Garrett. I was pretty sure the two had something going, but they were discreet around me. Both came from the old school of household staff, and that meant keeping romantic relationships to themselves. I wouldn't have minded, but it seemed I couldn't help the standoffish air that kept my staff at a distance. Probably for the best.

I climbed behind the wheel and started the car, then

pulled away from the airport. The narrow lane that cut through the field was empty, as it usually was, and a rabbit darted across the road as I headed towards Charming Cove.

When I'd received an invitation from Lionel Sparrow to compete to win his Garden of Enchantment, I'd known I needed to participate. Though I specialized in property renovation, a magical location like the garden would be the jewel in the crown of Hawthorne Enterprises.

There was no question that I'd win the competition—I'd never met anyone more powerful than me. And I wanted the garden. Badly.

I'd already contracted with teams of workers to turn the place into a botanical garden and event facility. Dozens of new jobs would be created, and something beautiful would be built. In addition, I'd made arrangements with companies overseas to sell some of the most valuable plants. The profits would make Hawthorne Enterprises the most successful business in the UK, a goal I'd worked towards my entire life.

The fact that it was located right outside of the hometown of the girl I'd met eight years ago was entirely inconsequential.

"Lying wanker," I muttered to myself. Of course it had something to do with it. I'd tried to get her out of my head— she certainly wouldn't want to take up space there, if her reaction the last time we'd parted was any indication.

But I'd found it impossible. For years, she'd haunted me. If I had the opportunity to see her again while competing to win the garden, it was a bonus too big to pass up.

I had the option of staying at one of my properties twenty minutes down the coast—a castle hotel that had become a leader in the hospitality industry in the southwest —but I didn't want to be so far from the action.

Or Aria.

I still had a soft spot for the town where I'd met her, the woman who'd pierced me through the heart even though she'd been too young.

"Aria." Her name rolled off my tongue like honey, as sweet as she probably tasted.

I had the memory of her face burned into my mind— stormy gray eyes, full lips, and skin as pale as cream. The memory of her lavender scent still intoxicated me, made worse by the recollection of her skin burning into my fingertips when I'd touched her arm.

We'd met when I was twenty-one, and she'd been too damned young. By the time I'd turned twenty-four and she was still on my mind, I'd started to feel like a lecher every time I thought of her lips. The age gap had become downright pervy, since I was remembering her younger self. I'd tried to force her from my mind, and it had worked.

Mostly.

My willpower was incredible, but not that incredible.

On dark and lonely nights—of which there were too many—she still drifted into my thoughts. Four years ago, I'd caved and used my magic to see an image of her face in the present day. I still felt guilty about it, but at least I was no longer lusting after a seventeen-year-old. Instead, she was at least an adult.

I barked a bitter laugh. If someone was handing out awards for weak efforts, I would be the winner. "Get it together, man. She probably won't even be there. And if she is, she'll still hate you."

I focused on the view outside the car window, watching as the land dipped down to the sea. It glittered in the distance, a brilliant blue that should have been impossible.

I reached Charming Cove, slowing as I drove through the human part of the village. The streets were as narrow and lovely as I remembered, and it was easy to find the turn onto Foxglove Lane, where all the magical people lived. I made my way to the bed and breakfast I'd booked, a quaint little building about halfway down the street. It had been built of stone that had been painted white long ago, and had a dark slate roof. Hundreds of flowers tumbled out of window boxes, and purple shutters gave it a whimsical feel.

The owner, Mrs. Aspen, had agreed to rent all four rooms to me, even though I wasn't bringing any staff along. As much as I wanted to stay close to the action and not off in a distant estate like a grumpy nineteenth-century earl, it was still hard to imagine sharing a little house with more than just the proprietor.

I found a parking spot on the street right in front of the house and pulled the car in. As I stepped out, a great shaggy dog came up to greet me. He had floppy ears and a sooty black coat speckled with green grass.

I rubbed his head. "Been having a nice lie-down in the garden, have you?"

The dog gave a low woof.

"Careful, he bites." A gray-haired woman came out of the front door, wiping her hands on her apron as she strode towards me.

"Mrs. Aspen?" I asked.

She nodded, then tilted her head to the dog. "And that's Lucifer."

Lucifer looked up at me with liquid brown eyes, then pushed his head back into my hand for another scratch. I obliged, then looked up at Mrs. Aspen. "He bites? Really?"

She shrugged. "If he wants to. But you must be a devil like him, so he's taken a liking to you."

She wasn't the first person who'd called me a devil, and she likely wouldn't be the last. But if the Sea View B&B featured a host who insulted the guests and a dog who liked to bite, then I wasn't surprised it had been easy to book the place out.

"Come on, I'll show you to your room." She gestured for me to follow. "But don't think I'll be carrying your bags. This isn't one of your fancy hotels, and you'll not be getting that kind of service. Not for a hundred quid a night." She chuckled to herself.

I felt my brows rise. Not because she knew who I was. That wasn't surprising. Most people recognized me. But because she thought I'd ask her to carry my bag. Mrs. Aspen couldn't have weighed more than six stone.

I gave Lucifer one last rub, then grabbed my bag and followed her into the quaint house. As I stepped inside, I couldn't help but look behind me to see if Aria might be walking down the street.

CHAPTER

FOUR

ARIA

I SPENT the day helping Gran with the shop. The chores were endless, and some of them seemed unnecessary. The gleaming wooden floors were already polished to a shine, and the herbs hanging from the ceiling were as tidy as bridal bouquets waiting for the big day.

I was pretty sure she wanted to remind me of what I was fighting for, but there was no need. As soon as I'd stepped into the shop, I'd remembered. The first floor was only the start of it, with its ceiling of herbs and shelves filled with sparkling glass bottles and charmed objects. Wands formed a beautiful spiral design on the south wall, each marked with a tiny tag that displayed its unique properties. Gold, silver, and copper cauldrons were stacked neatly by the stairs leading to the first floor, and the old hearth burned merrily despite the warm summer day. It didn't overheat the house, though. Gran would never stand for that.

Merlin, the cat who had lived here for nearly eighteen years, wouldn't have it any other way. He was a chubby black tom with a white heart on his nose and green eyes that could see straight through to your soul. I rarely made eye contact with him, largely because he saw something within me that required therapy. Hell, he was probably right.

I'd just finished cleaning the front window when Gran poked her head out of the back of the shop. "It's nearly dinnertime, but I imagine you want to clean up. Do you want to stay in the attic?"

I looked up, as if I could see through the floor to the small room at the top of the house. I had lived in that room in my later teen years. As charming as it was, with its views of the sea and pale yellow wall, I'd rather have my own place. But my plants needed a home ASAP, so it would have to do.

"That'll be great, Gran. Thank you." I gave the window one last polish, then stepped back to admire my work.

Through the gleaming glass, I could see the street out front. A few people walked the path that overlooked the sea, and I could see the water shimmering in the distance. A lone figure passed by the window, and I blinked, surprised.

Tabitha pushed her way into the shop, then gaped at me. It took her only a second to gather her wits, and then she squealed and threw her arms around me.

"You're back! Praise Hecate and Loki and Circe and the Dagda, you're back!" She pulled back and grinned widely, her curly red hair pulled up into a magnificent pile on her head. With her lightly freckled cheeks and brilliant green eyes, she looked like a movie director's idea of an Irish super-model. "I've missed you, you potato, and I'm glad you've come to your senses and come home."

I grinned back at her, so glad to see her that my heart felt like it could burst. Her makeshift insults had always been my favorite. "I've missed you, too. And you're right, I am a complete potato for leaving."

"A moldy one, at that." She grabbed my arm and spun so that she could face the door. "Just wait until you see Catrina. She's basically twenty-five now."

"*You're* basically twenty-five," I said.

"Twenty-six, but I feel forty-six, what with raising that monkey monster." The love in her voice overrode the monster thing, of course. Tabitha adored her niece. She'd done so even before her sister had died six years ago. But once she'd become Catrina's mother, it was like she'd exploded with love.

Tabitha pointed to the door. "And here she comes."

A seven-year-old with pigtails and an expression of grim determination stomped towards the shop, her glittery pink jumper proclaiming her to be the Most Magnificent Mermaid. A cloud of magic sparked around her that made me slightly wistful.

"What took you so long, young lady?" I could hear the smile in Tabitha's voice, even though her expression was stern.

"Will Bellows was outside, and he's a right tosser. He was throwing rocks at a squirrel, and I had to show him a thing or two about what happens to tossers like him."

"A tosser, is he?" Tabitha raised a brow, then side whispered at me that it was Catrina's new word. "If he was throwing rocks at a squirrel, it sounds like you did the right thing."

A look of satisfaction crossed the girl's face. "Let's just say the squirrel isn't the only one with a tail right now."

A laugh escaped me, and it clearly took Tabitha everything she had not to burst our cackling.

"As long as the tail goes away soon," she said, clearly doing her best to sound like a responsible adult.

"It will." Disappointment flashed on her face. "I haven't worked out how to make it permanent yet."

"You'll get there," I said, unable to stop myself from joining the conversation. There was such love and joy between the two of them that I wanted to be a part of it. Now that I was home and amongst people who loved me and whom I loved back, it almost felt like I'd been starving in London—slowly withering away in the busy, anonymous rush of the city.

Catrina's gaze went to me. She'd been so enraptured by the memory of giving her nemesis a tail that she hadn't seemed to have noticed me. Her gaze went from my short floral dress and leather jacket to the boots that I wore. "You're Aria."

I nodded. "How did you know?"

"Aunt Tabitha says you're her cool friend in the city, and that having a cool friend like you makes her cool by default."

Tabitha grinned. "It's faultless logic."

I pursed my lips and nodded thoughtfully. "I am pretty cool, that's true." Actually, I didn't feel very cool at all, especially now that I was back home. But I couldn't blow

Tabitha's story out of the water, and I wanted the kid to like me. Because *she* was actually the cool one, and also because I didn't want a tail.

Catrina gave my thin leather jacket a look. "I like *that*," she said, touching the sleeve.

The leather wasn't suited to Charming Cove, and I found I wanted to shed London like a snake shed its skin. "Yeah?" I took it off and handed it over. "It's yours."

"Really?" A broad grin split her face, and she took it. When she put it on, it was big, but not ridiculously so. I'd always been tiny, so it fit pretty well.

Catrina held out her arms and inspected herself. "Will Bellows won't know what hit him next."

I wasn't sure Will Bellows was going to make it out alive. I shared a look with Tabitha, and she grimaced as she said, "I'm probably going to have to apologize to his mother."

"Hey, chin up." I punched her lightly on the shoulder. "I happen to remember you giving someone a tail once. And she said it would disappear."

"One can only hope."

Gran appeared on the stairs that led up to the flat she kept on the first floor. A huge smile lit up her face, and she raised her arms for a hug. "My monster girl is here!"

Catrina roared like a dragon and hurtled towards Gran, jumping into her arms. Gran swung her around, appearing far stronger than a woman in her late seventies should be.

"What's for dinner?" Catrina demanded. "It had better be terrifying."

"Eyeballs and intestines, obviously." Gran set her down,

then waved at us before leading her up the stairs to the kitchen.

I grimaced and looked at Tabitha. "Eyeballs and intestines? Is there something you're not telling me about Catrina? Like, maybe her father was a ghoul?"

I said the last bit quietly, since no one knew who Catrina's father was.

Tabitha grinned but spoke just as quietly. "Spaghetti and meatballs, and it's for the Ghoulish Girls' Night. Gran and Catrina do it once a week while I go out and try to get laid."

A small laugh huffed out of me. "At least you're honest about it."

"Honest, but not lucky. That's the problem with living in the same village you grew up in. I've got only two choices for a weekend fling: the weirdo who runs the movie rental place and my own version of Will Bellows."

I smiled at the memory of the boy Tabitha had gifted with a tail back when we'd been ten. "Hang on, there's still a movie rental place? Wasn't it just horror flicks?"

"Yep. No one has gone in there in almost a decade, and Calvin's still trying to make it happen."

I remembered Calvin as a guy who abhorred showers but loved movies where women got chopped up, so I wasn't surprised to hear about Tabitha's dry spell. He was obviously not an option, and it was impossible to have sex with a man after you'd seen him with a tail, even if you had been ten years old.

"Anyway." She grabbed my hand and tugged me towards the door. "Now that you're in town, it looks like my luck is changing. You're coming out with me."

I held my ground. "I can't. I just got here, and I haven't even unpacked my plants."

"Your plants? That's your priority?" She arched a brow. "Don't let Catrina hear you say that, or I'll lose my cool-by-association cred."

"Hey, plants are cool." I gestured around the shop, waving at the bottles of potions on the north wall. *I* might not use them to make potions, but it was possible. "Look at what they can do."

"Fair point. But I don't care. You've been gone too long, and I'm entitled to some bestie time. I'm cashing in my chips, and you're going to make up for it. With *dancing*."

"Oh, you wouldn't."

"Of course I would."

"Vicious."

She grinned, and as much as I didn't want to go dancing, I couldn't help but smile back. It was crazy how we hadn't spoken in years, and yet things immediately fell back into place.

She bumped my shoulder with hers. "Anyway, when you come with me, I'll be able to tell you about your new place. Unless you want to sleep in the same twin bed you did as a teenager? I assume that's where Cici put you."

"How'd you know that was my fate?"

"Duh. Gran would obviously try to put you up there. She wouldn't want you to go far."

"You've really got a place for me?"

"Yep. But you've got to come dancing with me to find out more."

"Yeah, yeah. You had me with the bestie thing. But do I

need to change? Charming Cove hasn't suddenly got a dance club, has it?"

"As if. We're going to The Sea Shanty."

Of course we were. It had been our favorite place as teenagers, and I was pretty sure it still would be. The pub itself was old and cozy, with an excellent steak and ale pie and a fire that hadn't stopped burning since 1602. The walls had been covered with nautical regalia, and it was said to be haunted by a female pirate who was still out to cut off the balls of the sailor who had stolen her ship. But it wasn't the interior that we loved—it was the garden overlooking the sea where bands sometimes played and old barrels had been turned into tables for our pints.

Tabitha looked up towards the kitchen and shouted, "We're headed out. You girls good up there?"

"Of course!" Gran shouted down. "Now get out of here. You're a buzzkill."

Tabitha shot me a look. "You see why I need to get out once in a while?"

"Between Gran and Catrina, you definitely need a break."

Tabitha looped her arm through mine and escorted me towards the door. "I wouldn't trade them for anything."

Now that I was home and could see them for myself, I couldn't blame her.

CHAPTER
FIVE

ARIA

THE SUN DIPPED towards the horizon as we walked towards The Sea Shanty. The quirky old buildings lined the street on our right, and the sea stretched out to our left. An ice cream van drove by, music jingling. The pub was hopping as we slipped inside, and it was like going back in time. Going back in season, actually, considering that the fireplace was burning merrily.

The small wooden bar was so different to the one I'd worked behind in London. Half a dozen leather barstools sat in front of it, and the old-fashioned taps for Real Ale gleamed, their brass polished to a high shine.

"I forgot how nice this place is." I whistled low. "I wouldn't hate tending *this* bar."

Tabitha shot me a glance. "Not a fan of London bars?"

"Not really."

"Well, you're in luck, then, because I'm not going to yell at you about ditching me to go to that hellhole. Not tonight, at least."

"Thanks." I deserved it, but she was a good enough friend to cut me a break. "I owe you a beer for that, at least."

"Make it a Jail Ale, and we're even. Actually, make it a hundred. But you can pay in installments."

"Beer for life sounds reasonable."

She arched a brow. "A hundred beers isn't beer for life."

I grinned and threw an arm around her neck to hug her close. "I'm going to find you a hottie to hook up with, I swear."

At that, the three older men who sat at the bar turned around to look at us. From the goofy expressions on their faces, they might as well have been Larry, Curly, and Moe.

"Oops, I was too loud, huh?" I stage whispered.

"I've been trying my luck with Tabitha for years," said the older man on the right.

Tabitha laughed. "Oh, give it a break, Morris. We all know you worship the ground Margot walks on and have done for forty years."

Margot still ran the tea shop that I loved, and Tabitha was right. Morris had been making moon eyes at her since I'd been a kid. I gave him a friendly nod and approached the woman who ran the bar.

"What'll it be?" She grinned, her dark hair glinting beneath the golden lights that were strung from the ceiling. She wore a T-shirt emblazoned with The Sea Shanty's logo, a female pirate holding something questionable in her hand. It was impossible to see exactly what it was, but I had an idea.

44

"Two Jail Ales." I scanned the selection of snacks pinned to a post behind her. "And two cheese and onion crisps."

"Coming right up." She smiled, then filled the pints and handed them over, along with the crisps. "Last two packs."

"Thanks." I took them and paid, then handed Tabitha her glass and nodded towards the outside. "Shall we?"

She hooked her arm through mine. "Let's hurry. Good tables go fast on Fridays."

"What's on Fridays?"

"Dancing, silly."

"Oh, right. The dancing." I didn't know what local band would be playing, but there was a fifty percent chance of there being flutes involved.

Outside, we found one of the old barrel tables on the front row, facing the ocean. A soft breeze blew across our faces, ruffling the flowers that popped out of the grass in front of us. I kicked off my shoes and pulled off my socks, loving the feel of the soft grass beneath my feet. Tabitha tapped her pint glass to mine. "Health and happiness."

"Health and happiness." My grandmother had taught us the toast, and I still said it every time I had a drink.

The first sip went down like heaven, and I finished the pint in no time.

Tabitha's brows rose. "Looks like someone has had a long day."

"You've got no idea."

"Tell me about it."

So I did. We fell right back into our old rhythm, and it felt amazing. Three pints later, and the sun had set. I'd eaten two more bags of crisps and decided to call it dinner, and my mood couldn't have been better. It was even good enough to get me out on the dance floor with Tabitha.

As we walked out, I eyed the band. Two fiddlers and...a flute. "Of course there's a flute. How do you even dance to a flute?"

"Like a court jester?" Tabitha asked. She did a little jig, and I almost died laughing. When she finished her jig, she winced. "Not sure that was the sexiest move I could have pulled. Do you think I might have had a bit much to drink?"

"I think you've had just the right amount." I pulled her into the center of the floor, which was a wooden platform built over the grass, and we joined the other dancers. Fortunately, these kinds of bands were usually headliners for community dances. All that was required was a bit of good humor and a willingness to be spun around by a farmer or local artist at high speed.

We laughed and danced as the stars came out overhead, and by the time the first set was finished, I was ready for another drink. Tabitha and I stumbled off the dance floor, breathless, and I offered to go in for the next round.

The pub itself was nearly empty, which was no surprise, considering how pretty the night was. The owners had set up a table in the garden, selling wine and bottled beer, but Tabitha and I were Real Ale purists. If it wasn't pulled straight out of the cellar, we didn't want it.

There was only one person standing at the bar, a man who was so tall that he made me feel like a child by comparison. His broad shoulders strained at the dark jumper he wore, and I felt my gaze drop to a butt that was so perfect, I was pretty sure he'd stolen it from Michelangelo's *David*. I yanked my gaze away from his butt, feeling like a right perv, and looked at his head. Dark hair brushed his collar, inky black and shiny in the dim light of the pub.

But it was his scent that caught me. An evergreen forest and a hint of spiced soap.

I stilled like a rabbit caught in the headlights, heart racing.

It was him.

It had to be. I would know his scent anywhere. And there weren't many men who were built like oversized versions of classical sculptures.

I should run. I should definitely run.

Holy tits, I was such a coward.

Why the hell should I run from him?

He should run from *me*.

In front of me, he paid the bartender for the beer, clearly having no idea that a mad little melodrama was happening behind him.

Before I could decide what to do—run, or grab the soda gun and spray him like a real adult—he turned.

When his gaze landed on me, he went still as a statue. If he would just take off all his clothes and strike a pose with his left leg out, then he really would look like *David*.

Focus, idiot.

I wanted to say something scathing. A dozen ideas were right at the tip of my tongue, bursting to escape. And yet, the tension that wrapped around me was so tight that it sealed my lips closed. We stood ten feet apart and in a pub with a waitress staring at us, and yet my mind was right back in the rain at Grandad's tower. I was seventeen again, and he was leaning over me, his stormy gaze on my lips as his fingertips brushed my arm.

I'd had some flings in the past nine years, but nothing had ever felt like that moment with him, where an otherworldly energy had overtaken us.

Right now, in this pub, he seemed to be feeling it, too. His gaze was riveted to my face, something deep in his eyes that I couldn't identify. Regret? Longing?

No, I was fully insane to think that. It's what I wanted to see in his eyes, not what was really there. His grip tightened on his pint, the muscles of his forearms standing out in stark relief against the hem of the navy jumper he wore.

I forced my mind away from the perfection of his forearms—*forearms, for fates' sake! I was losing it*—and blurted, "What are you doing here?"

He looked down at the beer in his hands, then up at me. "Getting a drink?"

"Are you serious?" His words drove all the warm and sexy feelings right out of me, for which I was grateful, and replaced them with an annoyance so deep it felt like it came from the center of the earth.

The bartender's voice sounded from behind him. "And he tips well, too."

I leaned around him to look at the bartender, who grinned at me. Hearing that he was a good tipper just deepened my annoyance. He wasn't allowed to be decent in *any* way. Not after what he'd done.

"Whatever." I stalked by him and set my empty pint glasses on the bar, studiously ignoring him. "Two more Jail Ales, please."

"Coming right up." The bartender turned to pull the pints, and I stared hard at the crisps behind the bar. That wanker had better leave, or I didn't know what I'd do. Scream at him? Throw bags of crisps at him like an insane banshee?

Why not both?

As if he had no idea that he was taking his life into his hands, he leaned against the bar beside me. His gaze burned into the side of my face, but I refused to turn and look at him.

"You're Aria." His voice rumbled low, and I hated how it sent a little shiver through me.

I couldn't keep staring straight ahead like I was afraid of him. The last thing I wanted was for him to think he had the upper hand. So I turned to him and arched a brow. "You remember?"

"I never forgot." There was something deep in his voice, something loaded, that sent another little shiver through me. No one should be allowed to have a voice like that. Two shivers in less than two minutes. It was unacceptable.

I needed to make sure he knew where he stood so he'd quit with that shiver-inducing tone. "Yeah, well, I haven't forgot, either. You're dead to me."

He winced, and a shadow crossed over his face. It looked a hell of a lot like regret, but he wasn't allowed to feel regret. Not after what he'd done.

"I take it you're still angry about that."

I laughed, a bitter bark that hurt my throat, and turned back to stare at the crisps. "Of course I am."

"Then I'm sorry. Very genuinely. I didn't intend to hurt anyone."

49

The worst part was, I believed him. He *did* sound sorry, and like he hadn't intended harm.

"I *told* you what that place meant to me, and you still went ahead and did it." The words bubbled up in my chest, threatening to spill all over him like acid. I wanted to burn him with the force of my hurt and anger.

But the bartender delivered my drinks. It was for the best. Now wasn't the time. *Never* was the time. I needed to move on and bury him in the dirt of the past.

"Thank you, Cori." I took the drinks and forced a smile, realizing that she had probably heard the entirety of our conversation.

Good. I wanted her to know that at least someone thought he was an asshole.

Beside me, Callan laid a twenty-pound note on the bar. "For her drinks."

"Oh, no. You don't get to buy me drinks." I shifted to push the note back at him, but he'd already turned and headed towards the door.

Damn it. I wasn't going to chase after him.

"Whatever," I muttered, turning back to the bartender. "Keep the change, obviously."

She snapped up the note and grinned. "Obviously." Then her smile faltered. "I don't know what's going on between you two, but that was some serious energy."

"Evil energy."

"Ha, right. I'm not sure anyone would call that evil." Her gaze moved to the door, which had just shut behind Callan. We were alone in the pub now, and she looked back at me. "Seriously, though, did you see the way he looked at you? He wants you. Like, with the fire of a thousand suns. I don't know what he did to you, but if I were you, I'd let him make it up to me."

"Pass." I shrugged. "But if you want to get screwed and then screwed over, I suggest you go for it."

"It might almost be worth it. He's Callan Hawthorne. *The* Callan Hawthorne."

"Well, *the* Callan Hawthorne can go to hell, as far as I'm concerned." I raised my glasses at her. "Thanks for the drinks."

"Anytime."

I turned and left, hoping that Callan had fallen off the cliff. When I walked outside, I found that he hadn't. Pity.

He stood at the far end of the garden that overlooked the sea, staring out at the waves like a damned earl or duke or whatever, surveying his estate. It was just like him to act like he owned the whole ocean.

I looked for Tabitha and found her thirty feet away from him, glaring at him with venom in her eyes. She knew the story, and since she was my ride-or-die bestie despite the fact that I'd ditched her when I'd run away from Charming Cove, she would hate him until the day she died.

I strode to her, passing multiple tables of people who were whispering excitedly while pointing to Callan. Of course he was a celebrity here. He was a celebrity everywhere —he was on the cover of the damned *Magic Mirror*, for fate's sake.

Tabitha's gaze moved to me as she approached. "You okay?"

"Fan-freaking-tastic." I handed her a beer. "Do you want

to switch to straight vodka after this? Because I'm thinking that's a great idea."

She took a swig of her beer, then laughed. "I think we should stick to beer. Although I'm happy to go throw this on Callan for you, if you want."

"That would be great, but you know I don't believe in wasting beer." I took a sip of mine.

"Yeah, but extenuating circumstances and all."

"I'm thinking it might be better to throw him into the sea."

She shook her head. "What would *actually* be better would be beating him in the damned competition. He'll really hate that."

I stilled. "Hang on, what?"

She turned to me. "The competition. It starts tomorrow, remember, and it's the perfect place for you to get your revenge."

I held up my hands. "Whoa, there. You're telling me that he's in the competition for Lionel Sparrow's garden?"

"Didn't your gran tell you?"

"No." I scowled. Gran knew how much I hated him. We'd even talked about him in the car! Was that what she'd meant when she'd said we needed to keep an eye on the competition? I'd thought she'd meant because he and she were two of the most powerful magical beings in the UK.

"She's a crafty one," Tabitha said.

He's in the competition.

The idea kept hamster wheeling in my mind. There was no way I could compete against him. I couldn't handle being around him, but that wasn't even the main problem. He would kick my arse. Like, wipe the floor with me from day one.

He was freaking Callan Hawthorne! Everyone knew how powerful he was.

"Yeah, I'm out," I said.

"You want to go home?" She looked at my nearly full beer, her brows raised.

"No, I'm out of the competition. No way I'm letting him beat me."

"Then don't let him beat you."

"Tabitha, it was already a hilariously long shot that I could win this thing. I didn't stand a chance from the get-go, but I wasn't going to ignore a direct request from Gran." I nodded towards Callan. "But this? No way in hell can I beat him. And I'm not going to give him the satisfaction of beating me."

Tabitha's face fell. "You can't quit."

"Oh, yes, I can. And I'm going to."

CALLAN

WELL, that had gone poorly.

What had I thought I was going to accomplish by coming to the local pub? That I'd see her and win her over?

I'd been right about seeing her, but the idea of winning her over was now downright laughable. I could feel her gaze on me, hot and angry, but I didn't dare turn to look at her, even though I was desperate to see her face again.

She was even more beautiful than I remembered, with her stormy gray eyes and luminous skin. She was a *lot* angrier, though. I'd known she'd cared for the place, but I hadn't realized how much. I'd always been laser-focused on my goals, often to the detriment of other parts of my life, but had clearly missed something, because she was still holding on to that anger after all these years.

I was going to have to convince her that building The Keep Café at the tower had actually been a good idea. She probably hadn't been there. If I could get her to see that it hadn't ruined the beauty of the place, but just modified it, maybe she wouldn't be so angry. It was beautiful now, after all. One of my greatest accomplishments, and I knew the townspeople loved it. The café and bar made a mint—far more than I'd ever anticipated.

But how was I going to convince her that The Keep Café had been a good idea if she didn't want to be around me?

That was a serious stumbling block to my plan, and I had no idea how to get past it.

"So, it's the famous Callan Hawthorne."

A man's voice sounded from behind me, and I turned. He was probably about five years younger than me, with sandy blond hair and the sun-browned face of someone who spent a lot of time outside.

I held out my hand. "Nice to meet you...?"

"Reggie Hopper. I saw you watching Tabitha and Aria. Be careful of those two."

"Oh?"

"Tabitha gave me a tail once." He grimaced, and I wondered if he'd deserved the tail. Probably had. "And that Aria is a bit of nightmare with her magic. Just as likely to blow something up in your face as she is to create a worthy spell."

I frowned, feeling my fist clench tightly. I looked down at it, frowning. What the hell was I going to do? Punch the guy for his insult? Before I could respond, he continued.

"I don't know why she's bothering to compete in Lionel Sparrow's competition for the garden. She doesn't stand a chance."

"Wait, Aria? She's competing?"

He nodded. "That's what I hear."

That was it, then. If she competed, she would have to be around me. I'd have the time to find a way to convince her that The Keep Café wasn't the abomination she thought it was.

Reggie was looking at me expectantly, as if he thought I would join in on talking shite about Aria and Tabitha.

"I'm glad she's competing," I said. "She'll be worthy competition."

Reggie laughed, and something in me snapped.

I reached up to grip his shoulder, just tightly enough to let him know that I was the one to be worried about. It helped that he was a good six inches shorter than me.

"Don't ever speak that way about either of them again." I imbued my voice with enough power to make the air shiver around us. It wouldn't hurt Reggie, but it would scare the hell out of him.

As expected, his face turned white. He nodded frantically.

I released my grip and gave him a few not-so-friendly pats on the shoulder. "Good talk. Have a nice night, now."

He scampered off, and I turned to stare back out at the sea. It looked like it had been a good idea to come to the pub, after all.

CHAPTER
SIX

ARIA

I WOKE with a hangover that felt like it just might kill me. Bright light streamed through the windows, burning through my closed eyelids, and my head pounded like the Edinburgh Tattoo. A hundred kilted men were playing thier bagpipes between my ears, and it made me want to roll over and sleep forever.

"I'm going to die." Tabitha's groan sounded from the other side of the room, and I turned my head to look at her.

She was sprawled on the other twin bed, half out of her clothes and with her arm flung over her eyes.

"I think I might already be dead," I croaked.

"No, we're alive. This hurts too much to be death."

"Fair point." I dragged myself upright, regretting the last two vodka shots of the night. I'd rage-pounded them, which was never a good idea, and it was time to pay the price. "I need coffee."

"Same."

"Does Margot still make her rocket fuel?" It'd been the hangover cure that had seen us through the last year I'd lived here. Tabitha and I had been old enough to party, and we'd taken full advantage.

"She does. I'll give you a million quid if you go get me one."

"You don't have a million quid."

"But I do have a place for you to stay that isn't your childhood bedroom, and I'll show it to you today."

"Good point." I swung my legs over the side of the bed. "Anyway, you've got to check on your girl."

"True enough, although I'm sure she's awake with your gran now."

I could hear her, actually, shouting something about Oreo pancakes. As we'd sneaked in last night, Tabitha had stopped to check in on Catrina. She slept in the guest bedroom next to Gran's room on their Monster Nights, and the space had been decorated perfectly for a seven-year-old. Tabitha said it was her favorite night of the week, and I couldn't blame her.

As Catrina's and Gran's voices filtered up through the floorboards, I made my way to the little bathroom and looked into the mirror.

"Holy tits, I look like the kraken." My hair was a wild mess around my head, and my eyes were reddened.

"I'm sure you can pull it off," Tabitha said as she passed by on her way to the bathroom downstairs.

A small laugh huffed out of me, and I bent over to splash water on my face. I was going to have to tell Gran that I was no longer competing, and in order to do that, I needed to get rid of this damned hangover.

It didn't take me long to change my clothes and get my hair into a bun that at least hid how insane it had got. A pair of big sunglasses hid my disastrous eyes, and I sneaked out of the house before Gran could see me.

The day was a signature Charming Cove day, bright and beautiful, and I squinted behind the sunglasses. Several people walked down the street, coffees in hand, and a team of local volunteer gardeners tended the flowers that bordered the coastal path. Every one of them smiled and waved at me, and it took everything I had not to grimace back at them when I tried to return their smiles. From the confused looks on some of their faces, I might not have managed.

Finally, I reached Margot's coffee shop and ducked inside. It was as cozy and pretty as I remembered, with the divine scent of coffee and fresh pastries filling the air. I breathed in deeply, inhaling the rich scents of butter, sugar, chocolate, and fruit.

"Heaven," I murmured. There had been nowhere in London like this place, not even the bakery I'd worked at, and now that I was home, I couldn't imagine leaving.

An older couple sat at the little table by the window, each drinking a cup of tea as they devoured their novels. Margot bustled out from the kitchen in the back, wiping her hands on her apron. When she spotted me, a broad grin appeared on her face. "Aria! It's been an age, lamb. I'm so glad you're back!"

"Margot. I'm so glad to see you." And I meant it. Margo was one of my favorite people in Charming Cove, and not just because she made the best coffee in town.

"So, I heard from your gran that you're here to save the shop." She smiled. "Save us all, even. We need that shop here in Charming Cove."

The hope in Margot's voice made me cringe. There was no way I could save the shop because I was quitting the competition. Even if I stayed in, I didn't have a chance in hell of winning. But the hope in her voice killed me. I couldn't bear to take it away from her. Not yet.

"I don't know if I'll win, but I'll try my best." *Liar.*

"I have faith in you, lamb."

Oh, now that was even worse.

"I assume you're here for two of my Rocket Fuels?"

I grimaced. "Do I look that bad?"

"No, but Morris said he saw you and Tabitha down at the pub last night, and I know how you two used to go out on the lash." She turned and bustled towards the big espresso machine on the back counter. "Let me get those started for you."

"Thanks. Can you add a latte for Gran, please?"

"Sure thing."

I looked towards the glass case that contained her amazing treats, knowing I would have to show some self-restraint and only get one. The last thing I needed right now was to compound my hangover with a sugar coma. As my gaze ran over the delights, I caught sight of a furry black and white creature standing on its hind legs, paws glued to the glass. "What the hell are you doing here, Boris?"

I'm your familiar, dummy. Of course I'm here. I go everywhere with you.

"You weren't around to help me clean the shop yesterday."

Well, not everywhere *everywhere. That would be creepy.*

"And of course you're not creepy."

Never. He looked back at the pastries, then up at me. *I'll have a triple espresso and a chocolate croissant.*

"With what money?"

Your money, obviously. I'm a badger. I don't have money.

"Yeah, that's not how this is going to work."

I'm your new familiar. You have to do as I say.

"No, I don't."

Fine. But don't you want to be on my good side? I can poop—or not poop—in some very inconvenient places. He looked pointedly at my shoes.

"Oh, my God, this is a stick up, isn't it? You're robbing me."

He shrugged a little shoulder. *I feel like that's an ugly word, but whatever you say.*

"You fight dirty." I had to stifle a laugh.

It's why I win.

Fair enough. I could already tell that Boris was a little terror, but I liked him.

I called out his order to Margot and added on a couple extra pastries.

She chuckled as she said, "I'll have that right out, lamb."

I looked back at Boris, who was grinning at me with his little badger teeth. "See? Happy now?"

Ecstatic.

"Now get out of here. I don't want Margot getting cited by the health inspector."

Moi? He pointed a little paw to his chest. *I have impeccable grooming. I'm actually an asset to this establishment.*

"I see half a dozen badger hairs on the ground next to you, and I'll tell you right now that no one wants that on their food. Now go outside, and I'll bring you your breakfast.

He harrumphed. *Fine. But it had better be hot.*

"I wouldn't dream of delivering anything but the best to you."

Good. He lowered himself to four feet and turned to waddle out the door. I closed my eyes. Seriously? I'd been back in town less than twenty-four hours, and this was how my life was going.

When the bell above the door rang, I opened my eyes.

Callan stood in front of me.

I looked up at the ceiling as if looking towards the Lord in heaven. If he was up there, he was playing tricks on me. "You're a sick bastard, you know that?"

Callan frowned, and I realized he'd heard my words and thought I was talking to him instead of whatever maniac oversaw my life lately. Good. The sentence had absolutely no context and made me sound a bit mad, but I liked the idea of having him off his feet.

I turned back to the counter, hoping that Margot was almost done with our coffees. Unfortunately, she'd disappeared into the back of the café.

Callan appeared next to me, and his low voice sent obnoxious shivers through me when he spoke. "It must be fate that we keep running into each other."

"Or you're stalking me."

"Just good luck. I'm staying at the B&B next door."

I frowned, turning to him. "Mrs. Aspen's place? No one stays there—her dog bites. Shouldn't you be at some mansion in the countryside that you stole from orphans?"

"Sadly, the orphans kicked me out."

I felt my lips twitch. "Was that a joke?"

"I've been known to make them. Occasionally." A self-deprecating smile pulled at the edges of his mouth, and I hated that I found it charming.

"Whatever." I turned to see if Margot had come back, but she hadn't.

"What's good here?"

"Everything." I shot him an annoyed glance. "Seriously, though, I get why the orphans would boot you out. But shouldn't you have crawled back beneath some billionaire rock by now?"

"Billionaires live under rocks?"

"No, but they should. No one should have that much money to themselves. It's downright wrong."

He smiled. "Then you'll be happy to know I'm not a billionaire."

I was pretty sure that wasn't true, and even if it was, he was still rich as Croesus. "Oh, poor baby. Are you trying to survive on your hundreds of millions? How ever do you manage?"

"Hundreds of millions?" Margot asked as she walked out

of the back. "Who has hundreds of millions?" Her gaze landed on Callan and her eyes widened. "It's you!"

"Um." Callan clearly had no idea what to say.

"Didn't you donate most of your fortune?" she asked. "That's what I read in *Witches Weekly*."

"Um..." Clearly, he felt awkward as hell. "Would you believe I spent it on a fleet of sports cars painted with scenes of my favorite films?"

I felt the tiniest laugh try to escape my lips, and I bit it back.

"No." Margot crossed her arms. "I know what I read in *Witches Weekly*."

He just smiled and said, "Your shop smells amazing. Can I have your three favorite pastries and a coffee to go?"

He was sidestepping the question of donating millions of pounds to charity. Billions, maybe. And yet, he had definitely done it. I could read it on him like I could read a billboard.

Callan Hawthorne was decent. Like, fundamentally decent. And yet, he'd taken my grandfather's spirit from me —sort of.

"You're a good sort, Mr. Hawthorne." Margot turned from him and filled a pastry bag with my order, then handed me the bag and a little paper tray of coffees.

I handed her the money. "Thanks, Margot. You're a gem."

"Enjoy, Aria. And I'll be thinking of you tonight. Sending you all the good wishes I can."

Tonight was the start of the competition. The opening ceremonies, as Gran had said. Did Margot know Callan was competing? Probably not, because she wouldn't be so hopeful about my chances if she did. He would definitely

have huge plans for the garden that wouldn't involve contin-
uing to sell all the stock to a little potion shop.

I turned, ignoring Callan, and headed for the door. Boris
was waiting for me on the other side like a mini mobster
waiting for his mark to pay up. I handed him the coffee and
croissant, and he nodded. *Thank you.*

"That was unexpectedly polite," I said.

He looked at me, clearly offended. *How rude. I'm* always
polite.

"Ten minutes ago, you threatened to poop in my shoes."

I would never do something like that.

"Sure." I shook my head, unable to help the smile that
tugged at my lips, and headed down the street.

I'd only gone a few steps when Callan appeared at my
side, matching his pace to mine. I glared up at him. "What
are you doing? Weren't you supposed to be getting pastries?"

"I'll go back for them."

"That doesn't answer the question of what you're doing."

"Would you believe me if I said I enjoyed your company
and wanted more of it?"

"No."

"It's the truth." He said it so simply that I believed him.
For a second.

"You bailed on coffee to come tell me that?"

"I bailed on coffee to say I'm glad you're in the
competition."

"What, so you can beat me?" I shifted the coffees in my
hand and picked up the pace.

"No, so I can spend more time with you."

He sounded genuine, but I had such a hard time believing

him. It didn't match the image I had of him. He was the wealthy, powerful Callan Hawthorne; the guy who had so easily walked away when we'd first met. "Did you ever ask yourself whether I might want to spend time with you?"

"I don't need to. I know you don't." There was the slightest hint of regret to his voice. "But I'm hoping to change your mind."

"No way in hell."

"I can convince you that the renovations to the tower were a good idea."

I almost barked out a bitter laugh, but managed to keep it in check. I couldn't see my grandad's spirit there anymore, not now that so many people were around, so he didn't stand a chance of convincing me. "You're too much, you know that?"

"What do you mean?"

"You have everything. Wealth, power, looks." Shit. I regretted adding that last part. "Anyway. You have everything. And everyone, according to the gossip on the news about your endless cycle of girlfriends. You can't have me, too." Double shit. The last thing I'd said had come out weird. I hadn't meant it like *that*, and I glanced up at him to see if he had picked up on my words.

There was the briefest flash of *something* in his gaze before he looked out towards the sea. Finally, he said, "But you are competing?"

"No."

"Think you can't beat me?" There was the faintest hint of teasing to his voice, and I hated that I liked it.

I knew I couldn't beat him, but my pride couldn't allow

me to let him think he could get the better of me. "Oh, I know I could beat you."

"Then prove it. Compete for the garden."

Compete for the garden. How I wanted to. I wanted to win for Gran and prove that I wasn't a screwup with my magic. I wanted to beat him.

But I sucked at magic, and I didn't want to be anywhere near him.

I hated that I was waffling so hard.

"Well?" he asked.

Fortunately, the conversation was over because I'd reached the shop. I pushed open the door and turned to block the entry. "It looks like I've reached my stop. You'd better go back and get your breakfast before Margot sells out."

"I hope I see you at the competition tonight."

I just shook my head and shut the door in his face, satisfied by the sound of it clicking shut.

CHAPTER
SEVEN

ARIA

"Is that you, Aria?" Tabitha called from the kitchen upstairs. "If it is, you need to get up here pronto. I'm about to expire on the spot like an avocado left on the counter."

I grinned and took the stairs two at a time, carefully balancing the tray of coffees in my right hand. The smell was the only thing keeping me going at this point, and I didn't dare lose a drop. When I reached the kitchen, I found Tabitha and Gran at the table by the window, with Catrina standing on a stool at the counter. The girl was up to her elbows in flour, and she shot me a huge grin and said, "Breakfast biscuits!"

"Sounds amazing." I distributed the coffees to Gran and Tabitha.

Tabitha grabbed for it with a grateful smile, then took a big gulp. "You are a lifesaver."

"Coffee delivery is my specialty. If you need CPR, I suggest you go elsewhere."

She grinned and sipped again.

"So, did you girls have a good night?" Gran asked in a singsong voice that said she knew something.

"What do you think you know?" I demanded.

"Well, I might have heard that a certain handsome, wealthy mage was at the pub and that you two exchanged some words." She smiled like the cat who got the cream.

"That wanker," I muttered. The bartender had been the only other person in the place, and she had clearly ratted me out to the gossip network. "Freaking small towns."

"I've always said that if you're going to curse, you need to commit," Catrina said, though she stopped short of fully correcting my cursing.

I felt my eyes widen, and I looked at Tabitha.

She shrugged. "What can I say? She's a girl who knows her mind."

"And Aunt Tabitha says that as long as I get good marks and I'm nice to animals and I don't curse in inappropriate places, then I'm doing fine."

I shrugged. Sounded like good advice to me. I took a bracing sip of coffee, then looked at Gran. "Did you know that Callan Hawthorne is competing?"

"I—ahhh." She gave a guilty smile. "I might have, yes."

"Gran, come on. Really?"

"I know you hate him, and I didn't want you to drop out of the competition."

"Well, you're out of luck, then, because there's no way in hell I'm going to compete and let him beat me."

"That's not the spirit I raised you with." She shot me a disapproving glare.

"No, but you also taught me to pick my battles and be true to myself. Apparently, true to myself is turning tail and running from a battle I definitely can't win." Even as I said it, the idea prickled.

"Now, I know that's not you," she said. "And I also know you would never let your old gran lose the shop."

I laughed. "Old gran? Don't you think you're laying it on a bit thick?" She was dressed to the nines and would soon be having her afternoon cocktail before going swimming in the sea. There was nothing old about my gran. All the same, she could benefit from a break.

"I stand by my words. I don't want to lose the shop, and you can save it."

"I don't want to lose it, either. But honestly, a little bit of retirement would do you good. You've got more than enough money, and you need to put your feet up."

"I'll put my feet up when I'm dead."

I tilted my head back and groaned. "You'll be the death of me, Gran."

"Of course not." She reached out and squeezed my hand, and I squeezed back. "I know you can win this, Aria. I've asked my sources, and they've made it clear that you are the only one who can do it."

Her *sources* were a combination of tea leaves and crystal balls that I wasn't sure I trusted, but she sure did. They'd never been wrong before—at least, not that she'd told me—and she seemed convinced that they weren't wrong now. Except *I* hadn't asked these sources, so I didn't believe them.

"I'm still not competing. I don't stand a chance of winning, and I don't see why I'd put myself through that. We can find another way to get the supplies we need for the shop." Even as I said the words, I knew that it wasn't true. Lionel Sparrow's garden had ingredients that could be found nowhere else in the UK, and they were vital to our bestselling potions and spells.

Before Gran could point this out—which I *knew* she would—Catrina appeared at the table, a plate of perfectly baked biscuits in her hands. They smelled like buttery, chocolatey perfection. She held them up, a proud smile on her face. "Your breakfast."

"Thank you, monster." Tabitha took the plate from her and pressed a kiss to her head.

"Now, don't give yourselves a headache off too much sugar. I'm going to watch cartoons." She turned and skipped towards the living room.

Tabitha set the plate down on the table and looked at me, her gaze serious. "We need you to win this, Aria. Your Gran is sure it has to be you, and so am I. Your magic was wonky in the past, but we'll help you. Together, we can do this."

Together, we can do this.

The words made something tighten around my heart. Love? Longing?

I'd been on my own so long that I'd forgot what it was like to have family like this. Friends. A community. One of the reasons that I'd run from this town was because I'd hated how it had reminded me of my crappy magic. But I'd been young then, full of rampaging teenage emotion. What if I could change how I saw myself, and how the world saw me?

No longer the dud, but the woman who won the Garden of Enchantment?

The idea was so glorious and ridiculous that it made me laugh. "I don't stand a chance, and you guys know it."

"We don't know anything of the sort," Gran said.

"And it's not just Gran who needs this place," Tabitha said. "I do. And Catrina does. It's the most stable thing she's known since her parents died."

I poked her shoulder lightly. "No, *you're* the most stable thing she's known."

"Fine. Then it's the most stable *place*, and you've seen how she loves it."

Tabitha wasn't wrong. The girl lit up with her love for the old shop, and I could still remember what it felt like when I'd been a child here. In a world full of magic, this place was the most incredible. It had been everything to me as a kid. Could I really just let it go if I had a chance of saving it?

"Come on, Aria," Tabitha pleaded. "You're the only one who has ever stood up to Callan Hawthorne, and the only one who isn't afraid of him. You'll throw him off his guard."

"I hate him."

"And you can use that to beat him. We need this."

From out in the shop, I could hear Catrina singing a little song about faerie dust. And there was no way my grandmother could lose the place. She didn't say it, but I knew it was the last thing she had of Grandad's. It had been his as much as hers. The tower had been my way to connect with him, but the shop was hers.

I looked down at my coffee cup. Even Margot, who ran the teashop, said she was counting on me.

I sighed. "Fine. I'll do it."

"Good!" Gran crowed. "It's about time you got some sense into you."

"Sense?" I wasn't sure I'd call it sense, but I couldn't back down now.

∽

Aria

LATER THAT AFTERNOON, Tabitha took me out to the place that would become my new home.

"I don't see why you won't at least give me a hint of where we're going," I said as we walked down the seaside path away from town. We were about twenty feet above sea level, on the small, rocky cliffs that broke up the waves as they crashed below.

"We're almost there. Honestly, it's so close I'd be wasting my time even talking about it."

We'd been walking for ten minutes, so she was wrong about that. But since she was nice enough to be giving me a place to live, I probably needed to chill on the interrogation.

As we came up over a hill, I spotted two white cottages on the downslope. They were only about fifty meters apart, with beautiful gardens surrounding each.

Tabitha pointed, a proud smile on her face. "There. You get the one closer to us."

It was slightly smaller than the other, with whitewashed stone walls and pretty blue shutters that bordered sparkling windows. Pink, purple, and yellow flowers spilled from the window boxes, and more flowers clustered around the perimeter of the house. A small stone patio on the back over-looked the sea, and the chimney promised warm fires in the winters.

It was so pretty that it almost hurt to look at.

"We live in the other one," Tabitha said. "I bought them a few years ago. The big one came ready to live in, but I've been renovating the smaller one to rent it out. But then you showed up!"

"Tabitha." Shock made my voice come out shaky, and I turned to her. "They're beautiful. Perfect. How could you ever afford them?"

Neither Tabitha nor I had had any money when I'd left town. We'd been teenagers. But *this*. These houses were small but incredible. The view, the charm, the privacy. They had to have cost her a fortune.

She shrugged. "After you left, I wasn't wasting as much money down at the pub."

Guilt pierced me. I knew she was joking, but we had been like sisters, hanging out every night. I'd felt her loss keenly, but I'd had the distraction of the city and trying to make my own way.

She gripped my arm. "Hey, chill on those dark thoughts, okay? I know why you had to go, and I supported it. And I've been happy as a clam here in Charming Cove. That state-ment about the pub was just a joke."

"Yeah, well, I owe you." I looked at the houses, loving what I saw. I knew that as soon as I got into that little cottage, I'd never want to leave. "But I don't have a job yet, and I have no savings. You need to rent that place out to someone who can pay."

She grimaced. "And have a stranger living so close to Catrina and me? No way."

"But you just said you renovated it to rent."

"Yeah, but I'm still going to be picky about who I rent to. Right now, there's no one else that I want to live next to except you. So I'll wait until you get a job. Anyway, what are best friends for?"

"You're too good to me." I looped an arm around her neck and squeezed.

She hugged me back, then grabbed my hand and pulled me into a run. "Come on, you have to check it out."

I ran after her, laughing as the wind blew my hair back. It carried the scent of the flowers that tumbled around the front path up to the house, and I couldn't believe my good fortune. The sea that sparkled behind the building was so pretty, it could have been on a postcard, and the house itself was the same.

The front door had been painted a brilliant blue to match the shutters, and Tabitha opened it with a flourish.

The first thing I saw within was the wide windows overlooking the ocean. The view was enough to take my breath away. My plants would love it here. There was just so much light.

I stepped inside, noting the old wooden floorboards that gleamed with polish. To the right, a cozy living room was positioned around an old stone fireplace. Bookshelves bordered it, filled with the kind of fiction that Tabitha loved —romances, mysteries, and thrillers.

LINSEY HALL

"Okay, I admit I've been using it as a spillover library," Tabitha said.

"It's perfect." The squashy white couch and armchairs surrounded a gorgeous yellow and blue rug, and I could just imagine cozying down for a nice long read in the winter as the fireplace flickered away.

I turned to the kitchen and dining area, which was part of the same room but positioned in the corner of the house that overlooked the sea. It was as quaint and pretty as the exterior, with wooden counters and a white table that was pushed up against a wide bay window. A bench sat in the window, allowing one to eat at the table or relax against the side and look out at the view.

Tabitha pointed to a door at the left. "There's a bedroom over there, along with an ensuite. And a smaller bedroom on the other side of the house."

I threw my arms around her. "It's too perfect to believe. Thank you so much, and I'll pay you a million pounds for it as soon as I get it."

She laughed and hugged me back. "I'll hold you to that. Now come on, let's make tea and check out the back garden."

CHAPTER
EIGHT

ARIA

EARLY THAT EVENING, after unpacking my belongings and getting my plants situated in their gorgeous new home, I joined Tabitha, Catrina, and Gran for the walk to the Garden of Enchantment. We could have driven, but I needed to burn off the energy, and Gran swore the walking kept her young. Since she was moving a heck of a lot faster than I was, she was probably right.

"You ready for this?" Tabitha asked in a quiet voice as Catrina skipped ahead to join Gran on her power walk along the country lane.

"You know I'm not." I looked to the left, spotting a fat, fluffy sheep in the field next to us. The creature stared impassively at me, chewing on a clump of grass. I pointed to him. "That guy knows what's up. I'm supposed to be the champion of Seaside Spells, but he's more impressed with his grass."

"Clive is a real foodie. To him, there is nothing more impressive than grass."

"Clive? You named the sheep?"

"I see him on my runs. He's a good cheerleader."

I looked back at Clive, who kept chomping away, staring balefully into the distance. "Sure."

She grinned and nudged me. "You've got this, Aria. Whatever old Mr. Sparrow throws at you, we'll help you. It's about time you claimed your magic."

"I've been trying to claim my magic for over a decade and haven't had any luck yet, and you know it. What will make this time different?"

"Because you have *got* to win." Her voice was serious, and so was her gaze when it met mine. "I don't know why your magic always blows up in your face, but I do know you're powerful. You can do this. I believe in you."

The sheer intensity of her voice made my eyes prick with tears. I turned to watch Catrina and Gran skip down the narrow road between fields. "I don't know what Gran is taking for energy, but I need some of it."

"That woman is a goddess."

I nodded. "Truth."

We reached the Garden of Enchantment about ten minutes later. There was no sign marking Lionel Sparrow's property, but everyone in town knew exactly where it was. For one, you could feel the magic from miles away. It sparked against the skin like champagne bubbles popping inside a flute, and it smelled like the most glorious assortment of flowers and greenery.

Ancient oak trees bordered the garden, and we stepped onto the narrow path that led between them. The sun was beginning to set, and fireflies danced around us as we walked. A few brave rabbits peeked out from behind trees to watch us go, and a collection of red squirrels sat on a branch overhead and chittered angrily.

"Sounds like they don't like company," I said to Catrina.

"I just have to win them over with peanut butter." She pulled a little packet of the stuff from her pocket, along with a spoon. After loading the spoon with peanut butter, she went to the tree and started to shimmy up to the branch.

"Hey, Catrina, we don't have time for that," Tabitha said.

Catrina turned to Tabitha, making the most impressive puppy dog eyes ever seen. She could have melted the heart of a stone-cold tax accountant. "But please, Aunt Tabitha? It will just take a minute."

"We're early, dear," Gran said. "Surely we have a minute."

Tabitha sighed, but it was clear she couldn't resist her niece's desire to befriend the local rodents. "All right. Five minutes, Catrina. If they aren't your besties by then, you're out of luck."

"Oh, I only need three." The confidence in her voice was something to aspire to.

"You go on," Gran told me. "We'll catch up soon."

Part of me hated the idea of going in there alone—surely everyone knew what a dud I was when it came to my magic, and losing the shield of Tabitha and Gran would suck. But it was exactly that part of me that had to be ignored. If I wasn't good with my magic, at least I could be brave.

"Good luck, Cinderella," I called up to Catrina as I passed under her branch.

"I'll have a new dress by dawn, just you wait," she said.

The sweet confidence in her words bolstered me as I made my way through the quickly darkening forest to the clearing in the middle. Everyone knew where the heart of the Garden of Enchantment was located. We had our local Samhain celebrations there every year, and it was a party no one wanted to miss. I hadn't been to one in years, obviously, but I'd never been to a party even a fraction as good while I'd lived in London.

As I walked through the iron gate that had been swung open to permit entry to the garden, I felt a rush run through me. There was something just so incredible about this place. Even the air felt different—more alive.

The garden looked just as it did on the night of the parties. Glowing lanterns had been hung from the street, and Lionel Sparrow had somehow convinced all the fireflies to float in the air, moving in perfect swirls that made the sky look enchanted. Heavy blooms hung from bushes in every color of the rainbow. Lionel had spent his youth traveling the world in search of the rarest and most wonderful potion supplies. He'd spend the last fifty years in this garden, creating a wonderland with the fruits of his travels. It didn't matter where the plant had come from—he'd created the perfect ecosystem for it with his magic.

But unlike at the parties where I'd reveled with Tabitha until dawn, the clearing was mostly empty. The opening ceremonies were closed invitation—at least, that's what Tabitha had told me—and only the competitors and their chosen few were allowed to come.

Across the clearing stood three other people. Immediately, I recognized Serena, a witch from my school days who had been a real wanker about my magic. There had been one instance where I'd tried to do a spell in class and it had literally blown up in my face. I hadn't had eyebrows for a week, and she'd insisted on calling me Uncle Fester.

Two men stood next to her, but I didn't recognize them. One was a guy in his forties, and the other was younger than me. On the south side of the clearing stood a cluster of people who had to be the friends and family of the competitors who'd already arrived. There were only about a dozen of them, and they chatted with each other as they waited.

Should I go over and talk to the other competitors? Probably. It would be the mature thing, after all. I took a deep breath and stepped towards them. Before I'd made it more than a meter, someone appeared to my right. I recognized her as Serena's friend from school, and the group that I was heading towards shouted their greetings to her.

"Lilac!" Serena crowed, holding out her arms.

Well, shit.

They'd ignored my arrival but welcomed her like a long-lost sister who'd just returned from war. I couldn't exactly go over there now—not after they made it clear how they felt about me.

I shouldn't be surprised I was standing here on my own, like the kid who got picked last for dodgeball, but it still stung. I was pretty sure I even heard someone whisper the word *dud*.

I raised my brows at them. *Oh, it is* on.

I wanted to dredge up whatever tiny bits of magic I had and fling it at them like a monkey threw poo.

Oh, real mature, Aria.

Scowling, I vowed to act like an adult.

At my side, a small, furry body appeared. Boris. He looked up at me, then over at them, then back up at me. *Want me to shank them?*

I stifled a laugh. "Shank them?"

Yes. Shank them.

"Where did you learn that word?"

What? I'm a tough badger. I've been around.

I had no doubt, given the fact that he'd lived in a dumpster in London while doing Gran's spying. "I don't buy it. You saw it on Netflix, didn't you? Some documentary about prison."

Fine, yes. But I still know how to do it.

"Thank you for the very kind offer, but I'll pass. For now." I smiled down at him.

You know where to find me.

I actually didn't, but he'd already scampered off.

"What's the reason behind that smile?" Callan's voice sounded from beside me, and I looked up to see him staring down at me.

I didn't want to tell him that I was smiling at the retreating form of my wannabe murderer familiar, so I just shrugged, then looked at the other competitors to see that their expressions had morphed from amused pity to downright awe. It was like they were looking at a superhero or the pope, depending on which side of the religious spectrum they landed on.

"Do people always look at you like that?" I asked.

"Often." I could hear the grimace in his voice.

"Not a fan?"

"Would you be?"

"It's better than the looks I usually get."

"What do you mean?" The genuine curiosity in his voice made me want to share. I hated how he got under my skin like this. The loss of my grandad's tower had been the foundational moment of my youth—and it had been the bad kind. *He'd* been responsible. And yet, here he was, being all kind and charming and *interested* in me. Gran had said that he hadn't realized what he was doing when he'd built his stupid café at the tower and that she forgave him, but it was hard for me to believe that. I'd told him what that place meant to me.

Hadn't I?

It didn't matter. Even if he was interested in me, he was interested in every woman he met. I'd seen pictures of him on the news with so many different women that I could no longer count. I was just one of a hundred.

"I'm glad you came," he said, when it was clear I wasn't going to answer his question.

I looked up at him, annoyed. "How can you be so decent now when you were such a dick when we were young?"

"Age has been good to me?"

"Whatever." I turned back to the stares of the people who were still gawking at us. He had a point that aging could really change a person, but I didn't want to think too hard on it.

Catrina, Tabitha, and Gran arrived at that moment. They veered around us and went over to join the other family members, and I gave Tabitha my best murder eyes for not coming to save me.

She just grinned back.

I nodded towards the cluster of spectators. "Who are yours?"

"Don't have any."

"Oh, so the competition's not that big a deal to you?" Of course it wouldn't be, and I didn't like the hint of bitterness in my voice.

"It is. I'd have brought someone if I had them to bring."

Huh. "Really?"

"Of course."

"What about all your girlfriends?"

"I only have one at a time, and I don't have one now."

"But you usually have one."

"True. But I wanted to be unencumbered when I came here."

This wasn't what I'd expected. Even if he didn't have a girlfriend at the moment, I would have expected him to have people who would want to see him compete. Family or friends or something. He was Callan Hawthorne, after all. And yet, when I looked at him, I could see that he was telling the truth. I tucked the information away for another time.

I looked towards the other competitors, who were now

gossiping together. Lilac worked for her family's import and export business, which focused on moving magical items around the world in a way that would make the most profit. There was no way they'd continue to sell all their ingredients to a local shop like Mr. Sparrow had. They'd want to optimize their money by sending the plants abroad. We wouldn't be able to match those prices, I was sure.

"Do you know who that guy is?" I nodded at the tall, pale man who stood next to Lilac.

"Terry O'Keene. He runs a chain of potion shops based in Portsmouth. They've expanded to four different cities in the last few years."

"And what about—"

Before I could ask him about the other man, the sound of trumpets filled the air. For the briefest moment, I felt like I was back in medieval times, about to watch some idiots in iron suits try not to fall off their horses as they attempted to poke each other with big sticks. But instead of knights, a slight old man danced out from the shadows between the trees, a big grin on his face. He wore a tweed suit accented with a brilliant blue scarf, along with red glasses. His white hair was wild around his face.

His obvious good nature and joy for life reminded me of my grandfather. They'd been friends, and Mr. Sparrow had always been kind to me. I'd liked him as a kid, but I liked him even more as an adult. Now, I could fully appreciate someone who danced to the beat of their own drummer. And with my grandfather lost, he was one of the last few connections to him that I had.

"Welcome, competitors!" Mr. Sparrow called. "I'm so

glad you could make it." His gaze scanned the crowd. "I see some familiar faces and some not so familiar faces, but I'm delighted that you all accepted my invitation."

Invitation? Gran hadn't mentioned an invitation. Had it specifically said my name?

"There will be three rounds to these competitions," he said. "The winner—chosen by me and me alone—will inherit my legacy." He spun in a circle as he gestured dramatically to the plants all around us. "There are over seven hundred species in this forest, and I need to know that the winner will take care of them as I would."

Seven hundred species. Just the idea of it made my head spin. Plants and potions had always been my favorite kinds of magic, and even a dud like me could appreciate what Mr. Sparrow had here.

"For the first competition, I think it's important we get to know each other a little. It's also vital that the winner be able to work with others. Much of this business is about connections and community, and we need someone who understands that."

I winced. Considering the fact that I'd ditched Charming Cove when I'd been eighteen, I wasn't starting out on great footing. There was a low murmur from the small crowd of competitors near us, and I glanced over.

Yep, they were looking at me.

I stuck my tongue out at them, because it was the mature thing to do and I always did the mature thing. The shock on Serena's face was enough to make the childish action worth it.

I turned back to Mr. Sparrow, catching his gaze on me.

Shit.

He didn't look mad, though. He looked almost...delighted?

At least I hadn't pissed him off. Maybe he was a weirdo like me.

Mr. Sparrow raised his hands as if to emphasize how important his next words would be. "The first competition will involve pairing you up and presenting you with a problem to solve."

Pairing us up?

I glanced between Mr. Sparrow and Callan, not liking the look in the old man's eyes.

"The first pairing will be Serena and Evan. Serena is our local apothecary, and Evan has come all the way from Bristol, leaving behind a charming shop on the magical high street that caters to all sorts of supernatural needs."

I felt the last little balloon of hope deflate inside of me. If Evan had his own shop, that meant that every person here had a plan for the garden that would leave us out in the cold. No one would continue our contract.

"The second pair will be Lilac and Terry, who are—" My head buzzed loudly as Mr. Sparrow introduced the other pair. I should be listening to get as much info as I could about the competition, but it was impossible.

There was only one other competitor left, which meant Mr. Sparrow had just paired Callan and me. I could feel the mage's gaze on me, and the warmth of it made heat rise into my cheeks. If I'd had any control of my magic, I would have poured ice water over myself right now.

"And finally, Callan and Aria, the last pair!" Mr. Sparrow's voice cut into my thoughts, and I looked up at him. He grinned with delight, and I swore I saw something spark in his eyes that looked a lot like mischievousness. He'd known me ever since I was a kid, and I knew he was aware of how I felt about Callan. And yet, it seemed like this was all part of some plan.

I scowled at him, but he ignored me and continued talking.

"Each pair will receive a riddle that is concealed inside an envelope."

Oh no. I was terrible at riddles—like, comedically terrible.

Mr. Sparrow waved his hand, and three skinny vines rose up from the ground. Each gripped an envelope at the terminus of the vine, and they snaked their way towards us. When one of the vines stopped in front of me, I reached down to take the envelope.

"This is your only clue to finding the plant that I require. There are no prizes for being first to find the plant, but to continue to the next round, you must bring it to me by sunset in three days' time." With a flourish, he bowed.

The other competitors started chatting as they opened their envelopes, and the entire ceremony was clearly over. I gripped the envelope and charged towards Mr. Sparrow.

He watched me approach, his eyes sparkling with interest.

I stopped in front of him. "You know exactly why I'm coming up to talk to you, don't you?"

"Aria! It's been too long, my dear. We've missed you here in Charming Cove. It's been empty without you."

"Well, I'm back now. And I'm begging you to give me a new partner."

He chuckled. "Not an ice cube's chance in hell, my girl."

"Why?"

"I know what I'm doing." He tapped the side of his nose. "It's all part of the plan, you see."

"What plan?" I didn't like the sound of this.

"Oh, it will become apparent to you eventually." He looked up at Callan. "You're lucky I partnered you with the most powerful witch here. Don't waste the opportunity."

Callan nodded, and I looked up to see a seriousness in his gaze that I hadn't expected. He almost looked like he agreed with Mr. Sparrow about my power. Except there was no reason for either of them to think I would be any good at magic.

"Now, I'm off to my bed. Good luck!" Mr. Sparrow spun on his heel and marched away through the garden, his steps spry for someone so close to retirement.

I looked up at Callan, finding his gaze on me.

"On one hand, I'm sorry we're paired together because I know you don't want it," he said. "On the other, I was hoping this would happen."

"Why?"

A smile tugged at the side of his mouth. "I want to win you over."

"Unlikely." I looked down at the envelope and peeled it open. An elegant script spelled out the riddle.

· · ·

I run on four feet but have no fur. My top is green, and gold are my sides. Into the waves I surge, what am I?

"Huh." I shook my head. "I freaking hate riddles."

"I have no idea what that means." He leaned over me to see the riddle, his scent wrapping around me like a warm embrace. I wanted to say it was unwelcome, but part of me liked it.

Idiot.

Gran, Tabitha, and Catrina approached.

"Well?" Gran asked. "What's the riddle?"

I read it out loud to them, but everyone appeared stumped. Catrina pulled on one of her pigtails, her brow furrowed. "I'm usually quite good at these, but I've got nothing."

Tabitha laughed. "Well, I'm usually terrible and I've also got nothing."

"Same." Gran shook her head. "We'll have to consult the books."

"Are you allowed to have help?" Callan asked.

"He didn't say we couldn't," I replied. "And this is supposed to be all about cooperation."

On the far side of the clearing, the other groups stood in pairs about five meters apart. They had their heads bowed over their papers, and from the scowls on their faces, I didn't think they were any further ahead than we were.

"It's getting late," I said. "Let's get out of here."

"We'll meet in the morning?" Callan asked.

"Sure." But I didn't give him any details. I wanted to get home and get into Gran's collection of books to see if she had anything that might help us. I looked at my three companions with a loaded expression. "Shall we?"

CHAPTER
NINE

ARIA

IT WOULD HAVE BEEN a good first night in my new house except that dreams of the riddle had plagued me. We'd found nothing in Gran's collection and had eventually called it a night around eleven.

The sun wasn't yet up when I woke to the ring of my alarm. Mr. Sparrow had said we didn't need to be first to bring him the plant, but we would probably need all the time we could get, especially since last night had been a bust.

I dragged myself from bed and combed a hand through my messy hair. For the good of my fellow citizens, I should probably shower. But I felt the driving urge to keep going on the hunt.

I pulled open a drawer to get a fresh change of clothes, and the contents wiggled.

I screamed and lunged backwards.

Boris popped up, a bra draped over his head.

"What the hell are you doing in there?" I screeched, still trying to catch my breath.

Sleeping.

I grabbed my bra. "You can't sleep in my clean clothes." I held up the bra to inspect it and saw a dozen badger hairs attached to it. "Ugh. I'm going to have to do laundry now."

Rude.

I arched a brow. "Really?"

He shrugged. *And stupid. Badger hairs are known to be good luck. I'm gifting you with a bevy of good fortune with those hairs.*

"Bollocks." I dropped the bra to the ground and went to the other drawer, pulling out an old sports bra. It wasn't ideal, but at least it wasn't furry.

Don't tell me you're not showering. Boris wrinkled his nose.

"What? I smell fine." I grabbed the deodorant off the dresser's surface and ran it under my arms a few times. "And I'll make sure to stay downwind of people."

Sure, that'll work. Boris rolled his eyes.

Or I thought he did. Could badgers even roll their eyes?

"Don't break anything while I'm gone. And get out of my clothing drawer. You can sleep on the couch."

I'll sleep in your bed.

I whirled on him, imagining all the loose badger fur that would end up in my bed. "If you do, I won't be bringing you back any snacks."

His brows rose. *Oh?*

"See, I know how to speak your language."

He inclined his head. *Respect.*

I chuckled and left the room. It was too early for even the

coffee shop to be open, and I had no food in the new place. Still, I needed to get started if I wanted to solve this before I had to start working with Callan. I couldn't get rid of him as a partner, but I could finish this before I had to spend much time with him.

Since searching Gran's collection of books had turned into a bust, the next best place would be the local library. I'd spent hundreds of hours there as a kid, befriending the librarian, Mrs. Keith. My crappy magic meant that hanging out with the other kids wasn't always a great option, especially in the early teen years. Kids were vicious at that age.

Mrs. Keith had shown me where she hid the key for the nights when I just wanted to get away but needed somewhere to go. Hopefully, she still kept the key in the same hiding spot, and I'd explain myself when she arrived at a more reasonable hour.

The library was located on the street behind the main road, tucked into a beautiful little garden. It wasn't a big space, considering the fact that all the books were magical, and there just weren't that many of those. But it was a haven.

The two-story stone building looked just like I recalled, with a red door and matching geraniums in the pots on either side. The large oak tree that sat in the front garden hadn't changed, and I found the key hidden in the tree trunk, concealed by a spell that made the hole in the wood look solid. All I had to do was say the magic word—*abracadabra*, because Mrs. Keith had a sense of humor—and stick my hand right through the illusion of bark.

When my fingers closed around the keyring, I grinned. "Thanks, Mrs. Keith."

Funny how one could be gone from home for so long but slip right back into old rhythms upon return.

The door opened without issue, and I stepped into the small space. The floor above had been removed, so the bookshelves traveled all the way up to the roof. Two ladders rolled along the shelves, one on either side of the fireplace. Plants with long, trailing vines hung from the ceiling, and squashy arm chairs cluttered around the fireplace.

Maurice, the black cat with a white mustache, looked up from his bed in front of the fire. He'd been around since I was a teenager, and I grinned at the sight of him.

"Maurice!"

He meowed and rose to greet me, strolling over with the grace of a much younger cat. One of the best parts of magic was keeping our pets alive for longer, and I wasn't surprised that Mrs. Keith had used that magic on Maurice. We'd used it on Merlin, of course, and Mrs. Keith doted on her cat as much as we loved ours. Even the fire burned for him when she was away, though I was sure she'd put a safety spell on it.

Maurice rubbed himself against my legs, and I leaned down to give him a little scratch as I spoke aloud to the library. "I'm looking for any books about ancient riddles or plants. I'll be in the chair to the right of the fire."

Magic flared around me, tiny silver sparkles that swept through the air as they traveled from shelf to shelf, working to fulfill my request.

Maurice followed me to the chair, and I sank into it as the books piled themselves on the table at my side. Within seconds, I was lost within the pages, searching for the answers.

Mrs. Keith arrived a few hours later, a delighted little shout escaping her when she saw me. "Aria! I heard you were back."

I looked up, blinking my way out of my trance, then grinned.

She hurried towards me and gave me a big hug, and then the phone began ringing. "I'd better go take that, but let me know if you need any help. I'm so pleased you're back."

"Thanks, Mrs. Keith."

She bustled off, and I turned my attention back to my book. A few minutes later, I heard the bell over the door jingle when it opened, but I didn't look up.

"I see someone got an early start." Callan's voice dragged me from the book, and I looked up to see him holding a tray with two coffees and a paper bag that smelled like Margot's buttery, flaky perfection.

"How did you find me?" I reached for a coffee, and he handed it to me.

Callan might not be my favorite person, but I had no pride when it came to coffee. I'd take it from anyone.

"I stopped by your gran's place, since I figured you would go there to start. She said I'd find you here."

"Traitor," I muttered, then took a sip of the delightful concoction of coffee and milk.

"We are supposed to work *together*, you know." He sat next to me and picked up a book.

"About that..."

He looked up at me.

"I was thinking we could work apart, but towards the same goal."

"So, not working together?"

"We'd be even more efficient!" I reached for the bag and pulled out a Danish pastry. I saw that it was my favorite kind —apple cinnamon with pecans. "Did you ask Margot which ones I liked?"

He nodded.

I scowled, then bit into it. Why did the man have to be so thoughtful? I was trying to hate him, damn it.

"He'll know if we don't work together," Callan said. "And the point of this round is cooperation."

"Fine." I couldn't argue with that. "You can start with these." I picked up a pile of books and handed them to him.

He took them and started to flip through. I turned my attention back to the book, careful to keep my coffee and crumbs away from it. Time flew by as we worked, but every now and again, I felt his gaze on me. Why had he taken the chair *right* next to me? There was no ignoring him when he was this close, and I couldn't help but occasionally steal glances at him.

At one point, when his head was tipped down to look at the page in front of him, I remembered the exact moment I'd shown him the ancient carving of the ship on the tower wall. The awe on his face had hit me like an arrow then. We'd had something in common—a weird and wonderful shared love of old graffiti—and it had felt like a deep and true bond despite the fact that it was something small.

It was crazy that I could feel something so strong so fast, but there was just something about his energy that was *good*. Like, bone-deep good. And I liked it—a lot. It was one of the reasons I'd been so angry with him when he'd built at the tower. I'd thought he couldn't possibly do something like that to me.

We hadn't even known each other, and I'd built a fantasy around what kind of guy he was.

Idiot.

I shook the memory away and kept working.

By the time noon rolled around, neither of us had found anything. I set my book aside. "I'm starting to think the answer isn't going to be in a book."

"Good, because I'm starving."

"Did I hear someone say starving?" My gran's voice sounded from the doorway, which had been propped open to take advantage of the fine summer weather.

I looked towards her and smiled. "Hi, Gran."

"Come on, I have food almost ready at the house. Tabitha and Catrina will be there, too." She looked at Callan. "You, too, young man."

He rose, and as much as I wanted to scowl at my grandmother, I knew it would be childish. She'd forgiven him, and it wasn't in her nature to not invite someone over when they were standing right there during an invitation.

"We're done here," I told the library. "Thank you."

Magic flickered in the air, and the silver sparkles picked up the books and carried them to their places on the shelves. Maurice yawned and stretched, and I gave him a farewell scratch. Mrs. Keith appeared from the back room, a cup of tea in her hand. "Leaving already?" she asked.

I nodded. "I'll be back, though." Maybe not for this question, but for another, I was sure.

Gran, Callan, and I headed to her house for lunch. The

kitchen on the first floor was cheery and bright, with the windows overlooking the sea and the glass open to let in the breeze. Tabitha was already there, taking a tray of sandwiches out of the refrigerator.

"Will someone get Catrina? I think she's in the living room," Tabitha said.

"I'll do it." Anything to get some space.

I left the kitchen and went to the back, finding Catrina building a tower out of slender blocks that looked like they were made of ice. "Is that real ice?" I asked.

She nodded, her concentration fierce. "The trick is to use my magic to keep it from melting while I build."

I blew out a breath. "You're one strong witch, kid."

"Thanks, I know." She smiled up at me. "Lunch?"

"Yep. Come on." I reached down for her hand and pulled her up. "Say, since you're such a good witch and you have a talent for tails, what do you say you give our lunch guest a nice furry tail?" I definitely wouldn't be attracted to him if she could do that.

She laughed. "I'll see what I can do."

"Thanks." I gave her a quick side hug, and we went to the lunch table. Gran, Tabitha, and Callan had already sat, leaving two chairs open. Catrina raced to the one next to Gran, leaving me between Tabitha and Callan. Of course.

I sat next to him and helped myself to some sandwiches and lemonade. "This looks amazing, Gran. Thank you."

"Just a little something." She pushed a salad bowl at me. "Here, try this. It's got artichokes."

"Slime hearts." Catrina grinned.

"That's what you call artichokes?"

LINSEY HALL

"If it gets her to eat them, then yes," Tabitha muttered to me.

I grinned and took some salad, then passed it to Callan, who still didn't have any on his plate.

"Thank you." There was the strangest look on his face.

"You okay?" I asked. "If you don't feel well, you can lie down in the living room."

His gaze flicked up to mine. "What? Why would you think that?"

"Oh, you just look a little...weird."

"Yeah, like you've never had lunch with a family before," Catrina said.

"I, ah...haven't." He looked between all of us, seeming to realize he'd just said something that was possibly a bit revealing.

"I knew I was right," Catrina said. "Why not?"

"I didn't have a family like this when I was a kid. And now I'm an adult, so I mostly eat alone."

"That's sad." Catrina frowned.

"It's all right." He grinned, and it really did look like it was okay. That, or he was a good actor. He looked at my gran. "This is a wonderful lunch, Cici. Thank you so much for having me."

The sincerity in his voice made Gran blush, and she waved a hand at him in that kind of floppy-wrist wave that women did when they said things like, "Oh, stop, you charmer!"

Gran stopped just short of that, though.

I watched him as I chewed on my sandwich. The beginning of this lunch had thrown him for a loop, and I didn't like

100

the fluttery weirdness it made me feel. I didn't want him to like my family so much, though. It made him even more a part of my life.

Catrina broke my train of thought when she muttered a few words and grinned at Callan. I looked towards him, wondering if I would see a giant peacock tail behind him.

Instead, his jumper had turned a brilliant pink.

Catrina giggled at him.

Callan looked down, surprise on his face morphing into a stifled laugh. He looked up to meet Catrina's gaze. "Was this you?"

She nodded. "I thought you would look good in it."

He grinned. "I think I probably do."

The worst part was, he *did*. Somehow, the hot pink made his eyes look more blue and his hair more black. And his confidence and good humor just added to his appeal.

"Maybe you should redo my entire wardrobe," he said.

"I'll consider it," Catrina said. "For a price."

"You'd better make it high. With talent like yours, you shouldn't be undercharging."

She beamed, and I couldn't help but like him. Damn it. He wasn't supposed to be likable.

"What about the tail?" I whispered at Catrina.

She grinned. "Only the worst of the worst deserve tails."

Callan's laugh broke through our whispers. "You tried to get her to give me a tail?"

I looked at him and shrugged. "I wouldn't have had to ask if my magic were any good. I'd have done it myself."

He looked at Catrina. "I hope you would have given me

something dignified. Like a stallion's tail. None of the curly pig tail malarky."

Catrina gasped in mock horror. "I would never."

"Thank you." He nodded solemnly to her. "I'm glad you agree I'm worthy of a stallion tail."

I looked between him and Catrina. Dang it, he was charming. And he fit in so well with my weird little family—a family that I was just getting back to.

"Have you always been such a talented witch?" he asked.

"Yes." She grinned. "Speaking of! I just remembered I have an answer to your riddle, though I have no idea what a lizard has to do with plants."

"A lizard?"

"Lizards have four feet but no fur. Green tops and gold sides. And they swim. There's a tropical variety in the Pacific just like that. We learned about it in school."

I frowned and leaned back. It could be a lizard, but she was right. I had no idea what a tropical lizard had to do with plants. Unless...

"What if the riddle means the place and not an actual lizard?" I asked.

"Ah." Understanding lit Callan's eyes. "The plant must be native to the Lizard."

The Lizard was the most southerly part of the British mainland, a peninsula with grassy tops and golden beaches that stretched out into the waves.

"I know a local witch there," Gran said. "She might be able to help you determine which plants are special."

"Thank you, Gran." I looked at Callan. "It's about a two-hour drive from here. If we get started soon, we'll be there before dark."

He nodded. "I'll get my car. You pack a bag. We'll probably be there overnight." He looked at Catrina. "Good job, young witch. You're going to be very impressive when you're older."

"I already am very impressive."

"True. My apologies." He stood and bowed sightly to her. "Thank you for the makeover." He looked at Gran. "And thank you for the wonderful lunch."

He strode from the room, all casual confidence.

Tabitha whistled low. "If he didn't look at you like the sun rises and sets on you, I'd be all over that."

"What?" Catrina asked.

"Nothing, dear. Let's walk Aria home so she can pack." She looked at my gran, who was already using her power to float the dishes to the sink. "Thank you for lunch, Gran."

Gran nodded and smiled, then looked at me. "Let me write down my friend's address for you, my dear. And I'll ring Matilda so she knows to expect you."

"Thanks, Gran."

As the three of us walked down the path towards our houses, Catrina turned to me and said. "I like him."

"Yeah, he's a pretty good one, I suppose."

"Then why don't *you* like him?"

"Long story, kid. But thanks for the pink sweater."

She winked. "Next time, bring me a really bad one, and I'll give him a tail. But not Callan. He's too decent."

She was right, and I had a hard time reconciling the

current him with the younger one who had destroyed the place I loved most.

Catrina skipped off to chase the butterflies down the path. When she was far enough away, Tabitha leaned in and said, "He was looking at you like he wanted to eat you. Seriously."

"I didn't see that."

"No, he's too clever to let you see. But he does want you."

"Nah." And if he did, that was just who he was. A ladies man. I didn't want to be one in a long line of girls who fell for his looks and charms.

"Yeah. And you're going to see it soon enough. The question is...what are you going to do about it?"

"Nothing."

"Really?"

"Really. Although I do wish that Catrina had given him a tail. It would have made ignoring him much easier."

Tabitha laughed and looped her arm through mine.

CHAPTER
TEN

Callan

THIRTY MINUTES LATER, I drove up to the charming white cottage where Aria lived. It was postcard perfect, with the sea sparkling blue behind it and green grass bright in the sun.

It suited her perfectly. How long had she lived here? Had she grown up here?

My interest in her was too keen. I was never this interested in anyone, and it felt strange.

I pulled into the drive, parking the car as she ran out of the house. She set her bag on the ground and turned back to shut the door, calling over her shoulder, "I'll be right there!"

A furry little body waddled out of the house behind her, short and plump. A badger?

I climbed out of the car to collect her bag, hearing the low tones of her voice as she spoke to the animal. When I reached her, the badger was chattering back, though I couldn't understand what it was saying.

Aria was rolling her eyes, though.

I didn't interrupt their conversation, just leaned down to pick up the bag.

"You don't need to do that," she said.

"I don't mind." I headed back to the car, letting her finish with the badger.

After putting her bag in the boot, I climbed into the driver's seat. She climbed in a moment later, her hair still damp from a shower. The scent of her washed over me, making something tighten deep within. She looked beautiful, her cheeks still pink and her eyes bright.

She started to shut the door, but the furry little badger scampered up into the car and clambered over her lap, heading to the back seat.

"I said you had to stay home, Boris."

The badger gave a bored hiss and curled up. I looked back at him, but he'd already closed his eyes. Clearly, I didn't merit a greeting. Fair enough.

I turned to Aria. "We have company?"

"Looks like it." She leaned against the headrest. "That creature will be the death of me."

"He's your familiar?"

"Apparently." She shrugged. "Just met him a few days ago, though he'd been keeping an eye on me for a few months at the request of my gran."

"Sounds like a good familiar." I pulled the car away from her house.

Behind me, the badger made an approving noise.

"He likes you," she said. "Good luck."

A small laugh escaped me. "Good luck?"

"He's a handful. I hope you have a lot of snacks."

"Why?"

"To keep him calm."

Fantastic. An overly excitable badger was in my back seat. This couldn't possibly go wrong.

I looked over at her, unable to stop myself from stealing a glance. She'd grown more beautiful in the years since I'd met her, and it was impossible not to peek.

"Eyes on the road, mister."

"Right." I looked forward. I should be embarrassed, but I wasn't.

As we approached the main road, she handed over a slip of paper. "This is the address Gran gave me."

At the stop, I typed the address into the satnav, which gave us an estimated arrival around six p.m.

The countryside was beautiful out this way, all rolling green hills and clusters of trees. Quaint little houses filled tiny towns, and stone bridges crossed over rivers. Eventually, though, the beauty of the scenery wasn't enough to keep me distracted from the question that had been on my mind since lunch. "You said your magic wasn't any good. What did you mean?"

She shot me a glance out of the corner of her eye. "I don't really feel like sharing, to be honest."

"I just find it hard to believe that your magic might not be any good. Not just because a familiar chose you—which they only do with the strongest witches, by the way—but because power vibrates around you."

She frowned at me. "Really?"

I nodded. "I feel it. Don't you?"

She shrugged. "I feel like I always feel."

From the tone of her voice, I tried to guess what she meant. "Which is not powerful?"

"Not magically, at least. And that's the end of twenty questions."

I didn't want it to be the end. I wanted to know more about her—*everything* about her. "What if I answer one of your questions in return?"

"Sure, that would work. If I were actually curious about you."

I could feel her stare on the side of my face. "Really? You're not even a little curious?"

"Nope." I could hear the smile in her voice.

"It's a long ride. And it's boring."

"It's beautiful." She gestured to the field of wildflowers to our right.

"I'll play terrible music."

"Like what?"

"Something with a saxophone."

"Ugh, you wouldn't." It was one of the things I remembered about her—though who was I fooling? I remembered everything she'd said the day that we'd met. One of the old inscriptions carved into the fortress wall had looked like a saxophone, though it couldn't have been, given its age. But she'd confessed to hating the saxophone with the fire of a thousand suns.

"Oh, I would be delighted to play non-stop saxophone for hours. I have no problem with the instrument."

She groaned. "Fine. You want to know about my magic?"

"I do."

"It sucks, that's what. Ever since I was a kid, all I can do is make things blow up."

"Do you know why?"

"Not a clue."

I still found it hard to believe. Maybe something had happened to her. Because there was power all around her. She lit up the air with it. True, I had a particular skill for sensing this kind of thing, but anyone should have been able to feel it.

"Okay, time for my question." She turned her body fully to look at me. I wanted to meet her gaze, but I couldn't take my gaze off the road. "You seem like a decent guy. How could you have built at the tower like that when I asked you not to?"

A heaviness settled over me. I should have expected this question, and it was important we have the conversation. "For one thing, I didn't realize you were serious. The way I was raised..."

Hell, this was harder than I'd expected to talk about.

"What about the way you were raised?" she prodded.

The words felt stuck in my throat. But she'd shared with me, so it was only fair.

"My mother died before I could know her. Car crash. That left just me and my dad, and he was"—I searched for a word that was accurate but not overly cruel—"a cold man. The only things he valued were business and growth, and I grew up trying to impress him. When I was younger, all I wanted was for him to notice me."

Once I started talking, the words spilled out of me. I'd never said these things aloud. Hell, I'd never really even thought them. They'd drifted around in my subconscious, but I'd never lingered on them. I'd been afraid of what I might find.

It wasn't great, apparently.

"That sucks," she said. "But it's still not a great reason for why you laughed when I begged you not to build."

"I'm sorry about that, I truly am." I pulled the car over to the side of the road so that I could look at her. This was important, and it deserved my full attention. "The laugh was not one of humor or derision. It was surprise, I promise. I came from a world where nothing stops progress, and I was shocked. That's all."

She sighed, her gaze searching mine.

My heart thundered in my chest as I waited to hear what she would say. I didn't have much more than a sincere apology in my arsenal. True, I could try to charm her, and I would. But this was the important stuff, and only the truth would fix things.

"I believe you," she said. "I do remember that it wasn't much of a laugh, and certainly not malicious. But anything at all was so painful, considering what that place meant to me."

"What *did* it mean to you? It was more than just a beautiful place full of ancient carvings in the stones, wasn't it?"

"I told you what it meant." She glared. "That's why I was so upset when you laughed."

"Actually, you didn't tell me."

"I...didn't? Really?"

"No. You yelled about it being special and ancient and

that it was the most important place in the world, but you didn't say why, exactly. And then you stormed off."

"Huh." She slumped back against the door of the car. "Really?"

"Really. I remember it like it was yesterday."

"So do I, except I was so angry and hurt that it's kind of a haze. I just remember the feelings."

That wasn't great for me, since they were resoundingly bad feelings.

She gave a weary laugh and tilted her head back against the window, closing her eyes. "I really should have stuck around to finish the conversation, huh? Would you have changed things if I hadn't stormed off?"

"Maybe? I have no idea. It was so long ago, and I was a different person. I want to think I would have, but I don't know." I paused a moment, trying to get a read on her. I wanted more information, but didn't know if now was the time to push for it. I decided to go for it. I wanted to know everything about her and couldn't wait a moment longer. "What *did* that place mean to you?"

She tilted her head to the right to look out the windscreen. "My parents died when I was young. I was raised by my grandparents. You've met Gran, but Grandad died when I was sixteen. He used to take me to the tower, and when he died, his spirit would appear there."

Oh, shit.

I'd done something *really* bad.

Dread uncoiled in me as I spoke. "And the construction around the tower would mean he wouldn't reappear. It would be too busy."

"Exactly."

I'd taken her grandad's spirit from her. Guilt yawned wide inside me. "I am so sorry, Aria."

"Yeah." She nodded, then looked back at me. "Thanks. I guess."

She didn't sound particularly enthusiastic, and I couldn't blame her. What I'd done, unwittingly or not, had been terrible for her.

She shook her head and brushed her fingertips over her cheeks. "It's done. And for what it's worth, I believe you didn't mean to do it. And that things might have been different if I'd handled it better. I was just...a bit of a mess back then. With my wonky magic and the fights at school, I was always at the boiling point. My temper would get the better of me sometimes, and that's what happened with you. If I'd kept control and explained more fully without getting so worked up, maybe things would have been different."

"Don't." My voice was sharper than I wanted it to be, and her head swung towards me. "Don't blame yourself. It was my fault. I started construction so quickly that you didn't have time to come to your senses and return to talk."

"That's true." She gave a weary laugh. "We were both hotheads moving too fast."

"I really am sorry."

"I know." She looked back towards the road. "What happened to your father? I've never seen him mentioned in the papers, and you're different than you were back then. Because he's gone?"

"Maybe. And yes, he is gone. He died shortly after we

met, and eventually, I realized I was barking up a tree that had no cat in it."

"What do you mean?"

I wanted him to love me. Nope. I couldn't say that. Not out loud. "I wanted to prove myself to him. In those first few years after his death, I was in a frenzy to prove that I could be what he wanted me to be. But eventually, I realized that if he was going to be proud of me, he would have told me so before he died. I couldn't prove anything to someone who was dead."

"Shit, that's sad."

I laughed, a slightly bitter sound. "It is, isn't it?"

She nodded.

"That mentality hurt more than just me—it hurt you, too. I can't help but wonder who else I hurt along the way."

"Is that why you gave away so much of your money? To make amends for all the aggressive businessmanning you've done over the years?"

I smiled. "Businessmanning?"

She grinned back at me. "It's a perfectly acceptable verb. Just go with it."

"Maybe that's why. But also because I agree with you. No single person should be in possession of that much wealth when the rest of the world suffers so much." I looked around at the car, which was arguably far nicer than it needed to be. "I should probably give away more."

She shrugged. "I don't think you need to live like a monk. But I respect the attitude."

"Thank you." I laughed. "And good, because I've grown used to the convenience of money."

"Can't say that I blame you." She looked towards the road. "It's getting late. Should we go?"

I nodded and turned on the car. As we drove towards the Lizard, I couldn't help but think that things might actually be getting a little better between us.

CHAPTER
ELEVEN

ARIA

WE ARRIVED at the Lizard around seven, slightly delayed due to our conversation on the side of the road. Things felt better, though. I was still angry with him—it would take time for that to fade fully. But I was more angry with myself.

I suspected that my subconscious had known I'd had something to do with everything that had gone wrong back then, and it had been one of the reasons I'd run away to London. I'd wanted to run away from my own mistakes as much as I'd wanted a fresh start away from the kids who had called me a dud all my life.

About a mile from the Lizard, Callan pulled the car onto a lane that was overgrown with brambles and branches. The early evening sun gleamed warm gold on roses that grew wild along either side of the rustic road. Callan slowed as we bumped our way down the lane towards the house at the end.

He stopped the car in front of it, and I could do nothing but stare. It was a ramshackle old Victorian with beautiful trim that looked like icing on a cake. Chipped paint in shades of pale blue and green gave it a fairytale feeling, and the many windows glittered in the sunlight. Baskets full of plants hung from the wrap-around porch, spilling colorful blossoms towards the railing. And yet...

"That is *definitely* haunted," he said.

"You took the words right out of my mouth."

Despite the pretty trappings of the house, there was a darkness to it that was impossible to miss. In one of the upper windows, I caught sight of a ghostly white figure peering out. It disappeared almost as soon as I saw it.

I pulled the phone from my pocket and dialed Gran.

She picked up on the second ring, and I demanded, "What the heck is this place, Gran?"

A laugh sounded in her voice as she answered. "It sounds like you've arrived. Interesting, isn't it?"

"That's one word for it. How many ghosts live there?" Gran knew I hated ghosts. They were different than spirits. Not always scary or mean, but more likely to be. And most importantly, they could impact the mortal world.

"Maybe a dozen? Matilda will have the final count."

"I can't believe you sent us to a ghost house."

"Haunted house, dear." She tutted. "And it's the only place to get your answers. You'll be fine, though. Matilda is a very powerful witch. And you're with Callan. He'll protect you."

I shot him a glance to see if he'd heard, and he nodded. I grimaced, wanting to sink into the seat. More than that, I wanted to be able to protect *myself*.

I couldn't, though, because of my crappy magic. It was another reason I hated ghosts. Most witches had no trouble with them. I was an exception, of course, being unable to banish them.

A figure appeared on the porch and waved. Her pink tracksuit matched her lipstick, which looked great with her brilliant white hair.

"Okay, Gran, I've got to go," I said. "Matilda just walked outside."

"Have a nice time, dear. And good luck!"

"Good luck finding answers, or staying alive?"

"Answers, silly."

"Sure, sure." I hung up and looked at Callan, resignation filling me. "We might as well get a move on."

We climbed out of the car, and he beat me to the bags in the boot, swinging them over his shoulder with an easy grace. Boris, who had slept through the entire car ride, stirred from the back seat. His head popped up in the window as he took in the house. Through the glass, I could see his little eyes widen. Then he just shook his head and sank back down, curling up on the seat again.

"Even Boris thinks the place is too scary to go in," I whispered to Callan.

"Your grandmother is right. I'll protect you. Although I'm pretty sure you can protect yourself."

"I can." Most of the time. And I liked that he thought that way. Except when it came to ghosts, maybe I didn't need to be *quite* so independent. I wouldn't mind a little backup if any of the creepers got into my room tonight.

"Welcome!" Matilda shouted as we neared the porch. She waved us inside. "I'm so pleased to have you. Your gran told me all about you."

"I hope it was all good," I said.

She laughed. "Of course. Dinner is almost finished. Once I serve, we can start talking about this plant problem of yours."

"Thank you." I held out my hand to shake hers. "Aria, so we can meet officially.'

She smiled and shook my hand, then looked at Callan, her blue eyes glinting with delight. "Well, aren't you something?"

He smiled and stuck his hand out. "Callan Hawthorne. Nice to meet you."

"Oh, you charmer." She batted her hand at him, then spun and waved for us to follow her. "Come along, now!"

She led us through a cluttered old house that was so clean, it sparkled. She might have a lot of things—antiques, mostly—but she took care of the place.

"I've lived here all my life," she said over her shoulder, as if she could read my thoughts. "It's a lovely home."

"Haunted?" I asked as she led us into an ornate old dining room.

"Oh, definitely. Mostly nice ghosts, though."

"Mostly?" That wasn't what I'd been hoping to hear.

"Just avoid Ralph. He's a miserable old bugger."

"Ralph. Got it." I needed a drink.

She gestured to the long table that had been laid with

three place settings. A candelabra flickered in the middle of the table, and I felt like I was in some kind of play about the nineteenth century.

"Take a seat, and I'll bring out the meal." She bustled away to what I assumed was the kitchen, and I sat.

Callan put our bags in the corner, then took the seat across from me. There was no wine on the table, unfortunately. When Matilda returned from the kitchen, she carried a teapot that wafted a sour smelling steam.

"I've got my special brew right here." She smiled. "It's a tea that will polish your auras."

Oh, crap. That stuff was gross. Gran had tried to give it to me once, and I'd barely been able to choke it down.

"That sounds wonderful," Callan said.

I looked at him. Couldn't he smell it?

From the look on his face, everything was going perfectly. Well, we did need her help, so it wasn't like we could be rude. Not to mention she was being kind enough to put me up, and I was broke.

I picked up my teacup and held it out, smiling as she filled it. I was going to choke this stuff down if it killed me.

She poured Callan's cup, then her own.

"Cheers." She raised her glass.

"Cheers." I mimicked her movements, then raise the cup to my mouth. The scent was enough to turn my stomach, and I fought the instinct to gag.

I can do this.

I put the teacup to my lips, wondering what was really so bad about an unpolished aura.

The first sip of the vile concoction had touched my lips

when Matilda laughed lightly. "Okay, you can stop! You passed."

Surprised, I looked up at her over the rim of my teacup. "Wait, what?"

"The tea was a test, darling. No one likes this stuff. But if you were polite enough to try to drink it, then you're worthy of my help."

That was some weird, old-school Miss Manners shit, but I just smiled and set the cup down. "Oh, thank goodness. I'm not a huge fan of that tea, to be honest."

Callan had already drunk some of his and was looking a bit green around the gills, but Matilda seemed pleased. "Your aura does look a bit brighter, Callan."

"Thank you." He smiled, and though he still looked green, good humor glinted in his eyes.

Matilda stood and went to the kitchen. Before she disappeared through the door, she called out, "Who wants a whisky?"

"I do," Callan and I said at the same time.

"Please," we added in unison.

I glared at him.

"Don't worry, there's probably plenty to go around," he said.

I rolled my eyes. That hadn't been why I'd been glaring, but I wasn't going to explain.

A few minutes later, Matilda returned with a tray full of decanters. She poured us each our beverage of choice— scotch for Callan and bourbon for me—and quizzed us about our lives and how we knew each other.

We managed to keep it civil, and I had the conversation

in the car to thank for that. Once she'd decided that she knew us well enough, she brought out an old-fashioned roast—chicken, veg, mash, and even Yorkshire puddings.

The scent was enough to make me salivate. Boris would love this.

The sound of scratching drew my attention from the delicious-looking feast to the window, where Boris stood with his paws on the glass, his gaze on the food.

Matilda followed my gaze and grinned. "Are we expecting a third for dinner?"

"I thought he wanted to stay in the car, but it seems his sense of smell is as impressive as his ability to shed a ton of badger fur."

"Oh, that's all right. A little badger fur is good luck." She rose and went to the window, opening it with a little grunt.

Boris tumbled through, then waddled to the table and hopped up into the chair next to me.

"Say thank you," I whispered.

He looked at Matilda and gave her the sweetest little face I'd ever seen. I didn't even know he could look that cute.

"Well, isn't he the communicator!" Matilda said as she filled a plate and then handed it to him.

The joy on his face made me grin.

Matilda filled her own plate, and then Callan and I followed. The meal was beyond delicious, so good that I wondered if it was enchanted.

"It's not," Matilda said.

"Can you read minds?"

"Just a bit."

"That must be difficult," Callan said. "I'm not sure I'd want to know what everyone is thinking."

"You're not wrong there. I can't say I love it, but I've learned to use it." She looked at me. "So, you're here about some plants."

"Yes. We're looking for something that is specific to the Lizard and very useful in potion making." Considering how close the Lizard was to Charming Cove, there had to be a reason that Mr. Sparrow hadn't collected the plant himself sometime in the past. "It's probably dangerous to get to."

"Hmmm." She leaned back in her chair and pursed her lips as she thought." "There are three options. Lion's Mane, Xyanthia, and Spotted Fiorella. None are particularly easy to find."

"Three isn't so many, though. We'll bring them all back if we can find them."

She looked doubtful. "When do you need to be back by?"

"Sunset, the day after tomorrow."

"I doubt you can get them all in time."

Damn. So we definitely needed to know which one.

"Can you describe them to us?" Callan asked. "That might help us narrow it down."

"I don't know much about them, to be honest. I just know their names because they cost a fortune at the local apothecary."

Hmmm. Not great.

"Would the apothecary know more?"

"Mavis?" She laughed. "She's away with the fairies most of the time, so no. But I'll do some asking around and see who might be able to help you." She poured herself another whisky and took a sip. "Who would like pudding?"

Boris raised a paw.

WHEN DINNER WAS OVER, Matilda led us to the second floor. The stairs creaked eerily on our way up, and even though the house was still impeccably clean, the air seemed to turn slightly thicker, as if there were a presence floating all around us.

She must have caught me looking a bit weird because she asked, "Are you all right, dear?"

"Just fine. You have a lovely home."

"Thank you. And don't worry about the ghosts. Only Reginald is a real problem."

One *real problem* was enough for me, but all I said was, "Oh, good."

"Here you are!" She stopped at two adjacent doors. Inside the rooms, I could see queen-sized beds and ornate old furniture in front of fireplaces that shared a chimney. "The fireplaces go right through to each other, so you can chat if you like. But otherwise, you'll have your privacy."

Chat though the fireplace? I leaned in further to see what she was talking about, and she was right! I could see right through to the other room, but my view was restricted to only a few feet above the floor.

"You're sure you don't want to share?" Matilda asked, wiggling her eyebrows in a way that was hilarious rather than creepy.

"Um, we're good," I said.

"All right, then. Sleep tight!" She turned and disappeared down the hall to her room on the first floor. I looked between the two bedrooms, trying to decide which one was the least haunted looking. Boris had departed after pudding—sticky toffee, which he had informed me was his favorite—and I assumed he was sleeping off his food coma in the car.

Since I couldn't tell which room was less scary, I chose the one on the right. "See you in the morning."

"Good night." Callan handed me my bag.

I took it and disappeared inside my room. As soon as I shut the door, the shadows seemed to stretch longer across the floor. The room was as spotless as the rest of the house, with pretty old furniture and a floral duvet that looked freshly laundered. The fireplace was laid with logs, and two armchairs sat in front of it.

Had this been the window in which I'd seen the ghost earlier? Shit. I should have paid more attention.

Maybe a fire would make the place more cheerful. At the minimum, it might cut out the noise of Callan getting dressed for bed. Through the open fireplace, I could hear the sound of clothes rustling. My imagination took flight, and it was impossible not to speculate on what lay beneath his perfectly fitted shirts.

Something glorious, I was pretty sure.

All right, that's enough, weirdo.

Time to light a fire and get some distraction.

I took the little bottle of matches off the mantle and struck one, then leaned down to light the kindling beneath the wood. I made a point not to look through in case I saw more of Callan than he wanted to show me.

The fire burst to life, crackling merrily as the kindling lit with a bright orange glow.

Immediately, a shadowy face appeared in the flames. The eye sockets were hollow, and the mouth gaped as it gave a silent scream.

I tumbled back on my butt, panting. The face disappeared, but the memory lingered.

Shit, had that been Reginald? It had looked like a man.

Maybe I should join Boris.

But it would be unforgivably rude if Matilda found out, and we might still need her help. Not that I'd want to be rude to such a nice person under any circumstances, but the fact that we needed her made me even keener to stay on her good side.

"It'll be fine," I muttered as I pulled out an old T-shirt and fresh underwear. I changed into them, then scrambled under the covers.

The bed was a heavenly nest of softness, and the fresh scent of the duvet was enough to calm my jangling nerves. I couldn't keep my gaze off the flickering fire, however, and my heart thundered as I waited for the skull to come back.

It didn't, but another figure did.

The ghost appeared to be that of a man in a ragged suit. He had the pinched face of a school headmaster, and the energy that cracked around him was distinctly dark.

"Oooh, no." I scrambled back against the headboard.

"Oh, yes." He grinned and floated towards me. Confusion

flickered across his face as he stopped by the bed. "Why haven't you banished me yet?"

"Um." *Because I can't?*

I didn't want to tell him that, though. He looked like the kind of ghost who might bite. That was a little-known fact about ghosts—they were biters. I'd found out the hard way.

"I don't feel like bothering," I said.

"Oh?" He arched a brow. "Scared of me, are you?"

"No. Bored."

His brows lowered, and his lips pulled back into a snarl.

Okay, this was definitely Reginald, and maybe that had been the wrong thing to say.

"I mean—" I fumbled for something to say that would keep the ghost from attacking. "Maybe I just want to talk."

"Talk?" He frowned, clearly confused. "I don't want to talk."

"Really? You're sure there's nothing on your mind?"

"Just the fact that you might be tasty."

Crap. He really was a biter. I scrambled upright to stand on the bed, heart thundering.

He lunged forward, hands curled into claws as he reached for me. Panic made me reach inside and gather up whatever magic I had. It resisted at first, then exploded out of me in a blast. The ghost flew straight through the wall and into the other room, leaving black scorch marks on the wall where he'd disappeared.

Crap.

Ghosts could go through walls without damaging them, but they had to *want* to go through. Reginald had been unwilling, and I now had left an unsightly ghost stain to explain to Matilda.

Damn it.

An angry wail sounded from the other room, and I sat bolt upright in the bed.

Shit, he was mad.

His transparent form appeared in the middle of the black mark on the wall, his face twisted into a scowl.

I reached for my magic, terrified of what my power might do if I tried it again. Could I blow over Matilda's whole house?

Maybe.

Nah.

But maybe?

Was it worth the risk?

Matilda had lived here since she was a kid. Damn it, I couldn't risk damaging it.

A knock sounded at the door.

"Come in," I squeaked. "Come in, come in, come in!"

Callan appeared in the doorway, and relief rushed through me, embarrassing in its strength. He looked at the ghost, then waved a hand and muttered a banishment spell. The ghost disappeared, and I sagged back against the bed.

"Thank you." Now that the ghost was gone, I realized how Callan was dressed. Or how he *wasn't* dressed, rather. He wore only a pair of shorts, and they weren't that much bigger than boxers. The fabric molded around his thighs, and I couldn't believe how thick they were. The muscles were clearly defined, even though he was just standing there and not even flexing.

"Do you climb mountains for a living?" I blurted.

"What?"

Oooh, shit. I'd really just said that. What the heck was up with my mouth around him? He made me feel safe, that was for sure, but that was no excuse for just blurting out whatever was on my mind.

"Do you fight ghosts for the living? Like, on behalf of living people," I babbled, trying to cover up my gaffe. "I just wondered how you got so good at it. I thought maybe you did it on the side, in addition to the work you do with your company." Holy crap, I was really going to town with this babbling.

He gave me a puzzled look, as if he thought I might be having a little stroke or something. Finally, he said, "Um, no."

He definitely wasn't buying the bull I was trying to sell him, but whatever. I'd done my best.

Unfortunately, I'd just caught sight of his chest. I'd been so distracted by his thighs that I'd missed that absolute work of art that was his upper body. It was all hard muscles and broad planes. The forearms that I'd been obsessed with in the pub had only been a hint of it. He really *had* stolen his body from Michelangelo's *David*.

I didn't know how long I'd been staring at him, and it was definitely time for me to change the subject. "So, uh, thanks for getting rid of that ghost."

"Sure." He nodded to the stain on the wall. "Your work?"

"Yeah."

"You really are powerful. You just need practice."

"That's not all it is." If it had just been practice, I would have got better. "But thank you."

"It's just the truth."

Maybe, but I had bigger worries right now. Like ghosts. Reginald might not be gone for good, after all. "Um, any chance you might want to camp out here? I can sleep on the floor." The words made heat rise in my cheeks. I shouldn't be scared of ghosts! I should be able to handle them.

And yet, I *was* scared of ghosts.

"You don't need to sleep on the floor."

"You will?"

"No." He shook his head. "But I also know how to keep to my side of the bed."

Huh. Share a bed.

Because of ghosts, of course. For no other reason, obviously.

Suddenly, I almost wished Boris were in my bed.

CHAPTER
TWELVE

CALLAN

I STARED AT ARIA, surprised by the words that had just come out of my mouth. I'd offered to share her bed to protect her from ghosts. Seriously?

But after the way she'd looked at me, it had been the first thing to pop into my mind. The heat in her eyes had been unmistakable, and I'd been unable to resist.

I should have just done the decent thing and slept on the floor. Or let her sleep on the floor, although the idea of doing that was laughable.

We were both adults, though, and it was a big bed. I'd stick a pillow between us, and it would be like she wasn't even there.

Ha. Like that was going to work.

Just the idea of sleeping next to her made something

130

tighten inside me. I definitely wasn't going to sleep much if she was that close.

Aria looked at the fireplace, brow creased, then back at me. "Okay. You can sleep in the bed."

The words hit me in the chest like an arrow.

"But stay on your side."

I held up three fingers. "Scout's honor."

"And put on a shirt."

"Absolutely." I turned and went back to my room, grabbing a T-shirt and pulling it on over my head. What I really needed was a suit of armor, but that wasn't going to happen.

When I returned to the room, I found that she'd already stuck a pillow in the middle of the bed. She sat upright, staring at me, then nodded approvingly when she saw the shirt. "Just be sure to fight the ghosts if they show up."

"I can do one better and show you how to fight the ghosts."

Skepticism flashed on her face. "I've already told you that I've tried practicing my magic, and it hasn't worked."

"I don't buy it. You're too powerful to be unable to control it."

"Well, I've never managed it before, and trust me, I've *tried*." Irritation sounded in her voice.

"You're just different, and different is powerful. But the usual training methods might not work, so let me help you."

She gave me a long look, then lay down and turned to face away from the middle of the bed. "I'll think about it."

"Good." I wasn't sure how I would help her, but I'd figure it out. My magic was powerful, and I had a gift for sensing the magic in other people. Surely I could use that.

"Turn off the lights and get ready to fight the ghosts," she said.

I grinned, flipping off the light switch and climbing into the bed.

Immediately, her scent washed over me, lavender and something that was intrinsically her. I resisted drawing it deep into my lungs—the last thing I needed was for her to realize I was sniffing her—and closed my eyes. As much as I tried to focus on falling asleep, all I could think of was Aria. I felt myself harden and shifted uncomfortably. Already, I wanted to get out of bed and do a hundred pushups to make this feeling go away. She was just so damned close, and she smelled so good.

I heard her move, twisting within the sheets, and squeezed my eyes tightly shut. Unless she made a move—which I sincerely doubted she was going to—this would be a *very* long night.

Aria

I woke to the sound of birds outside the window.

"Shut up," I groaned, snuggling deeper into the warm pillow beneath my head.

Except, it wasn't as soft as it should be. And how was it so warm?

Dread—and a little bit of excitement, if I were being honest—uncoiled in me. I opened my eyes.

Yep. I'd somehow moved the pillow out of the middle of the bed and climbed on top of Callan in my sleep. Well, not *on top* on top, but close enough. I had one leg draped over his massive thighs and my head on his shoulder. My arm fell over his chest. The soft cotton of his shirt smelled distinctly like him, along with the fresh scent of laundry detergent.

At least my show of physical affection wasn't totally one-sided—he'd wrapped an arm around me as well.

Maybe he'd come over to my side of the bed. That would save my pride, at least.

Without moving—because the last thing I wanted to do was wake Callan—I strained my gaze to see what side of the bed we were on.

His.

Of course. Just my luck.

How the hell was I going to get off of him without him waking? I really didn't want to get caught here.

"I can hear your thoughts going a mile a minute, Aria." His low voice was rough with sleep.

Twin bolts of embarrassment and desire shot through me.

"You're awake?" I squeaked.

"Have been for half an hour."

Shit. "Why didn't you move?"

"Didn't want to wake you." He hesitated. "And, not going to lie, this is very nice."

I drew in a deep breath, trying to slow my hamster-wheeling mind. I needed to get my shit together so that I could weasel my way out of this with the minimal amount of embarrassment.

But he was right.

This *was* very nice.

It was the most perfect morning—the sun was shining warm and golden through the window, and my room was actually a lovely shade of sunny yellow. With the ghosts gone, it was cheerful and bright.

But it didn't matter how much time I spent thinking about the niceness of the room. It was the feeling of Callan's hard body beneath mine that was my favorite part. I'd been going through a serious dry spell, but it wouldn't have mattered if I'd been getting lucky every night.

I'd never been this close to someone like Callan. His sheer physical beauty was a drug, and I'd taken way too much of it. It clouded my mind and heated my body.

I leaned up and looked down at him, hoping to see something on his face that would make me jump off of him.

Instead, I was so close to his full lips that I could see how divinely perfect they were. And his eyes...a brilliant blue that blazed with heat.

He wanted me as much as I wanted him.

Despite my anger, I wanted to climb on him and prove I was tall enough to ride this ride.

"Aria," he murmured, his voice still raspy with sleep. "If you keep looking at me like that, I'm going to kiss you. And I think I have morning breath."

"You actually don't," I whispered. And it was true, which was shocking. Then a horrible thought occurred to me. "Do I?"

He smiled, but his voice was rough when he spoke. "No.

Maybe Matilda enchanted the room to keep our breath fresh. To encourage us, I mean."

I thought of the witch who'd tried to goad us into sharing a room and smiled. "Would that be so bad?"

"No." His gaze dropped to my lips.

I could feel the rapid beat of his heart beneath my hand, and his breathing sped up. Mine did likewise, and I felt the heat surge through me. It clouded my mind, and knowing that he wanted me made the flames of desire rise higher.

He closed his eyes briefly, as if fighting some internal war, then opened them. "If you don't want me to kiss you, you're going to need to climb off of me. Soon."

I hesitated, then hesitated a bit more. It was enough time for Callan to reach up and cup the back of my head. He pulled me down to him, a low groan escaping his lips as they captured mine.

He kissed me with ravenous desire, like he'd been waiting years to do so. And he held me like I was something precious—gently but firmly, unwilling to let me go.

I'd never been touched like this before, and it made my head spin. My heart raced as he traced my lips with his tongue, and I opened for him, wanting more. More, more, more.

Beneath me, he shifted until I felt his hardness pressed against me. I shifted until he was in just the right spot, then let out a little whimper as he moved in a rhythm so perfect, it made tendrils of pleasure shoot through me.

"You're so damned sweet," he whispered against my lips, dragging his mouth down to my neck.

I tilted my head to give him better access, wondering how far I would take this.

All the way.

No question. I wanted him. *Badly.*

When he touched me like this, all my misgivings floated to the back of miming.

"Knock, knock!" called Matilda as she banged on my door.

I gasped and jerked back. "Holy crap!"

I climbed off of Callan, but not quickly enough.

Matilda charged in. "I hope you're decent, because I've brought tea!"

I looked up at her, still panting and definitely red-faced. She carried a massive tea service in her hands. When her gaze landed on us, she gasped. "Well, I never!"

I narrowed my eyes at her. Her surprise was totally put on. "Of course you have, you sly old cat. Are you spying for my grandmother?"

She shrugged and smiled, totally unrepentant. "I wasn't sure what I'd find in here, but I figured it was okay to come in since we're both girls." Her gaze moved to Callan, who was stretched out on the bed like a god. He'd pulled the blanket over his midsection, but even it couldn't hide the impressive bulge. "This is just an unexpected bonus."

"Sure, sure. You had no idea what you'd find when you barged in here. Especially since I imagine Callan's door is open and his room is empty."

She rolled her eyes. "Fine. The floors are thin, so I had my suspicions last night that he came to your room, but your gran insisted I check."

I tilted my head back and groaned. "Of course she did."

"Now come on, I've carried this tea all the way up here. You need to at least drink it." She bustled over to the table that sat by the chairs positioned in front of the fire and laid it down.

Callan rose from the bed, and I walked over to check out the tray. There was a delightful assortment of pastries, along with a large teapot with steam gently wafting from the spout.

"This looks beautiful, thank you." I took a flaky pastry filled with a brilliant red jam and bit in. An explosion of tart, sweet berries made me roll my eyes back in my head. "Amazing."

Matilda chuckled. "I just hope the young lad can make you look that pleased."

My gaze snapped down to hers, and I gasped. "Matilda!"

"I've seen—and done—it all before." She waved her fingers in a goodbye gesture and turned to leave the room. "I'll see you downstairs when you are ready. And don't rush. Certainly not on my account."

Callan and I shared a look. Her last sentence had *definitely* been loaded.

"I like her." He grinned and picked up a pastry, biting into it.

"I'm going to get dressed. Take your pastry to go."

He gave a little salute and grabbed two more, then returned to his room.

I finished my pastry, then another, and dressed as quickly as I could. I brought the tray and my bag downstairs and found Boris in the kitchen, already set up at the table with his own plate of pastries. Matilda fussed over him like he was her baby, and he looked pleased as punch.

"If I'm not careful, I think he might leave me for you," I said.

She rubbed his head. "He's welcome any time."

Just take notes, Aria. This is how familiars ought to be treated.

I laughed, then turned when I heard Callan's voice.

"Good morning." He was dressed in another perfectly fitted shirt that revealed his forearms, and I was once again stupidly entranced.

"I found some more information for you," Matilda said. "The florist in town is also a botanist. A real renaissance woman, if you ask me." She blushed slightly, and I wondered if she had a crush on this renaissance woman. "Anyway, if you go speak to her, she might have more to say about the plants. Help you narrow down which it is, that sort of thing."

"Thanks." I smiled at her, then looked at the clock. It was almost nine. "Do you think she's open now?"

"I'm sure she is." She scribbled something on a piece of paper and handed it to me. "That's the address in town— look for the florist shop with the green storefront. It's just a short drive away."

"Thank you." I looked at Boris. "You good here?"

I'm certainly not leaving yet.

I rolled my eyes, then looked at Matilda. "Do you mind a furry houseguest a little longer? Feel free to send me the bill when he eats the entirety of your pantry."

She ruffled his head again. "Oh, we'll have a lovely time. Don't you worry."

"About Boris? Never." That badger had no problem taking care of himself.

Callan and I left, climbing into the car in silence. I didn't know how to talk about the kiss, so I didn't. Anyway, there was no need to analyze it. We'd done it, it had been hot, and we wouldn't do it again.

Case closed.

I focused on the weather instead, which was a surefire way to forget how turned on I'd been this morning. As if.

Still, I tried, looking out the window to see what kind of day it would be. The sky was slightly overcast, but it gave the sea a stormy look that I rather liked. I opened the windows to appreciate the breeze as we drove to the little town.

We reached it in less than ten minutes and found a spot in front of a bakery. It was a quaint town, a bit smaller than Charming Cove, but just as nice. I moved to close the window, but the faint strains of a familiar voice caught my ear.

It was Serena. I'd know that nasal pitch anywhere since it was seared into my mind from my school days, when she'd taunted me mercilessly. I looked into the side mirror and saw her walking down the street with Evan, her partner.

I grabbed Callan's arm to keep him from getting out of the car and made a loud shushing sound. He stilled.

Serena's voice got louder as she approached. "I don't get it. We followed them here, but now what?"

I shared a look with Callan, whose eyes had widened slightly.

"They followed us here?" I whispered. "What jerks."

THIRTEEN

Aria

I couldn't believe that Serena had tailed us. That was cheating.

She had just reached the car and was passing by my open window. Her voice filled the space. "We just have to find them and see where they go."

Annoyance surged through me, and I pushed open the car door. I climbed out and shouted after her. "Find *us*, you mean?"

She turned around, shock widening her eyes.

"I heard everything," I said. "I can't believe you followed us. That's cheating."

She recovered quickly and shrugged. "So? He never said no cheating."

"It's kind of a given." I looked at Callan. "Right?"

"It's definitely assumed, yes."

Evan shifted, a distinct expression of discomfort in his eyes. It looked like he wasn't cool with the cheating, but also like he didn't have the balls to stand up to Serena.

"You couldn't even figure out that the clue led to the Lizard," I said, pointedly ignoring the fact that I hadn't figured it out either. "How could you possibly think you deserve to win?"

"The Lizard?" Serena frowned. "Our clue definitely had nothing to do with a lizard."

Evan rolled his eyes. "Not a lizard, Serena. *The* Lizard. The place we're at now."

"Still, I don't think it was pointing to a lizard."

I frowned. "Really?"

She shrugged again.

Callan leaned close to me and whispered, "Do you think we might have received different clues?"

"Maybe?" I looked between Serena and Evan. "Can I see your riddle?"

"No." Serena crossed her arms over her chest and glared.

"But you said you couldn't figure out the answer."

"So? I don't want you to know it."

She was driving me crazy. "But what if that's the point of all this? Mr. Sparrow said that we needed to cooperate. Maybe he didn't mean with just our partners, but with everyone."

"Then how do we win?" She shot me a look like I was an idiot.

"No one wins this round, remember? We just have to bring the ingredients to the Garden of Enchantment by Wednesday night. Eventually, we're going to have to beat each other, but not this round. If all our clues are different, that means we have to combine them to find the answer."

"I think you're on to something," Callan said.

Serena still looked suspicious, but Evan seemed impressed. He turned to Serena. "We should show her the clue."

Serena frowned, clearly wanting to be stubborn. "Fine."

Evan pulled the paper out of his pocket and walked towards me, handing it over.

"I want to see your clue," Serena said.

"It pointed us here, to the Lizard. You followed us, remember?"

"Still, I want to make sure you're not cheating."

"Coming from you, that's rich." I pulled the paper from my pocket and handed it to Evan, who brought it back to Serena.

I unfolded the paper he'd given us and leaned over it. Callan did the same, and I couldn't help but draw in a deep breath of his scent.

Sunlight sparkles as I shift; crashing, beating, the sand I lift. The moon's my master, so is the wind. What am I?

I looked back up at the pair as we exchanged papers again. "Well, it's definitely different. I don't know what it means yet, but we'll figure it out."

"Then you have to tell us," Serena said.

"Of course. We're cooperating, remember?"

"Right." She pulled her phone from her pocket. "I'd better call Lilac and tell her to get down here. We need to know her clue."

While Serena made the call, I texted the new riddle to Gran and asked her to run it by Catrina. With any luck, the little genius would know. When I told Serena that the ace in my pocket was a seven-year-old, she would die.

Serena hung up the phone. "She'll be here in a few hours. They're leaving right away."

"Have they figured out their clue?"

"She thinks it's about a plant, but no."

"Excellent. Could she text it to you? Then we can get started on figuring it out early."

Serena laughed. "There's no way in hell she'll tell me before she gets here. She doesn't want us to beat her to it."

No surprise that Lilac's bestie was as mistrustful as she was.

"All right. We'll meet at twelve-thirty. But where?"

Evan pointed to a pub across the street that advertised a back garden. "There. It's one of the only magic places in town. We'll be safe while we wait for Lilac. And we can have lunch."

"I told you to stop thinking with your stomach, Evan," Serena snapped.

Evan just rolled his eyes. Those two definitely wouldn't keep in touch after this.

"We'll see you there," I said, then grabbed Callan's hand and pulled him after me.

He leaned down to whisper, "You don't want to tell them about our botanist lead?"

I could hear the smile in his voice.

"Hell, no. If we learn anything, I'll tell them. I stand by my agreement to cooperate. But I'll spend as little time as possible with Serena, thanks."

"You have history."

"If you call constant bullying history, then yes." I realized I had tightened my grip on his hand, which made me realize that I *still held his hand*.

Like we were dating and headed to brunch together. I dropped this hand like it was on fire.

"I think I know the riddle," he said as we walked. "It's the waves on the beach."

"Ohhh." I looked at him, impressed. "You're right. I should have realized that was it. So we just need a plant that grows on the beach, then?"

"Could be."

"Excellent. There's the florist." I pointed to the pretty green storefront. "We can ask the botanist."

We crossed the street, and I looked in the window. Enormous displays of flowers in all colors were marked with price tags that made my eyes pop.

I nudged Callan. "You're rich. Would you pay that?"

He looked at the tags, his eyes widening. "I don't know much about flower prices, but that does seem steep."

I pushed open the door and entered a small room that smelled divine. I had an excellent nose for floral scents, but even I couldn't distinguish between the varieties here. A young woman bustled out from the door at the back, wiping her wet hands on her apron. Her wild dark hair was speckled with tiny flower petals, like she'd just been in a windstorm of blossoms.

"Sorry," she said, her tone a bit short. "We only do weddings by recommendation of former clients. Although you do make a lovely couple."

I frowned. "We're not here for that. We're here to see the botanist."

Her eyebrows rose as she looked us up and down, and I had a feeling she was looking for a trace of magic. "Ah, of course." Her tone immediately became more friendly. "We're trying to stay under the radar of humans, hence the expensive flowers."

"Of course." I wondered why the storefront was in a human town if that was the case, but I didn't ask. The last thing we needed was to offend the owner. "Are you the botanist?"

She laughed lightly. "Oh, I wish." She waved for us to follow her. "Come this way."

I shared a look with Callan, then we trailed after her through the door into the back. The room we entered was longer than it was wide, bordered on each side by large refrigerators full of blooms.

"Do you really do weddings?" I asked.

"No. But we need a reason for the humans to think we actually a make a living to be here, since we certainly don't sell any bouquets to them." She nodded to the arrangements in the cases. "We sell those to the magical community. Most are for potions, but a few are for social events."

She reached a door at the far end of the long room and pushed it open. A warm surge of air rushed over me as I stepped into an enormous old greenhouse. The ceiling was a domed masterpiece of iron and glass, with plants hanging from hooks high overhead.

"Whoa." The word rushed out of me on an awed breath. "This place is incredible." And old. It felt like it had been here a hundred years or more, and the construction style was like something from the nineteenth century. It had been invisible from the street, and I assumed they used magic to hide it.

"Now you see why we have to keep up the charade of the flower shop. The botanist refuses to leave this greenhouse."

"And why would I?" An older woman walked out from between two rows of tall plants. "My great-great-grandmother built this. It's the best in the country. The only way I'm leaving here is in a hearse."

I grinned at her, immediately reminded of my own grandmother. She wore tough canvas overalls and a floral shirt. Her long white hair had been tied up in a bun on her head, and she wore brilliant coral lipstick.

"This is amazing," I said, spinning in a circle to take it all in. Being in places like this filled me with energy and joy.

"You like your plants, do you?" the botanist asked.

"Do I ever." I stopped spinning and faced her. "You really do have something special here."

"Thank you, dear. I'm always happy when someone appreciates it." She took off her heavy work gloves and tucked them into her pocket. "Now, what can I help you with?"

"We're looking for more information about plants that are specific to the Lizard. Particularly ones that would be valuable to the magical community."

Her gaze went from me to Callan, then back again. "You're two of Lionel's potential heirs, aren't you?"

"How did you know?"

She gave a friendly scoff. "Everyone in the magical botanical community knows. He's got quite the garden there." A wistful look crossed her face. "Even more impressive than my collection here."

"Why didn't you compete?" I asked.

"And leave my home? Never." Her gaze moved to the younger woman, who stood by the door still, watching us. "And my granddaughter wouldn't leave the Lizard for ten million pounds."

"You know my heart isn't with money, Nan," she said. "I'm headed back to the shop unless you need anything."

"No, dear. You go on."

The granddaughter disappeared, and the botanist leaned a hip against one of the tables full of succulents. "You need information for a very valuable purpose, which means I'm going to need you to prove yourselves."

"Prove ourselves?" I asked.

She nodded. "At least one of you needs to prove yourselves worthy of information about such valuable plants."

"What are you thinking?"

She shrugged. "Impress me."

Oh, bugger. That was a tall order. I looked around the greenhouse. If we wanted info about plants, then I should give her some in return. But the idea that I might find something in her garden to impress her with was unlikely.

Still, I had to try. "Do you mind if I walk around?"

"Be my guest."

I walked between the rows of tables, searching for anything that might need my help. Callan followed, along with the botanist. The sheer amount of plants that she'd fit into this greenhouse was astounding, and almost everything looked to be in excellent health.

Except for a leafy green tree that wilted in its pot by the wall. I pointed to it. "What's that?"

"Honestly, dear, I have no idea. It was left on our doorstep, probably by someone who couldn't care for it, and I've been trying to bring it back to health, but I've had no luck. It's been quite the challenge, let me tell you."

"So it's like the stray dog of the plant world?"

"That's one way to look at it. Maybe it's a hybrid, maybe it's from a place I've never been. But I don't know what it is, and I don't know how to fix it. I've tried for months—everything I can think of."

This was my challenge, then. I approached it, inspecting every inch. There were no bugs on it, of course. The botanist would take care of any infestation she saw.

"Do you recognize it?" she asked.

"No. I've never seen it before." I rested my hand on the plant, hoping my instinct would kick in. I ran my hand from the leaves to the trunk, lightly dragging my fingers all the way down to the soil. I wasn't sure why I could do this—maybe it was magic, though it didn't manifest in the way magic normally did—but I was able to get a feel for what plants needed.

After a moment, it came to me. "Rocks. This should be planted in rocks."

"Rocks?" The botanist frowned. "But it arrived in dirt."

I stood and shrugged. "Whoever dropped it off on your doorstep might not have known what medium it wanted to be planted in. Maybe they bought it like this, planted in soil, and that's why it never did well."

"How can you tell?"

I shrugged. "I just can."

"You have a gift, my dear." She smiled, then waved her hand and muttered a few words. Magic flared on the air, and a pot of small pebbles appeared next to the tree.

We worked together to move the tree, and the more I handled it, the more I could tell it would be happy in its new home. When it was done, I stood and brushed off my hands.

"Go get that hose, please." The botanist gestured to the hose near Callan.

He turned it on and brought it over, watering the rocks. The liquid drained through quickly, as expected, but the plant already looked like it was perking up. Satisfaction surged through me, and I turned to the botanist. "I believe you'll have to water it daily."

The botanist grinned at me. "Well done. Now, tell me more specifically what you need to know."

"We're looking for more information about Lion's Mane, Xyanthia, and Spotted Fiorella."

The botanist chuckled. "He wants you to bring him a sample, does he?"

"How did you know?"

"Because he's too smart to go after them himself."

"Dangerous, is it?" Callan asked. It was the first time he'd spoken since we arrived, and I was surprised that he'd been content to stay in the background. A man that powerful rarely was.

"Quite," she said.

"Do any of them grow by the beach?" Callan asked.

"Lion's Mane and Xyanthia. One grows in the sea caves, the others at the base of the cliffs."

"Two?" I frowned, looking at Callan. "I wonder if we could bring both to be sure."

"Don't," the botanist said. "They require special accommodation once you have them, and if Lionel doesn't have it ready, the plant will die. He would hate that."

Damn. "Okay, then. We'll make sure we're confident we know which one he wants before we harvest it. Can you tell us more about them? And is there any chance you have a picture of them?"

"Wait a moment." She bustled off to the back.

In the sudden silence, I could hear the lazy buzzing of chubby bees. Butterflies filled the air above us, flitting around the blooms. I could feel Callan's gaze on me and turned to him. "What?"

"You light up in here."

"Uh." That sounded distinctly like a compliment, and I didn't know what to say.

"You really love plants, don't you?"

I shrugged. "They've always made me feel...I don't know...myself?"

"Yeah, I can see that." His gaze lingered on me, and I looked away.

"All right, here we are." The botanist's voice announced her presence, and I turned to see her bustle out from between two rows of citrus trees. She held a large book in her hand. "This should have what we're looking for."

She went to the table nearest us and pushed aside one of the pots, then set the book down and flipped it open to a page that showed an intricate drawing of a tiny, fluffy orange flower nestled amongst the rocks at the base of the cliffs. "That's your Lion's Mane blossom, but it's tiny, so you'll have to have your nose to the ground to find it."

"Wow." It really was little. "What about Xyanthia? Does this have a picture of that?"

"Sure does." She flipped to the back of the book. The section looked like it was about vines, and when she found the page marked *Xyanthia*, she stopped and pointed to it. "Strange little bugger."

I'd never seen anything quite like the little plant, which looked like a green octopus that grew on land.

"The Xyanthia lives in the sea caves on the Lizard. There aren't many of them, and they'll give you a real run for it."

"A run for it?" Callan asked.

She smiled. "You'll see."

"So you think this is it?" I asked.

She shrugged. "Maybe. Both are different and difficult to harvest. Both require multiple people, which is probably why Lionel Sparrow hasn't done it yet."

"That proves your theory about working together," Callan murmured.

I nodded. Lionel was clever. "Is there anything else you can tell us?"

"Not really. You've got enough to go on, now. Rough locations and how to get them." She snapped the book shut. "I can't be making it too easy for you, now can I?"

"I wouldn't object." I grinned at her. "Thank you, though. When I'm not on a time crunch, do you mind if I come back and visit you? I'd love to know more about your collection."

A genuine smile creased her face. "Of course, dear. I always love a fellow enthusiast."

"Thanks." Warmth filled me. This wasn't the first time I'd been glad I'd returned to the southwest, and it wouldn't be the last.

"Let me draw you a map," she said, before bustling towards another part of the greenhouse and retrieving a piece of paper and pen. She bent over a table and quickly scrawled a little image, then handed it to us.

"Thank you." Callan took it. "We are in your debt."

"Of course." She smiled. "I'll come calling one day, you can count on it."

"I look forward to it." He inclined his head in a polite goodbye. "Until then."

I waited until he'd turned, then said. "I'll catch up with you outside, okay?"

He turned back. "Are you all right?"

"Yes. I'd just like to ask if I can use the loo, if you insist on being so nosy."

He nodded. "I'll be outside the front door."

I watched him go, then turned to the botanist. "I don't actually have to use the loo. I was wondering—are you looking for any new customers?"

Her brows rose. "For what?"

I blew out a breath. "Everything. Well, not exactly everything, but I'm looking for a supplier to replace Mr. Sparrow if I don't win this competition. My gran's potion shop will fold if we can't replace what he sells us."

Shadows crossed her face. "Oh, my dear. There's no one in the entire UK who can sell you what Lionel Sparrow did. Not even if you go to multiple distributors. His garden just has too much. Not to mention, there's been a surge in the popularity of potion shops. Every greenhouse and garden that I know of has a full customer list, including me."

Disappointment welled, but I nodded. "Thank you anyway. I appreciate it."

She nodded. "If there's anything else I can do to help, let me know."

I gave her a grateful smile, then turned and left.

CHAPTER
FOURTEEN

Callan

I WAITED for Aria in front of the shop, holding a box and a pot filled with dirt that the botanist's granddaughter had given me. She said it was so we'd have something to put the plant in when we recovered it, and I appreciated the thoughtfulness.

As I waited, I couldn't help but think of how Aria had diagnosed what was wrong with the plant that the botanist had spent months trying to nurse back to health. With just a touch, she'd realized what it had needed, and within minutes, it was already looking healthier.

Her talent was incredible. She truly had a gift for these things. As soon as she'd entered the greenhouse, she'd lit up from within. Her eyes had grown brighter and her smile wider. A happy glow had suffused her cheeks, and I'd never seen anyone so beautiful.

She stepped outside, and I dragged my thoughts from her beauty and asked, "All good?"

She nodded. "What next?"

"We need to practice your magic." She had power—it was obvious. We just needed to find out what was wrong with it.

"Now?"

"Why not now? We have a couple hours."

"Well, we've got to find this flower, for starters."

"There's nothing we can do until Lilac arrives and we get the rest of the information."

"But we should be preparing for that." She looked to the left, as if she didn't want to meet my gaze.

"Are you afraid?"

"What? No!" She glared at me.

"Then practice your magic with me."

"Ugh. You seriously want to do this now?"

"Why do you have such an aversion to it?"

She heaved a sigh. "Disappointment, maybe? It's never worked before. I don't want to face it again."

I hated that for her. "I can understand that, but there's power in you, Aria. A lot of it. And it will help you in this competition."

"Maybe." She rolled her eyes at the glare I gave her. "Fine, you're right. Where do you want to practice? I'm pretty sure I'm going to show you what a lost cause I am, but I'll do it just to get you off my back."

"Good. Let's go to the pub. Evan said it was one of the few magical places in town, so it should be safe."

"Lead the way." She gestured to the pedestrian crossing, which was still full of racing traffic.

I laughed. "Want me to get hit by a car before we start?"

"A few nights in hospital will get you off my back, at least." She shot me a grin to show she was joking, and I smiled back.

The traffic stopped, and the crossing's light changed. We started across, and I couldn't get her words out of my mind. "You're not a lost cause, Aria."

She looked up at me as she stepped onto the pavement on the other side. "Don't feel bad for me."

"I *don't*. I really don't, although I'd like to hex your former bullies. But I do feel like you have great potential."

"Sure, sure."

"I'm going to prove it to you." I walked towards the pub, which was only a few doors down, and pulled open the door for her.

She stepped inside, and I followed her into the cool interior. Like The Sea Shanty back in Charming Cove, it was the kind of pub that hadn't changed in a century. There was a small fire burning to the left and a gleaming wooden bar with leather bar stools in front of us. The interior was a bit larger, with darts in the corner and a tiny stage at the back.

The room was empty except for an older woman wiping down a table, and she looked up. Her graying hair was piled up on her head, and she scowled at us from heavily lined eyes. "We're closed."

I looked at the clock over the bar and saw that it was only ten-thirty.

She stood and propped her hands on her hips. "Don't open 'til eleven. No food 'til twelve."

"But you've got a garden at the back?" I asked.

"That's closed, too."

"Of course." I gave her my most charming smile. "I was hoping we could just spend some time back there. No need for drinks or food. Just a spot to sit."

"Sit?" She arched a brow. "Is that what you kids call it these days?"

A choked laugh escaped Aria, and I barely managed to hold mine back.

"I promise, no funny business," I said as I approached her, drawing out a wad of notes. "Perhaps we could rent the space. Just to cover your time and for your kindness in letting us use it."

Her gaze moved down to the money, and the scowl faded. "All right, then. I suppose I can make an exception."

I handed it over, and she grinned as she gestured to the back. "Door's that way. Help yourself."

"Thank you." I looked at Aria, who shrugged and followed me.

The walled garden at the back was a lovely space filled with wooden tables and umbrellas. Roses climbed up the rear wall, and metal artwork decorated the others.

"This is nice," Aria said. "I'd spend plenty of time here if this were my local."

"Your local is plenty nice."

"True enough." She grinned. "No pub is better than The Sea Shanty." She put her hands on her hips. "So, what are you thinking for this magic training session?"

"Why don't you tell me what you have a problem with?"

"Everything?" She shrugged. "I try to draw magic from the ether and manipulate it, and it almost never works. When it does, it's like it rushes into me and blows up whatever I'm attempting."

"Hmm." That was strange. Magic was generally more effortless than that. Magical beings were one with the ether and the energy stored within it. Not everyone had the same abilities—the ability to draw the magic into yourself was like a muscle, and some people were stronger than others. The more magic you could draw in, the more you could do. But it rarely blew up in our faces.

I approached her. "Do you mind if I touch your arm while you try to move the chair that's next to you?"

"Why?"

"I have a good feel for the flow of magical energy. Part of being a mage. I might get an idea of what your problem is."

She shrugged and held out her arm. "Knock yourself out."

I gripped her wrist gently, making sure there was contact between our skin. Warmth rushed through me and my breath came short.

Fates, I was just touching her wrist. It shouldn't make me feel anything. And yet, here I was like a randy teenager.

"You just want me to move the chair?" she asked.

I nodded. "As far as you're comfortable."

"Here goes nothing." She stared at the chair, her brow furrowed in concentration. I could feel her reach for the magic in the ether, but it didn't respond. That was odd. It should have come easily to her.

She pushed harder, and I felt the strain within her. What the hell was going on?

A moment later, a rush of magic plowed into her, reacting to her desire to move the chair and attempting to manifest it. The furniture flipped onto its back, crashing to the ground.

She gave me a weak smile. "Well, I moved it. Though I'm sure that wasn't what you were expecting."

"No, not quite. The ether doesn't respond to you, but you did eventually draw magic from somewhere."

"Wait, somewhere?" She frowned. "Where else could I have got it from? I always assumed it was just stubborn."

"It's not stubborn, and it didn't respond to you. But something did." I looked around the garden. There was magic in other parts of the world, not just within the ether. But the vast, vast majority of the magical population drew their power from the ether. It was almost unheard of to use other sources, and if that was her situation, I wasn't surprised no one had figured it out before.

"What are you thinking?"

"I'm thinking that you're different."

"We already decided that." She rolled her eyes. "Don't worry if you can't help me. I've made peace with it."

"I can help you." My voice came out harsher than I intended, but I didn't want her to think I was giving up on her. I turned to her, gentling my tone. "I'm sorry. I just hate to see you accept your situation. It can be fixed."

She glared at me. "*It*? Don't you mean me? You want to fix me. But maybe I don't need to be fixed. I'm not broken. I'm fine."

Shite. I'd really put my foot in it. "Of course you are. More than fine. I've never met anyone like you. I just mean—"

"Thought I'd bring you a bit of a treat." The waitress's voice preceded her into the garden, and she appeared a moment later with a tray of tea and scones. "Had this in the back and thought you might like a bit of refreshment."

Damn it. Her timing couldn't have been worse.

"Thank you," Aria said, walking towards her. She was clearly done with me for now. "You have impeccable timing."

"'Course I do." She set the tray down on a table and brushed her hands off on her apron. "Just let me know if you need anything else."

Aria gestured to the impressively laid tray. "Stay and share with us, this is so much food."

She *really* didn't want to be alone with me, apparently.

"No, no. The pub has been open a while now, and I have customers. You enjoy though." She bustled off.

Aria poured the tea without turning to look at me. "She really changed her tune."

"Aria, I'm sorry. I didn't mean to imply you were broken."

"Don't worry about it." She picked up a pastry and bit into it almost savagely. "I'm used to that kind of thing."

If I could kick my own ass, I would. I'd done the exact thing to her that all of her bullies had. It didn't matter that I'd been well intentioned. The pain she felt was the same.

Still, there was so much potential in her.

She finished her pastry and brushed off her hands. "Shall we keep practicing? Maybe it will get easier with time."

It didn't. Though we practiced until after twelve, she still struggled. It convinced me even more that she drew her power from somewhere besides the ether—we just needed to figure out where.

Before I could come up with a solution, the pub door opened again. Serena and Evan walked into the garden, and Evan's gaze landed on the tray. "Perfect! A snack is just what we need."

Aria gestured to the spread. "Help yourself."

"Lilac should be here any minute," Serena said.

Was it already half past twelve? Time had passed quickly while we'd practiced.

Evan joined Aria and dug into the food, while Serena walked over to me. A broad smile stretched across her face, and she sat on the table closest to me, crossing her legs so that her skirt rose a few inches.

"So, Callan, what makes you want to win the garden?" Her tone was distinctly flirty, and I caught sight of Aria's head whipping towards her.

Aria seemed to notice I was looking at her and turned to talk to Evan.

"Callan?" Serena prodded.

"Um, same reason as everyone, I suppose." I didn't want to be talking to Serena right now. Even more, I didn't want Aria talking to Evan. But I was an adult, and being polite was part of the territory. Unfortunately. "What about you? Any special reason?"

She said something that I tried my damnedest to pay attention to, but too much of my focus was on Aria and Evan as I tried to pick up hints of their conversation. Fortunately, Lilac arrived before I had to respond to Serena.

The woman charged into the garden alongside her partner, Terry, and stopped next to Serena. "All right, we're here as requested. What was the damned rush?"

"For one, you're now in the location in which you need to be in order to advance in the competition," Aria said.

"Fine." She rolled her eyes. "I just hate long-distance travel in the car, so I'm grumpy."

"Well, get it together," Serena said. "Did you bring your clue?"

"Yes, but we want to know yours first." Terry gripped a paper in his hand, and I had to assume it was the clue.

"Our clue was to come here to the Lizard," I said.

"Serena followed us," Aria added.

Lilac's eyes widened. "Cheater. Why didn't you give me that tip?"

"There can be only one winner, Lilac." Serena crossed her arms over her chest. "And it's going to be me."

Lilac scowled. "Oh, you little—"

I raised my hands and sent a blast of calming magic into the air, cutting off Lilac's words. "Let's focus on the problem at hand. Serena, share your clue."

Serena huffed, but she pulled the clue from her pocket and read the riddle aloud.

Lilac's gaze brightened. "Is it talking about waves?"

"We think so, yes."

"All right." She grinned widely. "So, we're looking for a flower near some waves." She flicked the paper that contained the clue against her hands, her gaze thoughtful. "You're sure about this working together thing, Aria?"

"I am. There's no way we'd be able to find the plant without combining clues."

"I suppose you're right." She nodded. "You're brighter than I thought you were."

"It's my magic that's iffy, not my mind."

"There's a difference?" The disdain in her gaze made my jaw tightened, and I glanced at Aria.

Shadows had entered her eyes, but she looked more annoyed than hurt. Thank goddess for that, because I didn't know what I'd do if Lilac's words had hurt her feelings. I couldn't exactly do damage to a witch for being mean to Aria, but the petty part of me wanted some kind of vengeance on her behalf.

"Well, I don't want to go with her." Serena looked at Aria. "She could jinx us."

"That's enough." My voice cut through the mean comments, harsh and fierce. "Aria is the reason we've come this far, which makes her the most accomplished one here. You can either be grateful to work with her, or we're leaving you behind."

Lilac and Serena looked at me, eyes wide and shocked.

"Uh—" Lilac couldn't seem to finish the sentence.

"All right, that's enough." Aria gripped my arm to make sure I didn't say anything else, but the look she shot me was grateful. "Lilac, read your clue."

"Fine." She looked down at the paper. "Legs of green and roots so deep, to the shadows of the cave I keep. What am I?"

"It's the Xyanthia." Aria grinned. "I think I know where we need to go. Let's get a move on."

CHAPTER
FIFTEEN

ARIA

CALLAN'S WORDS still echoed in my head. He'd defended me. Quite vigorously, in fact. The looks on Serena's and Lilac's faces would keep me going for a while, actually. I grinned at the memory.

"Are you okay?" Callan murmured as we walked from the pub to our cars.

"That was nothing. But thank you."

"'Course." He glared at my schoolmates' backs. "Miserable harpies."

"I'm just going to make sure I beat them." I grinned, enjoying the fantasy. "Then they'll have to come to me for their potion ingredients." Oh, the idea was sweet. The petty part of me wanted to demand silly things in exchange for what they wanted. Spreading manure on the fields that grew the golden wheat used in Druid's Brew Wheat Ale, for example.

It was an unlikely fantasy, but a fun one.

We reached the car, and Callan got behind the wheel. I pulled out the little handwritten map from the botanist and inspected it. "It looks like you head south out of town, and we go almost to the end of the Lizard. We stop before the public beach. From there, we climb down to the beach and find the sea cave."

He nodded and pulled away from the street, expertly navigating through the growing holidaymaker traffic as we led the others towards our destination. The sun shone brightly overhead as we drove on the cliff road alongside the sea.

Callan found a parking spot off the road and pulled to a stop. "Do you think this is it?"

I pointed to the satnav on his dash. "Looks like we're still a few hundred meters from the spot where the holiday-makers go. So it's got to be."

"Good. I'd hate to have to keep people away in case there is visible magic."

"Agreed." The Lizard was a popular summer spot for people looking to enjoy the sea. With any luck, we'd avoid them entirely.

The other two cars pulled to a stop behind us, and we climbed out to meet them. The fresh breeze whipped my hair back from my face and blew the long grass that covered the fields across the road. I could hear the waves crashing on the beach far below, and the sea in the distance was a brilliant turquoise. The cloudy day had passed, and the sun gleamed bright against the water.

Lilac and Serena stuck close together as they approached, and I turned to walk towards the cliff. The sooner I found the path down, the sooner we'd be able to say our goodbyes.

Callan joined me, and we walked along the cliff, looking for the safest way down. When I got close enough to the edge to lean over and see the beach below, my stomach dropped.

"Oh, that's far." I stepped back, heart racing.

"Problem with heights?" Callan asked.

"I didn't think so, but there's a first time for everything."

"This would make anyone nervous," Evan said.

I looked over, not realizing that he'd approached. He looked a bit white around the gills.

"This is more adventure than I anticipated," I said.

"Me, too." He grimaced. "Gardening isn't supposed to be dangerous. At least, not this kind of dangerous."

"Feel free to drop out now." Serena smiled.

"I'm fine." His voice was as stiff as his posture.

"There are some rugged stairs that go down over here," Terry called from further up the cliff path.

We hurried towards him, and I spotted the stone steps that had been carved out of the cliffside at some point. Maybe by smugglers? It was well known that smugglers from hundreds of years ago had come ashore in Cornwall to sell their illegal gains, and some of them had carved stairs up the cliffs that led from the sea.

Whoever had made them, they were indeed rugged. Some were barely wider than my foot, with one side opening up to a steep drop straight down to the beach below.

I drew in a slow and steady breath.

Callan cupped my shoulder in a brief, comforting grip, and I hated to admit that it did make me feel a little better.

"We'll be fine." He shot me a smile. "This is nothing."

"For you, maybe. I've spent most of my life serving cakes, stocking shelves, and trying to sell things I can't mention in polite company. I'm not prepared for this."

"That I know is not true. You can handle anything." The confidence in his voice was unmistakable, and I looked over at him. It was reflected in his eyes.

"You really think so?"

He nodded. "I've got a feeling for this kind of thing. Now, come on. You're only going to get more nervous the longer you stand here."

"Right." I stepped forward. "Let's get this show on the road."

We lined up with Serena in the lead and Callan and me at the back. I was fine with it, honestly. Being at the rear meant there would be more people testing the steps before I came to them. And with Callan behind me, hopefully he'd catch me if he saw me lose my footing.

"Just keep your eyes on the stairs at your feet, but not the sea," he said.

"Roger that." I followed the others down the stone steps, my shoulder pressed so hard to the wall that I was pretty sure I'd rub my jacket raw by the time I got to the bottom.

Loose pebbles shifted under my feet, making my stomach lurch. I drew in a steady breath.

"You've got this," Callan murmured.

I chose to believe him and used the little boost of confidence to keep myself going. It wasn't like I had a choice, anyway. The stairs were so narrow that I doubted my ability to turn around and head back up.

The sound of the crashing waves grew louder as we neared the bottom, and I chanced a glance at the beach below. The brilliant blue sea slammed into the rocks on the beach, sending up glittering sprays of water. Though it was a sunny day, the wind and waves were fierce. I hoped they wouldn't give us too much trouble once we found the cave.

Finally, we reached the bottom. Cold sweat had covered my skin, and I wiped my face off with the hem of my T-shirt. Callan gave my arm a gentle squeeze. "Good job."

"Thanks. The fact that I wasn't sick all over Terry's back is one of my life's great accomplishments."

Terry, who had been walking in front of me, turned to look at me with a horrified expression. I just smiled and shrugged.

Serena and Lilac were already hurrying off down the beach in search of the sea cave, so we picked up the pace to join them. The cliffs rose tall on our right, and I couldn't help but glance at the base to see if I could spot any of the flowers we weren't actually searching for.

Of course I spotted a fluffy orange blossom immediately. But the point of this task wasn't to be easy, I reminded myself.

"Found it!" Serena called from up ahead before disappearing into the cliff.

We reached the opening into the cave a moment later and ducked inside behind her. It was fairly large and quite deep, probably the size of several shops on Foxglove Lane put together. The sunlight cast shadows inside the damp space, along with beams of light that highlighted several strange plants growing on the ground.

"There they are!" Serena ran towards one.

When she got close, the thing rose up out of the soil and ran away from her on legs made of roots.

She stopped dead in her tracks, stunned. "That little bastard."

"You can hardly call a plant a bastard," Evan said.

"I just did, didn't I?" She glared at him, then hurried after the plant.

Cold water rushed around my ankles, and I looked down to see that the tide had begun to rise. Fast. It went from my ankles to mid-calf in seconds.

"Callan!" I called. He'd gone a bit farther into the cave ahead of me. "The sea is coming in."

He turned, his eyes widening. In a heartbeat, he had his hand thrust forward and magic flowing from his palms. It pressed the water back out to sea, but the strain around his mouth deepened. "There's too much of it. I need help with this!"

Serena gave up chasing the plant and joined Callan, along with Evan and Terry. They used their joint power to hold back the waves that had started to fill the cavern.

I stepped forward, desperate to help but uncertain of how. "Should I—"

"No," Serena snapped. "You'll probably just make it rush in faster."

"The damned plant is running away from me, too!" Lilac cried.

"Trade with her," Serena said, her face creased with the effort of trying to hold back the waves. "Lilac, get over here and help us hold back the water!"

I sprinted towards the back of the cave, passing Lilac as she ran to help the others. I'd be lying if I said being unable to help them didn't feel like shit.

I'd just have to catch this damned plant instead. I needed to contribute *somehow*.

I caught sight of the plant halfway up the cave wall, far out of reach. My heart dropped. How the hell was I going to catch it all the way up there? The wall was too smooth to climb, and my magic wasn't reliable enough to carry it to me through the air.

I stopped below it, staring up. Behind me, I could hear the shouts of the others as they worked to hold back the water. I could feel their magic in the air, thick and potent. Power was finite, however, and they wouldn't be able to restrain the sea for long.

"Hey, buddy," I said quietly, figuring I might as well treat the plant like it was one of my own. They seemed to like me, after all. None of them could get out of their pots and run, but hopefully, this one wasn't so different. "Why don't you come down here?"

The plant stilled. I couldn't tell if it was thinking. I doubted it, since plants didn't have brains. But this one had some kind of instinct.

I tried to reach out to feel its magic. It was a weird skill I used with my own plants. If I tried to connect with them through the ether, I could feel if they were healthy or if they needed something. Maybe I could feel what this one wanted.

When I connected with the plant, it felt a bit different to my own plants. I couldn't tell if it needed water or fertilizer or even if it was healthy. But I could still feel it—almost like it pulsed with life.

"Come to me, pal," I murmured, holding out my hand.

The plant slowly moved towards me, and my heart sped up.

"Catch that damned plant!" Serena shrieked.

The plant hesitated, and I cursed her.

"Come on. I promise you'll be happy where I'm taking you."

That seemed to convince the plant. It jumped off the wall and landed in my hand. As soon as it made contact, it grew still. Not lifeless—just quiet and steady, the way plants always were. I closed my fist gently around the greenery, letting the roots dangle free, and raced towards the others.

The water at the mouth of the cave was now nearly as tall as they were, and their faces were strained with the effort of holding it back.

As I neared them, Callan turned his head, his gaze going immediately to me. "You've got it?"

I held it up, then nodded towards the water. "But how are we going to get past that?"

"I'll create a tunnel." He shifted, directing his outstretched hands towards the exit of the cave nearest the stairs.

Magic flared, and the water carved out a tunnel next to the stone wall. "Go. Hurry." He looked towards his companions. "The rest of you, too. I'll follow."

I looked back at him, worry clutching my chest. Would

he be okay? Was it even possible for one person to hold back this much water?

As soon as my gaze met his, I knew it was. He stood tall, his magic swirling around him, the power of it whipping his hair back. It lit up his eyes, turning them a nearly iridescent blue. The sight of him made my breath catch, and I had to force myself to turn and run.

I followed the others through the tunnel. Water dripped on my head, breaking away from the solid wall of liquid that threatened to crash in on me if Callan lost his grip. I glanced over my shoulder to make sure he was following.

I couldn't see him.

Fear lanced me.

Had the water got him?

No, because it still arced over my head, providing a safe passageway back to the stairs.

Up ahead, I could spot the tunnel exit. Bright sunshine beckoned me, and I sprinted out onto the beach, turning to look at the wall of water behind me. It had risen up around the cave entrance but not much further, which meant we hadn't drowned a bunch of tourists at the swimming beach a few hundred meters away. Thank fates for small favors.

Behind me, the others were racing towards the stone stairs. I waited for Callan, my gaze glued to the tunnel through the water.

When he ran through, I sagged with relief. He didn't stop going, though. He just grabbed my hand and pulled me along. "I don't know what will happen when I let go of the water, but we need to get out of here."

I gripped his hand and raced alongside him. We sprinted

towards the stairs, dropping our hold on each other when we reached them. I jumped onto them and started the trek upward.

"I can't hold it any longer," Callan said. His power faded from the air, and I looked back to see the water crash down. It rushed along the beach towards us, most of it diffusing out to sea. There was enough of it that it plowed into the bottom of the stairs, though, and I jumped in shock.

I lost my footing, feeling the briefest moment of utmost terror as I began to fall. Callan reached for me, grabbing me close to him. His arms wrapped around me, strong and secure, and I clung to him, panting.

"Are you all right?" he asked.

I nodded, my breath heaving as I tried to get myself back together. "Yeah." I still had the plant gripped in my hand, thank goddess. "You saved me."

"Nah. You would have probably bounced."

A surprised laugh escaped me. "Let's get out of here before this adrenaline is gone and I can't stand."

He nodded and released me, making sure I had my footing before fully removing his grip.

I climbed the rest of the stairs more carefully, focusing only on the rock right below my feet. By the time I made it up to the top, my breath was heaving so hard that I sounded like I'd run a marathon. My lungs and legs burned, and I almost crawled onto the grass.

"You've got it, right?" Serena demanded.

I looked up. "That's all you've got to say?"

"Duh. The plant is what we're here for."

I rolled my eyes. "Yes, I've got it. And we all lived, thanks to Callan."

"We helped," Lilac said.

"You guys are comedically awful, you know that?" I asked.

They both glared at me.

"Who is going to be responsible for the plant?" Terry's gaze was glued to it.

"Aria, no question," Callan said. "She's the only one who can keep it from running away."

Lilac and Serena grumbled, but even they couldn't argue.

"We'll meet at the entrance to the garden ten minutes before we're due to hand it in," I said. "All of us, together. That way, Mr. Sparrow will know we all played a role."

The others nodded begrudgingly, but it wasn't like they had a choice. This little plant had run from them so fast that they didn't stand a chance of bringing it to Mr. Sparrow.

I grinned. For the first time since the competition had begun, I actually felt a bit confident. Maybe I had a chance at this.

"Let's go," Callan said. "We could use a change of clothes and something to eat. Then we should get back."

Oh, right. I was dripping wet. In all the excitement, I hadn't noticed how badly the wave had soaked me. I'd been too busy feeling grateful to be alive.

My jeans clung to me as I trudged towards the car. The others hurried to their cars and drove off, leaving us alone. I was physically relieved to see their backs, and some of the tension left my shoulders.

Callan clicked the key fob in his hand, and the boot

opened. He withdrew the lidded box that the botanist had given me and opened it, then held out the base.

I looked down at the tangle of green vines and roots in my hand. "I'm going to put you in this cozy box with some dirt, and soon, we'll be at a place you'll like. Sound good?"

The plant didn't so much as move.

"I'm nuts, aren't I?" I asked Callan.

"No. There's a reason this plant likes you, after all. Maybe it's because you talk to it."

"I respect it, that's why." I gently laid the plant in the box, nestling the roots in the dirt. "All living things deserve respect. Plants included."

He shut the box carefully. "Well said."

Callan laid the box down in the boot and picked up his bag. I grabbed my own bag and went around to the side of the car that faced the cliffs. I opened both the front and back doors to create a makeshift dressing room and began to pull off my clothes.

The warm sun felt divine against my clammy skin as I peeled off the wet layers. As quickly as I could, I tugged on a fresh set, then looked up at Callan.

He was on the other side of the car, and his gaze met mine over the roof. His shoulders were bare, and I was immediately plunged back to the moment I'd realized I was lying on top of those same shoulders.

Heat rushed through me, annoying and tantalizing all at once.

I spun away from him and looked out to sea.

I needed to get myself together.

CHAPTER
SIXTEEN

ARIA

WE MADE the drive back to Charming Cove in silence. It wasn't because of awkwardness, though there was some of that. Mostly it was because I was exhausted, and the take-away fish and chips that we'd grabbed for lunch had put me into a food coma. We'd got the fish after picking up Boris, and he'd curled up on the back seat after eating his. It wasn't long before I fell asleep, and when I woke, we were pulling into the drive in front of my house.

I rubbed my eyes, staring groggily out the window. "That was quick. Thank you for driving."

"Thank you for ensuring that I was on the best team."

I grinned at him, unable to help myself. The strongest desire to invite him inside rushed through me. What could it hurt if we shared a drink?

"Aria." Callan's voice held a note of seriousness that

made me stiffen, and I looked at him. "I'm sorry about what I said at the pub—that I made it sound like I wanted to fix you. I never meant it to sound like that."

The memory washed over me, opening up a wound that hadn't closed since childhood. *That* was why I shouldn't invite him in. As much as I was starting to like him, he had the power to hurt me. I couldn't afford to fall for someone who was just going to leave when the competition was over.

"It's fine," I said. "I'm just sensitive, is all."

"Of course you are. People have been horrible to you. But you're incredibly powerful, and..." He hesitated, clearly unsure of where to go next. "I think you're great."

I blinked at him. "You think I'm *great*?"

He dragged a hand through his hair, a weary laugh escaping him. "That sounded ridiculous, I know. I'm not good at this kind of thing."

"What kind of thing?"

"Feelings."

"But you are constantly in the news with a different woman."

"Why do you think they're always different?"

"Ah, right." I supposed that made sense, but I had a hard time believing I was different. "Well, thank you for thinking I'm great." I was going to have to store that tidbit away for later and examine it. He really thought I was great? It was such a silly word, but even that was something to consider. I made him tongue-tied. *The* Callan Hawthorne, and I made him tongue-tied. "And thank you for wanting to help me with my magic. I do want the help. Especially after today."

"Why today?"

"Because I think I might actually have a chance to win this thing, and I'm probably going to need my magic to do it."

He nodded, his expression serious. "I'll help you."

"What? No joke about how you're going to win?"

"No, because I'm not sure I *am* going to win. Not now that I've seen you in action."

"Oh." I felt a smile pull at my lips. "All right, then."

I liked how serious he was about it—how he respected me and considered me a threat.

I liked it a little too much, in fact. The idea scared me into action, and I pushed open the car door and hopped out. "Thanks for the ride. I'll see you tomorrow."

I headed to my front door, realizing partway there that I was leaving my bag behind like an idiot. And my badger. *And* that damned plant we'd gone all the way to the Lizard for.

When I turned, I spotted Boris climbing out of the back seat and Callan opening the trunk and pulling out my bag and the box with the Xyanthia. He brought it to me, and I accepted it with a sheepish smile. "Ah, thanks. Later."

I didn't wait to see if he would say something. I just turned and headed back into the house as fast as my feet would carry me.

THE NEXT MORNING, I woke to the sound of someone banging on my front door. I stumbled out of bed and pulled on the old fake silk robe that I'd bought at Primark when I'd first moved to London.

I walked by Boris, who'd passed out on the couch as soon as he'd entered the house and clambered up onto it. At the door, I opened it to find Tabitha standing there. She held up a tray with a smile. "Some of Catrina's breakfast biscuits. I'll trade you some for coffee and gossip about your trip to the Lizard."

My stomach grumbled at the sight of them, and I snagged one. "Where's Catrina?" I asked around the biscuit, which tasted of buttery chocolate perfection.

"School. It's a weekday."

"Oh, right." I turned and walked into the house, heading towards the coffee pot in the kitchen. Tabitha followed, propping her butt on the table as I began to make the coffee. While it brewed, I watered some of my thirstier plants, pleased to see that everyone was settling in nicely.

"Well?" she prodded. "How did it go with Callan?"

"Let me have my coffee first, at least."

She groaned. "Fine, but then I want the details."

"You'll get them, I promise." When the coffee finished brewing, I poured two cups, then nodded to the back door that led to the stone patio. "Can you open that, please? We'll sit outside."

"Sure thing." She pulled open the door and carried the biscuits outside. I followed her, taking a seat at the little table and handing her a coffee mug. The sea breeze rushed over me, and the view of the Atlantic was beautiful. Red flowers waved in the grass between the house and the sea, and I smiled. "This place really is perfection. Thank you for letting me live here."

"Of course. Now pay me back by telling me all the deets."

"Right, right." I took a sip to brace myself. "We kissed."

"You what?" She squawked the words, then grinned. "How was it? And do you not hate him anymore?"

"It was amazing, for one. And I don't hate him. I used to. I still hate what he did, but it was miscommunication and a mistake."

"Miscommunication?"

"Apparently, I was so upset back then that I didn't actually tell him what that place meant to me. *Why* it was important, I mean. I just yelled at him and stormed off."

She grimaced. "That does sound a bit like the Aria I know."

"Exactly."

"Do you think he would have still built on it if you'd told him?"

"No? Yes? I don't know. I want to think he wouldn't have."

"Follow your gut."

"My gut says that the Callan of today wouldn't do it."

"Then that's all that matters, because that's the Callan you're dealing with." She picked up another biscuit and bit into it, chewing thoughtfully. "And you like him."

I tilted my head back and looked at the fluffy clouds overhead. "I think I might. At least a little."

"Well, if this isn't the development of the decade, I don't know what is."

"Yeah, yeah." I rubbed a hand through my hair. "But it doesn't matter. He's just going to leave when this is over."

"Maybe not?"

I shot her a look. "Come on. You've seen his life on the

news. Constant travel to exciting places with an endless stream of supermodel girlfriends. Charming Cove is nothing like that, and *I'm* nothing like them."

"First, we need to work on your self-esteem. Because you're right—you're not like them. You're better."

"Ha. I'm a witch with wonky magic who can't hold down a job." And if my self-esteem needed work, I was too old to fix it. I decided to change the conversation. "We were successful at the Lizard, by the way. We'll be bringing the plant to Mr. Sparrow tonight."

"We? You mean you and Callan?"

"And everyone else." I told her about the cooperative nature of the competition, and she grinned.

"You're going to win this one!" she crowed.

"I told you, there are no winners."

"Nah, there are winners. Maybe not officially, but when Mr. Sparrow hears the role you played, you're definitely going to get more credit than anyone else."

Hope flared in my chest. Even though it made me feel a bit silly, I couldn't help it. "I think I might actually have a chance at this, you know."

"Oh, I know. I've known all along, and so has your gran. There's a reason you were chosen to be champion."

"I thought my name was on the invitation."

"We'll, it was. That's true. But we would have chosen you even if Mr. Sparrow hadn't."

I rubbed my arms, nerves chilling me just a bit. Now that I thought it might be possible to win, it made me nervous. I rose. "I need to check on the Xyanthia we brought back. And some of my plants need attention. Then I need to get to the shop and see how Gran is doing."

"Good idea. Keep busy so you can't get nervous."

"How do you know me so well?"

She shrugged. "Time and distance don't matter when you're best friends."

THAT EVENING, I waited at the entrance to the Garden of Enchantment. Since it wasn't the opening ceremony, there would be no audience. I'd come alone, and I'd come early enough to ensure that I'd be the first one here.

I stood at the ornate wooden gate, the scent of the climbing roses filling the air around me. I closed my eyes and imagined what it might be like to own this place. To take care of it.

Amazing.

Not only would I save Gran's shop, but I would have a purpose in the magical community that I was capable of fulfilling. And I would *love* it.

"What are you thinking about?" Callan's voice cut through my fantasies, and I opened my eyes to see him coming down the path.

The dreams blinked out of existence in a moment.

I might now stand a shot at winning, but he was my biggest competition. And he was way more powerful than I was. His magic blew everyone else's out of the water.

How could I possibly beat him?

"What is it?" Worry echoed in his voice.

"What do you mean?"

"Your face went from wistful and happy to sad when I arrived."

I felt heat rise in my cheeks and didn't like that he could read me so well. "Oh, it wasn't you. Just thinking of some things I need to do at the cottage. Clean the toilet and things like that."

"That would make anyone sad, but I don't think that's what you were thinking about."

"Well, it's my secret to keep, isn't it?" I smiled at him to soften the words. I didn't want to start a fight, and it was easy to flirt with him. There was just something so natural and fun about being with him.

He stopped in front of me, so close that I could smell his evergreen and spice scent. When he spoke, his voice was low enough to send a shiver down my spine. "It is, but I want your secrets."

"Maybe one day, you'll get one or two. But not today." I heard footsteps coming down the path behind him and looked around him to see Serena approaching.

She arched a brow when she saw me. "So you really did keep up your end of the bargain and wait for us at the entrance."

"Of course I did." For one, I wasn't a liar. And for another, I wasn't stupid. The whole point of this part of the competition was to cooperate. If I betrayed my team at the end, I would hardly win.

"How is the plant doing?" she asked, stopping next to us.

"Fine. It's been normal since I put it in the box. Not trying to run away or anything like that."

"Good." She sounded a little bitter, though, and I wondered if it was because I'd been able to convince the plant to come to me and she hadn't.

Probably. She was used to being better at magic than I was. *Was* it even magic that I'd used on the plant? It had come as naturally as breathing, and magic never did that.

The others arrived as a group, and we walked through the gate and into the Garden of Enchantment. As soon as I entered, I felt that same wonderful rush I'd felt the first time. Like coming home and going on an adventure, all at the same time.

Lionel Sparrow waited for us in the center of the clearing where we'd met a few days ago. He wore another tweed suit, but he'd accented it with a brilliant blue scarf this time. He looked anxiously from person to person, his gaze finally settling on me and the box I held.

His eyes lit, and he threw up his hands. "You've got it!"

"*We've* got it." I approached him, handing over the box. "But be careful, it's a runner."

"Oh, I know. Only a select few would be capable of convincing it to come with them." His eyes twinkled as he looked at me, and it was obvious he knew that I was the one who'd retrieved the plant. "But it couldn't be done alone. That person would need backup to hold the water at bay."

"It was Aria who figured that all out," Callan said.

I heard Lilac hiss her displeasure, but ignored her as I turned to look at Callan. He hadn't had to say that, but I appreciated it. I smiled at him, and he just gave a little shrug as if to say *it's the truth*.

"Well done, lads and lasses," Mr. Sparrow said. "You made quite the team if you managed to get this little guy."

"Why *did* the waves rush in?" I asked. "I've never seen anything like that. Surely it's not natural."

"It was a spell meant to protect the plants. It only affects that cave, which is the one place these little darlings grow."

"How will you keep this one alive?" Callan asked.

"I'll show you right now. And it will also give you a little more insight into your next task." He turned and gestured for us to follow him. "This way, now."

We followed him from the clearing, taking one of the paths that led into the garden. Soon, we were in a part that I'd never visited before, and excitement made my skin tingle. I sneaked a glance at Callan, who'd come to walk alongside me, and he looked just as interested.

Up ahead, I spotted a bit of sparkle through the trees. As we neared it, I realized that it was the glass of a greenhouse glinting beneath the light of the setting sun. Just like the botanist's greenhouse, it was built of iron and glass, an ornate structure from a previous time.

Mr. Sparrow looked back to see me inspecting it and said, "You might be noticing that it's quite an old-style greenhouse. Nineteenth century, in fact."

"I was." I frowned at him. "I thought you started this place forty years ago."

"You have a good eye and a keen mind," he said, and I felt my cheeks heat.

"So why is the greenhouse so much older than the garden itself? Was it already here?"

"No, indeed. But I rather like the aesthetic of the older

greenhouses. I sought them out and moved them here when I built the garden. Many of my plants require habitats that cannot be found in Cornwall."

"Them? There's more than one greenhouse?" Callan asked.

"Oh, most definitely. There are twenty-four, scattered all over the property."

I felt my jaw drop. *Twenty-four.*

"Now, come along. We need to get this little fellow into his new home." Mr. Sparrow hurried ahead, moving spryly for someone his age.

The door to the greenhouse creaked as he opened it, and I followed him inside. I was moving faster than I normally would, wanting to be the first to see inside the greenhouse. In the past, I'd have stuck to the back of the crowd, but I couldn't help myself. I wanted to see it all.

I wanted *this.* The greenhouse, the garden, everything.

When I stepped into the glass structure, it was like walking into another world.

I was back at the Lizard, with sand beneath my feet and the ocean to my left. On the right, the entrance to the sea cave opened into the rock face of the cliff. There was no way he'd fit all of this into a greenhouse.

I gasped, unable to help myself. "Is it a portal?"

"No, we're still in my garden," Mr. Sparrow said. "It's a microclimate, created by magic. The interior space is expanded as well, though you will note that the cave isn't quite as big as it was back at the Lizard."

He was right about that. Now that my initial shock had

faded and I was looking more closely, I noticed that it was indeed a miniature version of what we'd seen at the Lizard.

The other competitors pushed their way inside the greenhouse, having to shove past me since I'd stopped dead in the middle of the doorway.

I shuffled to the side and asked, "Was it your magic that created this?"

"Some of it, though some of it belongs to my friends. I always need help with an operation of this size, which is why I emphasized cooperation in this first part of the competition."

He said he'd had help, but it had still probably been a lot of his magic that had made this place.

A thread of doubt crept through me. Would I be able to maintain something like this? How much magic would it take? It was one thing to have a gift for plants, but if I couldn't maintain their specialized habitats because my magic was too weak, then there was no point to me winning.

"All of the greenhouses on the property are microclimates for specific plants—some hold many plants, some hold only a few." Mr. Sparrow walked towards the cave entrance. "This one was built specially for this Xyanthia."

We followed him into the cave, and I realized that even the air smelled of the sea and cold, damp stone. It was darkly shadowed in the cave, but I could still make out Mr. Sparrow as he removed the plant from its box and placed it in a small hole that he'd dug. The leaves seemed to unfurl in a yawn, and I smiled.

"At least the water isn't rising," Lilac muttered.

Mr. Sparrow rose and dusted off his hands, then turned

to us. "Now, on to contest number two! You will each be assigned to a greenhouse, which you will take care of for three days. There might be problems you have to solve, so you'll need to be ready for anything. It is acceptable to have help from friends and family, since they would be there for you if you were to win the garden."

I grinned. I liked the idea of seeing more of these greenhouses.

Mr. Sparrow reached into his pocket and withdrew six small envelopes. He approached and handed one to each of us. "There's a map inside the envelope that will take you to your greenhouse. You may return tomorrow at nine a.m. to begin your task. The challenge ends at sunset on Saturday."

"Can we start earlier?" I asked.

He smiled. "I know you're excited, but no. The sun has nearly set, and it would be better for you to start in the daylight. And I would like to be here to greet you."

I nodded, vowing to be here before the gates opened.

"Thank you for retrieving the Xyanthia," he said, looking back at it fondly. "You may go."

The others murmured their goodbyes and left. I did the same and turned to follow, but Mr. Sparrow's voice stopped me. "Aria? Wait a moment, will you?"

I spun back to face him, happy to be able to talk to him some more.

"I'll wait outside for you," Callan said.

I wanted to tell him he didn't need to wait, but I was glad that he planned to.

The door shut behind him, and Mr. Sparrow spoke. "You

have a special talent, Aria. I can see it in you. *And* the Xyanthia allowed you to carry it. That is rare."

"Thank you."

"But you're going to need more. I know you've had trouble with your magic in the past. You're going to need to get past that if you want a chance at winning this competition."

I drew in an unsteady breath, not liking the words but knowing that they were right.

"Thank you," I said. "You're right."

"I know I am. I always am. Now go on to bed."

"Sure thing." I laughed and turned. "I'll see you tomorrow."

CHAPTER
SEVENTEEN

CALLAN

I WAITED for Aria at the gate, wondering what Mr. Sparrow had wanted to talk to her about. He should be congratulating her on a job well done.

All around, the garden came alive with nocturnal life. Small rodents scurried through the underbrush, and fireflies lit up the air around me. The night-blooming flowers began to unfurl, their brilliant blue and purple blossoms glowing beneath the light of the fireflies.

It really was a beautiful place. My plans for it would turn it into something spectacular, and it would be the crown jewel of Hawthorne Enterprises. There were already dozens of jobs in the making, and contractors who had cleared their schedule to start work on my vision once I won. My plans for this garden would catapult my company to the highest echelons of the business world, making us the most successful company in the UK. I'd worked my entire life for this.

And yet, guilt tugged at me.

Aria really wanted this garden, too, and she was perfect for it.

She appeared at the exit to the garden, distracting me from my dark thoughts. Her face glowed with that special something she'd got when she'd gone into the botanist's greenhouse.

"Everything okay?" I asked.

"Yeah. You didn't have to wait."

"I wanted to." I nodded towards the path that led back to town. "Walk you home?"

"Sure. I have a favor to ask."

"Anything."

"Anything?"

"Well, almost anything. I'd rather not prance through town in a pony costume, if it's all the same to you."

She laughed. "If I thought I could get you to do that, I would definitely ask. But it's less funny. I need help fixing my magic."

I looked down at her and smiled. "You know I think nothing about you needs to be fixed, but I can definitely help you unlock your magic. And we should start now."

"Like, *now* now?"

"You're going to need all the time we have."

"Agreed. Where to?"

We reached the main lane that led to her cottage. The cool night air blew in from the sea, smelling fresh and lovely.

The fireflies still escorted us, and the moon had risen higher in the sky, glittering on the waves far out to sea.

"We need a place with a lot of plant life," I said. "A variety of it is ideal. The garden would have been perfect, but it's closed now."

"My house?"

"Do you have a lot of plants?"

"I do indeed."

I grinned.

"What?" she asked. "You look like you expected that."

"I'm not surprised to hear it. You have a gift for plants, and I'm working on a theory."

"What kind of theory?"

"I don't want to say until we know more. But your place will be perfect." I could already see it in the distance, a little white cottage with the garden blowing in the breeze. She'd left a light on in one of the rooms, and the windows glowed with welcome.

She led me up the front path and opened the door, not bothering with a lock. I supposed this wasn't the kind of place that needed one, but still, I didn't like the idea that someone could be waiting for her in her house. "You should lock your doors."

"Here? Nah."

"I know crime is basically nonexistent, but it would make me feel better."

"Sure, city guy. I'll consider it." She flicked on the rest of the house lights and led me into a charming open living space. The kitchen was tidy except for an empty box of crackers on the floor, and Aria glowered and muttered, "Boris."

The badger was nowhere to be seen in the little living room or dining area, and he'd probably cleared out to do whatever badgers did at night.

She'd been right about the plants, though—she had a lot of them. They hung from the ceiling and sat on window ledges, all of them in perfect health. They gave the place a vibe similar to the Garden of Enchantment.

"This is great," I said, walking into the living room to inspect the corner where several plant stands rose towards the ceiling, each piled with a dozen pots.

"Thanks, I love it." She followed me towards the plants, running her hands over the ruffled green leaves.

"Have you always?"

She shrugged. "I liked them when I was a kid, but not any more than your usual child. It wasn't until I moved to London that I realized how much I missed being surrounded by nature. There's so much of it out here." She gestured towards the outside. "I collected these over the years."

"It looks great."

"Thanks."

"Ready to get started?"

"Yeah. Although I feel like its rude not to offer you a cup of tea or something."

"How about after the first round of practice?"

"There will be rounds?"

"Could be." I stepped back and gestured to the nook created by the plant stands. "Can you position yourself there? Close to the plants. Then try to move something in the room like a book or chair."

She nodded and stepped in to stand amongst the plants, then looked around. She pointed to one of the wooden kitchen chairs. "I'll move that."

I watched as she screwed up her face and focused on the chair. The chair tipped over, far more quickly and gently than the one at the pub.

I smiled. "How did that feel?"

"Better, actually. My control is still crap, but the magic came more easily."

"I had a feeling it might work."

Her brows rose in a look of understanding. "You think I do better in environments where I'm comfortable?"

I shook my head. "I think you draw your magic from plants, not the ether."

She frowned. "Is that possible?"

"Possible, but very rare. I'm not surprised no one figured it out if that's the case."

"I can't imagine my grandmother missing something like this."

"There are only a few witches in the world who still have this kind of power, and none of them live in Britain."

"I guess that explains it, but now that we know, how do I use it?"

"I don't know. But I know someone who might. I'll ask her, and we'll figure it out."

"Wow." She blew out a breath, then shot me an appreciative look. "Honestly, I wasn't expecting to get anywhere with this. I don't know what to say."

"No need to say anything. I'm just glad we might be getting our answers."

"Me, too." She looked vaguely stunned, her gaze distant and thoughtful. "Can I get you that drink?"

I wanted it—I *really* did. Since it meant getting to stay here with her a little longer, I would have drunk that terrible-looking blue stuff the teenagers down at the pub ordered by the case.

But the longer I stayed with her, the more I was going to want to kiss her. And now that I'd realized how perfect she was for the garden, and how important it still was that I win it, I felt the guilt starting to creep in.

This was getting complicated. "Thanks, but I think I'm going to head back to the B&B."

"Sure." She looked a little surprised, but she still seemed so distracted by the news about her magic that she said nothing else as she led me to the door.

I opened it and turned back to her to say goodnight, realizing that she stood far closer than I'd expected.

At this distance, I could see the flecks of gold in her eyes and the faint sheen on her lips that indicated she must have just run her tongue over them. The thought of it made me want to close my eyes and groan.

Instead, I stared at her like she was a feast.

"Callan?" Her voice was raspy as she looked up at my face. "What are you thinking?"

"That you look like a sunrise after a decade of darkness." The words that escaped my lips surprised me, and her as well. Her brows rose, and a flush filled her cheeks.

She looked so beautiful that it was impossible not to

imagine kissing her. When she leaned up and hovered her lips right in front of mine, I couldn't resist. I swept down and took her mouth with my own, sinking into the delicious softness.

A small moan escaped her, tightening something within me. I wrapped my hands around her waist and pulled her towards me. She pressed the length of her body against mine, and it took everything I had not to push her back into the room and kiss her until we were both breathless, panting, and naked.

Just the idea of what could happen next made me pull away.

Complicated.

This was complicated.

I released her and stepped back. "We're competing against each other."

She blinked, panting a bit. "Right. We shouldn't like each other. We're competing for the same thing." She shook her head as if to clear it. "And I'm already supposed to dislike you after what happened in the past."

"Do you?"

"No. But it would be easier if I did."

I felt a wry smile tug at the corner of my mouth. Now that I knew what it had meant to her, I still felt tremendous guilt about The Keep Café, but at least she had forgiven me.

"I'll see you tomorrow," I said.

"Tomorrow." As I walked away from the house, I felt her gaze on me. I wanted to turn back to look at her, but shoved my hand into my pocket instead. I withdrew the phone and called Seth, my assistant, and asked him to set up an appointment with the only other witch I knew who drew her magic from plants.

Aria

THE NEXT MORNING, I sat outside on my patio, soaking up the sun as the sound of waves crashing in the distance provided a backdrop to the calls of seagulls. A cool breeze ruffled the flowers in the garden, and their sweet scent filled the air. I stared down into my coffee cup, still groggy from a night spent tossing and turning with dreams of kissing Callan. None of this was going the way I'd expected it to.

So much was riding on me winning this competition. I actually had a shot at victory, and I had to give it my all. My gran depended on me. That shop had been in our family for generations. I couldn't be the one to lose it—especially not because I'd become distracted by wanting to kiss the man who was trying to beat me in said competition.

I just had to ignore how helpful and cool he was being. That was the only solution.

And I *definitely* needed to not kiss him. The whole kissing thing was a bad idea in too many ways.

From the edge of the patio, I spotted movement. I turned to see Boris trundling through the bed of colorful flowers, his little face looking tired.

"Big night for you?" I asked.

You don't even want to know.

"You sound like a lad coming back from the pub after a night out on the pull."

Isn't that what I am?

"Ugh." Had Boris been out trying to find a lady badger? I did not need to know anything more about my familiar's romantic life. Instead, I handed him my half-drunk coffee.

He sat back on his butt and accepted it, then raised it to his mouth. He was far more agile than I'd expected a badger to be, but maybe familiars had extra skills.

You're a life saver.

"Remember that next time you're tempted to sleep in my lingerie drawer."

Fine, fine. Your lingerie is safe from me.

"Good." I rose. It was time to get dressed and head to the Garden of Enchantment. Mr. Sparrow had told us we could show up at nine, and I was determined to be there five minutes early.

I chose my best gardening clothes—some old overalls and a plaid shirt that was thick enough to protect from most thorns—then tucked gloves into my pocket before heading out the door. Boris had already fallen asleep on the couch, and I left him snoring.

The day was gorgeous as I hurried towards the garden. It was impossible not to fall in love with my new life here. But if I won the garden?

It would be beyond perfect.

Determination filled me.

I'm going to do it.

I wouldn't let anything stop me now that I had a chance.

I reached the gate about five minutes before nine, finding

Callan already standing there. He was dressed in dark, sturdy trousers that made his butt look like a work of art. The gray shirt he wore was pushed up to his elbows, revealing the forearms that still had the power to entrance me.

Before I could get sucked in by too-sexy forearms—*get it together, idiot*—he turned. His smile was wide and genuine as he took me in. "Good morning."

"Ready to get started?" I asked, hearing the sound of the other competitors arriving. They chatted to each other, but I only had ears for Callan.

He nodded. "Looking forward to seeing what's in my greenhouse."

"Same." I pulled the envelope from my pocket and removed the map, though I'd memorized it last night before bed.

Mr. Sparrow appeared at the gates, his expression cheery as he unlocked them. He swept out his arm in a grand gesture. "Welcome!"

"Morning." Shoot, should I have brought him pastries or something? I wasn't above sucking up to win this thing, and I was now realizing maybe I'd missed a prime opportunity.

Ah, well, the opportunity had passed. I'd just have to prove myself in the greenhouse.

As we walked by Mr. Sparrow, he handed us each a set of keys. Callan stuck by my side as we entered the garden. A few minutes later, he took a path to the right. "Good luck," he said as he walked away.

"Good luck." I left the other competitors behind as I hurried down the path, taking the turns I'd memorized from the map. Eventually, I reached a greenhouse that was shaped like a dome. The structure was built of the same iron and old glass as the others, giving it an antiquated feel, and I couldn't help but fall in love.

The glass was steamed up on the inside, and my curiosity lit as I reached for the door and pulled it open. Heat washed over me, and I drew in a deep breath of air that smelled of soil, flowers, and foliage.

"Ah, heaven," I murmured, walking into the tropical wonderland.

The greenhouse that I had been assigned was a jungle, complete with massive trees, hanging vines, and colorful flowers of all varieties. Bugs and birds flew through the air, singing and buzzing as they worked. A monkey screeched from a few dozen meters away, though I couldn't see him.

I walked deeper into the jungle, my feet sinking into the moist ground, then spun in a circle to take it all in.

Mr. Sparrow had truly built the most incredible place I'd ever seen. This greenhouse had to be dozens of acres in size now that I was in it, and the magical microclimate he'd created was perfect for the plants. There were even rain-clouds above, though they hadn't released their bounty yet. The plants had everything they needed to sustain life—even insects for pollinating—and I couldn't imagine what Mr. Sparrow needed me for.

"I'll just have to find it," I said, hoping to psych myself up for the task ahead. There had to be some way to prove myself here.

I began to explore the garden, taking in the various plants and animals. I found a guide book near the door, which I read as quickly as I could, and then I began to

THE MODERN GIRL'S GUIDE TO MAGIC

explore. There was a huge section of the colorful meat-eating plants that were famous in the magical world for being used in multiple medications. They snapped at me, their purple petals surrounding white fangs that glinted brightly.

"Careful, now," I said. "Don't bite the hand that feeds you."

"I'd keep an eye on those," Mr. Sparrow's voice sounded from behind me. "They aren't very bright, but they are hungry. They will definitely eat the hand that feeds them."

I smiled and turned. "I'll keep that in mind. This place is so amazing, I can't imagine what I'm supposed to improve here."

"Oh, it will become apparent with time, I am sure." He smiled. "I just wanted to see how you were getting along and make sure that our resident monsters didn't get you." He nodded towards the plants, which were still snapping at me. "The Wizard's Butterwort are a bit more vicious than I anticipated when I brought them here."

"Have they been here long?"

He shook his head. "Only a few months. The transition period has been a bit rocky. It's been looking a little ill lately."

Maybe that's what I was supposed to help with?

Mr. Sparrow grinned. "Since you seem fine, that's all the help you're getting from me. I'll see you in a few days." He waved and turned, moving swiftly towards the exit.

I spent the next several hours mentally cataloguing everything in the greenhouse and taking note of things that I might be able to improve. A few things required photographs so that I could look them up later. And Mr. Sparrow was right, the Wizard's Butterwort was looking a bit peaky. I would have to do some research into that. By the time early afternoon rolled around, I realized that I was starving.

I left the greenhouse, careful to latch the door behind me, and headed towards the exit. Partway there, I hesitated.

I wanted to see Callan.

I also wanted to see his greenhouse. Though I was determined to keep things professional between us, I didn't want to lose this opportunity to see more of Mr. Sparrow's facility.

I found the path that Callan had taken and followed it, eventually stopping near a greenhouse that had windows coated with ice. All around it, the ground was frozen. The icy patches reached about ten feet out from the greenhouse, encroaching into the garden.

Callan appeared around the side of the building, his hair mussed and his jaw tight with exhaustion.

"Wow, you've got a problem," I said.

He nodded. "The climate control spell is malfunctioning. It's still cold in the greenhouse, but if the cold goes too far from the main building, it will begin to impact the rest of the garden."

I could already see where it had frozen several bushes that weren't meant to be so cold. "Do you have a plan?"

"Not yet. I managed to halt the spell, but I haven't been able to reverse it. I'll need to do some research tonight."

I was almost jealous that he had a concrete problem to solve. On the other hand, I didn't have the skills to solve a magical problem of that magnitude, so I should probably just be grateful that I wasn't him.

"How is your greenhouse?" he asked.

"Good. Maybe a little too good. I didn't find much I could fix." Had I missed something? No. I'd been thorough.

"I'm sure you will." He dragged a weary hand through his hair. "In the meantime, I have good news for you. I've found the location of the witch who has similar magic to yours. We can go visit her."

Excitement flared within me. "Really? Now?"

He nodded. "She said that it would be best if we came as soon as possible."

"What about the competition?"

"It will just be for the afternoon, and your magic is more important than any competition."

I wasn't sure if I agreed with him—there was so much on the line here—but the lure of understanding my magic was too great. And nothing was wrong at my greenhouse right now, so maybe I could afford a few hours to get some answers. "All right, let's go. But we have to be back by this evening."

"Great. We can have lunch on the plane."

"What do you mean, on the plane?"

"We have to go to Germany."

"Germany?!" I squeaked. "I can't go to Germany. I don't even have a passport." I knew it was weird I didn't have one, but I'd never had the opportunity to travel.

"You won't need one. I have contacts with private airports, and the plane is masked from humans by magic."

I blew out a breath. "Money really is something, isn't it?"

CHAPTER

EIGHTEEN

*A*RIA

C*ALLAN* drove us to the private airfield, which I'd had no idea existed so close to Charming Cove. There were no planes there except for a medium-sized one that looked really nice —not that I was any expert. *A medium-sized one that looked really nice* was the extent of my plane knowledge.

"I've never been on a plane before," I said. "I think I might actually be a bit nervous."

"Never?"

I shrugged. "Life in Charming Cove was quiet when I was a kid. Then I moved to London and had to make my own way. I never had any money for travel. Well, and I was always spending my money on plants."

He parked near the plane and turned off the car. "Don't be nervous. It's safer than riding in a car."

"I've heard that before, but it doesn't really help. We're going to be hurtling through the air in a pressurized metal tube." Just the idea of it gave me the shivers.

"Can I distract you with food?"

"Absolutely." I grinned at him. "There really is food on board?"

"Good food, even. I called ahead."

"Then lead the way." I climbed out of the car and followed him to the plane.

A man in a suit stood by the stairs that led up to the aircraft. He smiled and inclined his head at Callan. "Sir, good to see you again."

"Thank you, Trevor." Callan gestured to me. "This is Aria. She'll be flying with us today. Could you get her a glass of champagne as soon as you can?"

I looked at Callan, brows raised. "Champagne?"

"Do you not like it?"

"Oh, no, I love it." And I had a feeling that it would be the good stuff. "It's just that it's the middle of the day."

"We have to celebrate your first flight. And it will take some of the edge off."

I grinned at him. "I can't argue with that logic."

He gestured to the stairs. "After you."

I climbed up to the plane, stepping into a perfectly decorated living room. It didn't even look like it should be a plane except for the distinctly shaped windows. There was a couch in front of a coffee table, and a dining set with sturdy, beautiful chairs.

"I'll be right there with your drinks," Trevor said. "In the meantime, help yourself to the tray I set out." He waved towards a side table, and I felt my jaw drop at the sight of the cheese display. There was every variety imaginable, and some that I hadn't even considered. A bright pink one was particularly interesting.

"This is just too much." I turned to look at Callan. "You really live like this?"

He had the good grace to look at least a little bit uncomfortable. "Only sometimes. Normally, I just have a sandwich if we're flying during mealtimes."

"So this spread is for me?"

"I promised to distract you with food."

"Well, it worked." And it warmed my heart, too, as much as I didn't want to admit it.

Trevor appeared, two champagne flutes in his hands. He handed them to us and said, "I'll check with the pilot, but I think we'll be leaving soon. You'd best get a plate and find your seat."

"Thank you." I looked at Callan, who tilted his glass towards mine.

"Cheers?" he asked.

"Cheers."

"To your first flight."

I clinked my glass with his, then took a sip. Tart, cold bubbles exploded on my tongue, and I felt my eyes widen. "This is amazing."

"It's my favorite vintage."

The man had a favorite vintage. Of course he did. We really were on different levels.

I took another sip of the wine that tasted like the gods

themselves had brewed it, then walked to the cheese table. A whole table on an airplane, just for cheese!

This was heaven.

I piled my plate high with every delicacy there was, along with some gorgeous crusty bread. Callan did the same, and we took a seat at the dining table.

Trevor appeared from behind the curtain that I assume hid the kitchen and the entrance to the cockpit. "We'll be taking off momentarily. Please fasten your seatbelts."

I did as he asked, then looked at the champagne flute. Why not? I picked it up and tipped it back, downing the contents as quickly as I could. When I looked back down at Callan, he had a bemused expression on his face.

"What? I didn't want it to spill." I shrugged. "And you were right about the liquid courage. It'll help."

Trevor, ever perfect at his job, approached with the bottle. "Perhaps you should have some more."

"I think I should." I held out my flute and watched him fill it halfway. "You're a saint, Trevor."

He grinned, then returned to the kitchen. I took a few sips, then looked at Callan. "Was that totally embarrassing, what I just did?" I asked.

"I thought it was cute as hell, actually."

"I'm not sure how I feel about being called cute. Makes me sound like a kitten or something."

"Oh, you're no kitten." The grin he shot me was wolfish. "Or if you are, you've got claws."

"Good."

The plane began to rumble down the runway, and I gripped the stem of my champagne flute.

"This is the most intense part," Callan said. "Once we're in the air, it'll smooth out."

"What about turbulence?"

"A possibility, but you'll just have to down your wine if that happens."

"Glad to."

My heart spent the duration of our ascent lodged in my throat, but once we were airborne, everything really did settle out.

The plane ride ended up being enjoyable, though that probably had something to do with the hundreds of quid worth of wine and cheese I consumed. I would have drunk more of the liquid gold, but I wanted to be sober when we landed.

As the plane descended, I looked at Callan. "This part is going to be unpleasant too, isn't it?"

"Perhaps a bit, but it won't take long."

The plane bounced onto the runway, roaring along with a ferocity that shocked me. I squeaked and reached for Callan's hand, gripping it hard. He squeezed back.

"You said takeoff was the worst." I glared at him.

"It's a coin toss, really. And I didn't want you dreading the landing."

The plane slowed, finally stopping, and I let go of Callan's hand. I was still panting slightly, and my limbs were buzzy with adrenaline. "I hope you have another bottle of that champagne for the ride home."

"Two, in fact." He smiled.

"Good." I rose, my legs shaky.

Trevor went to the door and opened it, and when I

reached it, I saw that someone had already pushed the stairs up to the plane. I thanked Trevor and descended, grateful to be on solid ground.

The little airfield was just one runway in front of a forest. Dark shadows stretched between the huge hardwood trees, and I felt a thrill of excitement run through me.

Callan joined me and nodded to the car that waited a short distance away. "That's our car."

A driver stood next to it, waiting patiently with his arms crossed in front of his suited body. We walked towards him, and he opened the door for me. This was another new experience—being chauffeured by anyone except Gran or the City of London public transportation service was well outside the realm of my normal.

Callan shared a few quiet words with the driver, then joined me. Soon, we were off. There was a privacy screen between us and the driver, and I leaned towards Callan and whispered, "You really don't mind being driven everywhere?"

"Not a huge fan, actually. I prefer to drive myself. But this is quicker since he knows the way. There's too much as stake for me to risk getting us lost on the wrong road."

"Thanks." I appreciated that, actually.

The driver turned down a dark lane that led through the forest, and I looked out to see that the shadows were growing even darker. Beams of sunlight cut through some of the gaps in the canopy, and wherever they landed grew a profusion of colorful blooms. There was magic everywhere.

"Do humans know about this place?" I asked. There was

so much power here that even they would probably feel it, though they might not be able to identify it.

"No, and they're repelled by a spell that Gertrude cast."

"Gertrude is our witch?"

"She is. She's lived here for the last forty years."

I blew out a breath. That was a long time to live in a fairytale forest.

After about thirty minutes, the car slowed as it approached a cottage that sat in the middle of a clearing. Sunshine filled the space, making the green grass look extra bright.

I climbed out of the car, taking in the magnificent garden that surrounded the little thatch-roofed cottage. Roses climbed up the walls, and smoke drifted lazily from the chimney. A creek burbled by on the right.

A woman appeared in the doorway, grinning broadly when she saw us. She waved. "Callan! What a surprise."

He approached, and I followed. The woman was probably about sixty, with beautiful salt-and-pepper hair that had been piled into a high bun. She wore a flowing dress with a number of beaded necklaces draping to her waist. Her dark eyes were bright with friendliness as she reached out to hug him.

He embraced her back, though the movement was a bit stiff, as if he weren't used to hugging in greeting. It was no surprise. His life as a highflying businessman probably didn't involve a lot of hugs.

Gertrude pulled back and looked at me. The smile on her face widened. "Oh, my goddess, you're a plant witch!" She hit Callan playfully on the chest. "I can't believe you didn't tell me you were bringing one of my kind."

"Wow, you recognized me that quickly?" I asked.

She nodded. "Of course. A plant witch always recognizes one of their own. Unfortunately, there are only half a dozen of us in the world, so we don't run into each other often."

Only half a dozen? No wonder Gran hadn't figured out what I was.

"Come." She gestured for us to follow her inside. "Let's have tea and talk about this."

Her home was incredible. The main living area was like my cottage, with one room for kitchen, dining, and living. Every surface was covered with plants, some of them so exotic that I'd never even seen them in books. Sometimes, plants could make a place look cluttered, but not here. They were arranged in such a way that they fit amongst the décor perfectly. It was so cozy that I never wanted to leave.

She gestured to a back door. "Why don't you go out into the garden and take a seat? I will join you as soon as I have the tea."

We did as she asked, leaving the house and stepping onto a beautiful flagstone patio. The little creek had wrapped around the back of the house and ran right alongside the patio, murmuring as the water tumbled over shiny pebbles. Flowerbeds bordered the patio, their blooms exploding in every color of the rainbow. Fat, industrious honeybees went about their work, buzzing happily.

Though there was a cushioned patio set surrounding a fire pit, we chose to sit at the round wooden dining table. A sleek black cat had taken up residence in the middle, and I reached forward to give him a pet. He lifted his face and purred as I scratched under his chin.

"This reminds me of your home," Callan said.

"I was thinking the same. I guess we plant witches have something in common."

"Indeed we do." Gertrude's voice sounded from behind us, and I turned to see her walking out of her kitchen.

Behind her, a large vine carried a tray of tea towards the table. I couldn't see where it had originated from, but it stretched longer and longer until it was able to set the tray down.

"That's amazing," I murmured. Other witches could control plants, but I'd never seen one act as a helpful assistant before.

"It's easy." Gertrude smiled and flicked her hand. "I can show you how to do it."

"Can you show me how to fix my magic?"

"Hopefully." She gave a little shrug and poured the tea. "At the very least, I can tell you how to unlock it."

"I'll take anything you've got." I accepted the teacup she handed me with a grateful nod. "I have almost no control right now, and it's been a disaster. My whole life, in fact."

"I'm not surprised." She poured another cup and handed it to Callan. "We plant witches aren't like the others. We have the potential to be more powerful, but only if we have the support we need."

"What do you mean by support?" I took a sip of the tea, delighted by the floral flavor.

"You need someone to tell you what you are, for one. And how to unlock your magic."

"Unlock it? That's what you mentioned before, but I've never heard of that."

"Indeed not. The ether witches don't have to do it. There are so many of them, and they're taught from such a young age how to use their magic that they don't have the problems we do. But since there are so few of us in the world, and our gift isn't genetic, we don't have a way to find the others."

"So you think there are more of us than just half a dozen?" I liked the idea of that.

"I presume so, but they probably don't know what they are, either. No doubt they think they are failed ether witches, as we all do when we first come into our magic."

The idea that I wasn't a failed witch after all was heady stuff. It had been my identity for so long, but I was ready to shed it like a snake skin and start my life in control of my gift. "What do I need to do to unlock my magic?"

"At the full moon, you must go into a deep forest—one that has a great variety of plant life is ideal—and lay amongst the greenery. The place must be vitally important to you, though. It's key that you feel a connection with the land. If the place isn't right, then nothing will happen, but if it *is* right, then the power will react with the moonlight and flow through you. The rest will take care of itself."

"That's all?"

She laughed lightly. "It's not easy to find the right place. And it took you decades to figure out what you were. I'd hardly say it's been an easy journey for you. And once your magic has been unlocked, you will still need to learn to control it. Nothing about it will be easy, but you'll be on your way, at least."

"Thank you." I tried to infuse my voice with all the gratitude that I felt, which was hard, considering how much there was of it.

"Of course."

"The full moon is in three days," Callan said.

Fortunately, I had just the place for the big event. There was no question that it was the Garden of Enchantment. Every time I walked in there, I felt how special it was, and it had been part of my family's life for years.

A rose bush from behind her reached out, stretching a bloom towards her as if to be petted. She turned and ran her hand over the bloom, a frown appearing on her face. "Oh, that must be quite itchy, my darling. Let me take care of that for you."

She was talking to the plant like I did. I shared a quick glance with Callan, who looked just as interested as I felt.

Gertrude murmured a few words that sounded something like, "Pests be gone and out of sight."

A few moments later, the rosebud shivered in what appeared to be pleasure, then retreated to its spot in the garden.

"What just happened?" I asked.

"I suppose this can be your first lesson, and the most important. Not only are you able to draw your power from plants, but you can communicate with them. The rose bush had developed a small infestation of pests overnight, and it wanted me to get rid of them."

"So it reached out to you and told you?"

"Not with words, but I was able to understand the problem once I touched the plant. And the spell that I uttered wasn't necessary, precisely. You don't have to use words to manifest your desires, but I find that it helps me to focus the magic and my intentions."

I blew out a breath and thought back to all the times I'd touched one of my plants and had an instinct for what it needed, whether it was fertilizer or water or more sun. "That's incredibly cool," I murmured. "I love getting answers."

"I take it you've done something similar in the past?"

I nodded. "I just wasn't sure if I was right about what I thought the plants needed. I assumed I had an instinct for it. I didn't realize the plants were straight up *telling* me."

"Well, they are." She smiled. "And if you try hard, you can also tell *them* things."

"Like what?"

"To carry a tea set." She gestured to the tray on the table. "Or to grow along a path instead of away from it, though there is no guarantee it will listen. Plants still have will. But if you are clever and kind, they often want to do your bidding."

The possibilities were incredible. More than that, I had *answers*. That was the biggest thing.

"Thank you so much," I said. "Truly. I can't tell you what this means to me."

"Oh, darling, I was you once! I know exactly what it means." She looked at Callan. "I'm glad you found Aria and brought her to me. Thank you. Our numbers are too low as it is."

"Why is our magic different?" I asked. "My parents weren't plant witches."

"We don't know, honestly."

"Well, at least I now know what I am. And that's a hell of a lot." I grinned.

We said our goodbyes, and I was positively buzzing as we returned to the plane. The possibilities were endless now that I knew what I was. And when the full moon came in three days, the world would be so much different.

CHAPTER
NINETEEN

ARIA

THE NEXT MORNING, I awoke before the dawn. We'd arrived home so late last night that Callan had dropped me off shortly before midnight. I'd briefly considered inviting him in, then discarded it as the insanity that it was.

Now that I knew what kind of magic I had, I needed to win this competition more than ever.

Since Mr. Sparrow had given us keys to the gardens and our greenhouses, I could get in whenever I wanted.

Excitement shot through me as I rose, ready to see the greenhouse again. I had just turned on the shower when a knock sounded at the door. I shut off the water and hurried through the house, pulling open the door to reveal Gran, who had three grocery bags draped over her arm. "Gran? What are you doing here so early?"

"I wanted an update on the competition. And when Mr. Sparrow told me about the newest challenge, I knew I'd find you awake before dawn, ready to get there."

I grinned. "Then you also know I need to get a move on."

"Right, right. But you need a shower. While you do that, I will make you breakfast. I'll be quick as a sinner on his way past a church."

I laughed. "Thanks, Gran. You know I can't turn down your breakfasts."

Boris peeked his head into the house, squeezing past Gran's legs to trundle inside.

"Where have you been, mister? Out gallivanting again?"

You know it. He turned and sat on his butt, giving my gran his cutest expression. *Breakfast?*

"I don't understand you since you're not my familiar, dear," Gran said. "But I can assume you're asking for breakfast?"

Boris nodded.

"Then you've got it," she said. "Come keep me company while I cook."

I left them to it and went into the bathroom, showering as quickly as I could. Once I was clean, I pulled on another ratty gardening outfit. By the time I made it back out into the kitchen, Gran had assembled three bacon and egg sandwiches on rolls. She handed one to Boris, who downed it like a snake unhinging his jaw to eat a large rodent.

Ew. Not really the best thought for so early in the morning. Gran wrapped the other two sandwiches in paper and turned to me, a smile on her face. "Ready to go! I'll walk you to the garden."

"Thanks, Gran." Warmth suffused my chest, and I was once again grateful that I'd returned home. How had I gone without this for so long? The idea of returning to London was crazy now. Horrible, even.

Gran handed me my sandwich, then passed over a travel mug that had been filled with coffee. The side was emblazoned with the message, *Double, double, toil and trouble...I need coffee on the double.*

"I got that on vacation in Majorca." She grinned at me. "Had a wild weekend with the girls. *Wild.*"

"Oh, Gran." I couldn't help but grin back so widely, my cheeks hurt. I probably looked like a crazy person, but if there was one place you could look like a crazy person, it was with your gran.

We left the house and headed towards the cliff path that would lead to the gardens. Boris followed along, though I wasn't sure if he was coming for the company or the chance at a bite of one of our sandwiches.

Maybe both.

As we reached the main path along the cliffs, I bit into the delicious sandwich my grandmother had made. It tasted of childhood—warm and comforting and delightfully cheesy. To my left, the sea sparkled in the morning light. Waves crashed into the cliffs below, and seagulls squawked as they swooped overhead, clearly hoping for a bite. No way in hell was I sharing with them.

"All right now, tell me what's going on," Gran said. "I've let you eat some of your sandwich, now it's time to pay up."

I laughed and updated her on what we'd learned in

Germany. Her face filled with joy. "A plant witch? I've never heard of such a thing."

"I know, otherwise you would have figured it out yourself, I'm sure."

"Of course." She shook her head, clearly in awe. "My goodness. I am just so pleased, my dear. And this must be why all my sources said you were the perfect one for the job of winning the garden."

"I'm starting to think your sources might be right." I'd been skeptical of her tea leaves and crystal balls before, but maybe that had been silly.

She wrapped an arm around my shoulders and gave me a tight side hug. "Of course they are. They're never wrong, and *I'm* never wrong."

I decided not to remind her of the time she'd thought it would be a good idea to sell live butterflies. They'd completely overtaken the store, knocking over dozens of potion bottles—one of which had splashed on me and given me a pig's snout. It had not been a great day.

When we reached the garden, Gran and I stopped at the closed gate.

She pulled a little package from her bag and pressed it into my hands. "Lunch. And this is where I'll leave you. Good luck today. I know you can do it."

I wasn't sure what I liked more—the thoughtful lunch she'd packed me or the words of praise. Fortunately, I didn't have to choose.

I gave her a tight hug and murmured, "I'm sorry I left for so long."

"Me, too, but I know why you had to do it. You're home,

and that's all that matters." She pulled back and smiled broadly at me. "Now, go get them."

"Will do."

She turned and headed down the path while I dug the bigger silver key out of my pocket. I used it to unlock the gate, which swung open with silent grace. The garden spread out before me, beautiful and mysterious. As I stepped inside, I couldn't help the shiver of possibility that ran down my spine.

Mine.

It already felt like mine, even though I was a long way off from winning it.

Morning birds chirped as I made my way to the greenhouse that I'd been assigned. As I got closer, I realized that something was amiss. The windows weren't as foggy as they should be. My heart jumped into my throat, and I ran towards the building.

Was I having a climate control problem like Callan?

I reached the door and yanked on it, but it was still locked. Heart racing, I fumbled with the smaller brass key I'd been given. It clicked in the lock, and the door swung open. I darted inside, searching for whatever problem had made the climate go wonky.

In the distance, I spotted the flesh-eating plants chomping on the iron framing of the greenhouse. Wizard's Butterwort, Mr. Sparrow had called it. The fangs sunk into the metal and tore off bite after bite.

"Hey!" I dropped the lunch bag that Gran had packed me and ran towards the plants. "Stop that!"

The plants ignored me and continued to chomp on the

metal framing. Glass shattered and fell as the purple bastards tore into a new pane.

Had I not fed them at the appropriate time? No, the guide book had said that the greenhouse was self-sustaining, including these guys. Flesh eating for a plant meant that it caught bugs and ate them. True, these magical guys would also eat a person if they got the chance, but they subsisted happily on the bugs in the greenhouse. So they shouldn't be hungry.

Were the bugs all gone?

I looked around, catching sight of several flying out through the openings in the domed ceiling. Shit!

"Come back!" I cried, knowing that I sounded like an idiot.

Of course they didn't listen.

The plants must need something besides bugs. More iron in their diet? Could plants take iron supplements? Did they need them?

I reached out a tentative hand, hoping to use the skills that Gertrude had explained to me. I'd done it before with my own plants, but the stakes were higher now.

My fingertips brushed a smooth green stem and I got the briefest jolt of awareness before the flower whipped around and snapped at me.

Pain flashed as it took a little chunk out of my wrist. I yanked my hand back and stumbled away, panting. "You wanker!"

The flower seemed to grin at me, the petals pulling back to reveal sharp little fangs. I glared at it as I looked down at my wrist. Blood welled and dripped to the floor. It was a nasty wound.

The faintest sound of rustling leaves drew my attention to the Wizard's Butterwort. Every single blossom had turned its head and was staring right at me. *Could you stare if you didn't have eyes?*

Whatever the case, the blossoms were all moving towards me. *Fast.*

I turned tail and ran, sprinting through the greenhouse to the exit. When I reached it, I turned back to see that the plants hadn't been able to follow me all the way. They could stretch their stems a bit, but they couldn't pick up their roots and walk like the Xyanthia.

"Is it the blood that's attracted you?" I asked, cradling my hand. I knew they couldn't answer me unless I was touching them, but my plants liked it when I talked to them, so I figured I would try it here. "There's iron in blood. Maybe that's what you wanted?"

They didn't nod—it wouldn't be that easy—but they did continue to face me, which I figured was the plant version of staring.

"You need something, right?" I asked. "That's why you're eating the greenhouse. I'm going to figure out what it is."

They just continued to stare.

"Looks like I'm going to have to figure it out the hard way," I muttered as I stepped towards them. Maybe I could be quick enough to get my information without getting another bite taken out of me.

When I was about five feet away, a dozen blossoms snapped

at me, shooting farther than I'd expected. I lunged backwards, tumbling onto my butt and rolling away until I was cowering behind a collection of large pots that held fluffy green ferns.

Right. New plan needed. No way I was going closer to those plants without a better plan.

"Going that well, is it?" Callan's voice sounded from behind me.

I turned and spotted him in the doorway. "The day is a smashing success so far."

"I can see that." His gaze went to the windows that had been broken by the ravenous plants as they'd torn at the iron framing.

I pushed myself to my feet and brushed my clothes off, spinning to inspect the rest of my greenhouse. I'd been so distracted by the destructive little wankers that I hadn't checked on all the other plants.

Most of them looked okay—for now. At least the Wizard's Butterwort was only attacking the iron structure and not the other plants. But these guys lived in a steamy greenhouse for a reason. If I didn't get it fixed, the cool nights would wreak havoc on some of these plants. At least it was summer. I wouldn't have stood a chance if it was winter. Half of these guys would be dead by now.

"Is this what happened at your place?" I asked.

"No, there was no visible damage. Everything inside seems fine."

"Have you figured out what's causing it, then?"

"Not yet, but I have some ideas." He nodded towards the purple flowers that had turned and begun to chomp at the iron framing once more. "Do you know how to stop them?"

"No, and they're mean." I raised my wrist to inspect it. I was going to need a bandage.

A frown flashed on Callan's face, and he was at my side. "They did this to you?"

"You know what they say about gardening. It's not for the fainthearted."

"I don't think they say that." He looked up at the fanged purple flowers. "Though maybe they should."

"They definitely should." My mind raced, turning over ways to fix this damned problem.

"Let's get that cleaned up, then we can brainstorm."

"Together?"

"Why not?"

"We're competing *against* each other."

He shrugged. "So I'll kick your arse in the next challenge. But right now, I'd say we need each other's help."

"Fine, let's work together." He was right, anyway. I didn't know where to go from here, and the full moon wasn't for two days, so I couldn't count on it to give me extra skills in time to win this particular challenge. It looked like I could use all the help I could get.

I gave the ravenous plants one last look and followed him out of the greenhouse, stopping briefly to pick up the lunch bag that I'd dropped when I'd come in. A few yards down the path was a bench that had a perfect view of the plants that were chomping away at my greenhouse. I took a seat and watched them. Callan joined me, sitting close enough that I could smell the intoxicating scent that was intrinsically him.

"How's your freezing problem working out?" I asked as I

watched the little purple bastards eat my precious greenhouse.

"My containment spell is starting to falter."

"You can't fix it?"

He shook his head. "I can give it a bit more power, but it won't last much longer. I need to find another solution. What are you going to do about this?"

"I need to find a way to touch them without them eating me alive. Once I make contact, I bet I can figure out why they're doing this and give them whatever it is they want."

"Iron supplements?"

I laughed. "That's what I'm hoping. I'll just go down to the chemist and buy a hundred bottles and chuck them in there." I frowned. "But right now, I'm most worried about the other plants. Even summer in Britain isn't warm enough for jungle plants."

"I could help you with that." He gave the greenhouse a considering look. "If I use my magic to construct a second glass dome over the greenhouse, it will at least control the climate until you can determine what is wrong with the purple flowers."

"That would be an enormous help." I smiled at him. "You're sure you don't mind?"

"No. Especially if you're willing to come check out my greenhouse and see if you can identify my problem."

"Done." His help would buy me the time to figure out what was wrong with my plants, and maybe I could help him. "Is this something you can do right now?"

He nodded, then stood, lacing his fingers together to stretch. When he unlocked his fingers and raised his hands, his magic swirled around him. It blew his hair off his face and made his eyes gleam with iridescent intensity.

I turned to the greenhouse, gasping as panes of glass appeared from thin air. Mages were immensely powerful, and Callan was possibly the strongest of them all. Within minutes, a new glass dome had appeared. Notably, there was no iron.

"It won't last forever," Callan said. "Eventually, those plants might grow to reach it, but hopefully, they'll be deterred by the lack of iron. It should buy you a day or two, though."

"Thank you." The dome was beautiful, sparkling and bright in the midmorning sun. If only this could be my solution. But taking away the iron wouldn't solve the underlying problem. I turned to him. "Well, you've helped me. Now it's time for me to help you. Lead the way."

He led me towards his greenhouse, and my mind continued to spin with ways to fix my own problem. I was going to have to sneak up on the plants, probably.

When we reached his greenhouse, I noticed that the ice had spread even further from the structure. The problem had to be inside, though.

"Can we go in?" I asked.

He nodded and led the way to the door. It opened as smoothly as mine had, and cold air rushed out. I shivered and wrapped my arms around myself as I stepped inside.

A frozen tundra extended in front of me, harshly beautiful. Tall, snow-tipped pines filled the space, along with Arctic willow and bearberry. The silver-green leaves of the willow were beautiful beneath the sunny light, and the bright red bearberries glistened. My breath fogged in the air as I looked around.

"It all looks fine," he said. "I haven't found anything visibly wrong in the entire place. I've read the guide that was by the door and they all have what they need. No issues with the structure of the greenhouse. And yet the climate spell is failing."

"Hmm." I started towards one of the large trees in the middle of the greenhouse. "With plants, what you see on the surface is only half of it."

"Of course. The roots. I didn't think of that."

I reached the tree and pressed my palms against the rough bark. A sense of calm rushed through me. I'd always thought that the feelings were coming from inside me, but what if they were coming from the tree?

If that was the case, then this guy wasn't the problem.

I removed my hand and went closer to the greenhouse wall, choosing another tree to touch. He, too, seemed fine. Callan followed me as I went around the greenhouse, touching tree after tree. When I was at the tree closest to the greenhouse wall, I finally got something different.

"This guy is stressed," I said. "I think his roots are pushing outside of the boundary of the climate control. He's getting into warm soil, and he doesn't like it."

"And it's probably interfering with the climate control spell."

"I would think so." I looked around the greenhouse, noting that there were other trees close to the walls. "He's probably not the only one."

"I think you've found the problem." Callan sounded

impressed, and if I were being totally honest with myself, I liked it. "Now I just have to figure out how to fix it."

"That, I'm not so sure about. The spells that keep climate in line are above my pay grade. But I do know you need to get these trees under control before they get any bigger."

CHAPTER
TWENTY

CALLAN

I STARED AT ARIA, awed by her ability to read what the tree needed.

She really was the best person to win the Garden of Enchantment. She had a natural affinity for it. And not only would she be good for the garden, but the garden would be good for her.

I wanted her to win the competition.

It hit me in an instant.

There was no way in hell I could take the garden from her —if I even stood a chance of winning. At this point, I wasn't so confident. After seeing what she could do, it was clear that my odds of victory were far lower than I'd anticipated.

She was incredible, and I had to make sure she won. There would obviously be problems with the investors who expected me to deliver on my grand plans for the garden, but

I'd find a way to deal with them. And the jobs that were meant to be made? Those were harder to figure out, but money could solve that, too.

I pushed the thought to the back of my mind for later.

"Earth to Callan." She waved a hand in front of my face. "Are you there?"

"What?" I blinked at her, realizing that I'd drifted away from the conversion. "Yes, definitely."

"Then what was I saying?"

"Um." I searched my mind.

"It wasn't important. But you were clearly thinking about something else. What was it?"

"I was thinking about how incredible it was that you could diagnose what was wrong with my greenhouse by touching the tree." It was the truth, though only part of it. "You're the Plant Whisperer."

She grinned broadly. "I like that name."

"It suits you."

She looked back at the tree. "I can't believe that after all these years, I might finally be able to do magic. Like, proper magic."

"When the full moon comes Sunday night, you'll get to see what you're really capable of. My money is on it being a lot."

"I hope so. I really need to win this competition for Gran, and it would be great to have some extra power to do that."

"Why do you need to win for your grandmother?"

"Our shop gets most of our supplies from the garden, and there's no place else like it. There are potion ingredients there that we can't find anywhere else. And trust me, I've tried. The other places that sell them already have customers waiting." She shrugged and looked back at me. "Without those ingredients, our most popular products won't be available. The shop will close within months."

It was just another reason she needed to be the one to win.

She continued speaking, her voice slightly wistful. "And honestly, I just really want a chance to prove myself. It's fate that my worst bullies from my school years are my competition. Everyone has called me a failure my whole life, and I want to prove that I'm not."

Her words stole my breath. I wanted to hex the people who'd made young Aria's life hell.

But her words made one thing very clear: I could never let her know that I wanted her to win and that I'd do whatever it took to make sure she did. She needed to win this on her own.

"I think you've got a chance," I said. "As long as I don't beat you, of course."

She grinned. "Oh, I'm going to crush you, mage boy. Just you wait and see."

"I look forward to it."

She turned towards the door of the greenhouse. "I need to get started on figuring out how to fix my greenhouse. See you later."

She was gone before I could say anything. As I watched her walk away, I had to admit to myself that there was another reason I wanted her to win. *Because I want her.*

Not just for a night, though that was high on my list. But forever. She was unlike anyone I had ever met. I'd enjoyed the company of all the women I'd known, but Aria was different. There was just something about her that made me want to never be out of her presence. Her wit, brains, and beauty were enough to keep me enthralled for the rest of my life.

∼

Aria

As I HURRIED AWAY from Callan's greenhouse, I tried to banish the memories of flirting with him.

I liked him.

A lot.

And yet, he was the famous, powerful Callan Hawthorne. And I was a nobody witch who couldn't control her magic or hold down a job. It was crazy to think there could be anything between us. The thought just made me sad.

Fortunately, I'd arrived at our shop. I had no answers for those hard questions, and I needed to focus on figuring out how to fix my greenhouse.

I found Gran at the counter, sitting on her embroidered pink stool as she glared at a paper and muttered to herself.

"What's wrong, Gran?"

"Oh, nothing dear. Just trying to sort out this new potion." She put the paper and pen down, then removed her glasses and smiled at me. My chest filled with warmth just from looking at her. "What can I do for you?"

"I need help." I went behind the counter and grabbed the

small chair that was pressed into the corner, then brought it over to sit next to Gran. Once seated, I told her all about the ravenous Wizard's Butterwort that was eating my greenhouse, and how it seemed to be attracted to iron. "If I could just touch them, I could find out what they need and fix their problem. But they bite me as soon as I get close. They could take out a few chunks of me by the time I got the info I needed."

"Oh, we don't need that." She grimaced. "These sound like nasty beasts, if you ask me."

"No, they're just ill, I think. And I can fix them. But I need a way to get them to hold still long enough."

Gran tapped her chin, her expression going thoughtful. "I suppose we could give you an iron skin potion so that they couldn't bite you. Or at least their fangs couldn't get far."

"That could work." I looked for the holes in the plan. "Though there is a possibility they could squeeze me with their vines. I saw them really wrapped around some of the iron posts that support the greenhouse roof."

Gran shook her head. "That idea is out, then. I think we should assume they are capable of that." Her face brightened. "What if we tranquilize them?"

"It won't hurt them, will it?"

"No, we would use a mild sedative. It will take a bit of time to brew, though."

My heart fell. "How long?"

She blew out a breath, and it was clear from her expression that she was doing the calculations in her head. "I can have it for you by morning."

That didn't leave me a lot of time, since tomorrow night

was the end of the contest. But I also didn't have any other options. "Thank you, Gran. You're a lifesaver."

"Of course I am." She leaned forward and kissed me on the cheek. "Now get up and help me collect the ingredients."

I hopped up, my mood light. It had been a long time since I'd helped Gran brew a potion, but I'd always enjoyed it as a kid.

"To start, I'm going to need six bunches of mugwort, a jar of Elysian bloom, a clump of thunderweed, and two handfuls of watermint. Make sure the last is extra fresh. No wilting. Not even a single leaf."

"On it." I set about collecting the ingredients from the shop and back garden. The mugwort I could find hanging from the ceiling, and it was quick work to get a stepstool to reach it and a pair of scissors to cut it down.

The Elysian bloom was in the back store room, and that took a little longer to find. The shelves were stacked high and deep with hundreds of jars of ingredients. When I found the little jar of pink petals marked *Elysian bloom*, I realized that there was barely enough left, and this stuff was hard to come by.

"Damn it," I muttered, bringing it back to Gran. I wasn't going to have a lot of wiggle room if this was all the Elysian bloom we had. I handed it over to Gran. "How much extra of this potion will there be?"

"Not much," she said. "I'd have made you more, but I knew we were running low on Elysian bloom."

She didn't need to add that we got the stuff from Lionel Sparrow, and if we wanted more, I was going to have to win this competition.

"Now off you go," she said. "Get me that thunderweed and water mint from the back garden."

I did as she asked, hurrying towards the rear of the shop and the little door that led to our private garden. We were able to grow some of the things we needed ourselves, and thunderweed and watermint were two of those.

Warm summer air rushed over me as I stepped out into the walled garden. It was about eight meters wide by fifteen deep, with tall stone walls on all sides. Flowering vines climbed up the walls, and bees buzzed around the blooms. At the base of the walls, wild profusions of plants grew. Some flowered; some didn't. Others gave off intoxicating scents or strange fruits.

Sun streamed into the garden, and I immediately caught sight of Boris lounging in the hammock that had been strung up between two apple trees. He snored loudly, his furry belly rising and falling.

"Wake up, nerd," I called as I walked towards the little pond at the back of the garden. "It's time to get to work."

Boris snuffled and sat up, then glared at me.

"Come help me harvest this thunderweed," I said. "It grows in the trees around the pond back here."

He shook his head and didn't move.

"I need your magnificent climbing skills. You can just scurry up and grab some."

Badgers don't climb.

I turned to look at him. "Really?"

Really. At least not as high as that thunderweed.

"Sure you don't want to try?"

Yes. Very.

Damn. Looked like I would be climbing the tree today.

By the time I returned with the thunderweed and watermint, Gran had the cauldron steaming. She'd conjured a small purple fire beneath it, and the flames flickered like jewels as they heated the contents of the pot.

"Give it here." She held out her hand for the last of the ingredients, then quickly chopped them into the appropriate sizes and dumped them in the pot. A small flash of light exploded, and I shielded my eyes.

"That's a good sign," she said. "Everything is working."

"Now we wait?"

She nodded. "And practice."

"Practice what?"

"Didn't you wonder how you were going to tranquilize the plants?"

"I figured I would put the potion on the roots or something."

"Oh, no, my dear. You have to hit them with a dart from a blowgun."

"A blowgun? You're not serious."

"I'm deadly serious." She bustled to the other side of the shop and withdrew two of the blowguns that I knew we sold but had never tried out myself. "Now come on, we need to get blowing."

Oh, bugger. I was going to need a lot of practice. There was no way this was a skill I naturally had.

"This way, dear." Gran took the blowguns and darts and strode towards the back garden.

I followed her out, finding Boris once again asleep in the hammock. The sun had sunk lower in the sky, but it would still be a few hours before dark. Hopefully, that was enough time to become a blowgun expert.

Gran gestured to the little shed at the side of the garden. "See if you can find a barrel lid in there."

I headed for the small shed, which had been painted a beautiful sea-blue years ago but had since faded to something more mellow. Yellow sunflowers grew alongside the walls, their faces tilted up to the sky.

When I returned with a lid from one of the storage barrels we kept in the shed, Gran drew a marker from her pocket and marked the wood with several Xs. Then she took the lid and propped it in a tree so that it was about five feet off the ground.

"Now, this is how it's done." She raised a blowgun to her lips and blew out a breath, shooting the dart straight at the X in the center of the barrel. Within seconds, she'd reloaded and shot three more darts, hitting each X in turns.

I gaped at her. "Gran. I had no idea you were so good at this."

"Of course I'm good at this. And you will be, too, with practice."

"Maybe you could just come with me tomorrow and shoot the plant."

She shook her head. "You have to win this for yourself, dear."

I stared at her, wondering if she could read into my soul and see the deep desire to prove myself. Probably. She was my gran, after all. "But it's more important that we win the garden so we can keep the shop going."

"Is it?"

"Of course."

She shrugged. "I believe in you." She handed me a blowgun that had already been loaded with a dart. "Now, get to it. You still stink."

Gran had me out there for hours, blowing dart after dart. Tabitha and Catrina joined us after dinner, which Gran and I had skipped. Catrina, of course, was an absolute natural. She hit every X on the first try.

But I wasn't too bad, either. With any luck, I'd manage to tranq the plant tomorrow and find out exactly how to fix it. Except, even once the plant was happy, I would still have a severely damaged greenhouse.

"I'm going to need more help," I said, lowering the blowgun to my side. "Once the plants are fixed, I'll need to rebuild the greenhouse. But I don't have the magic."

Tabitha nodded. "You can count on us. How bad is the damage?"

"Really bad. Probably hundreds of square meters are missing by now."

"That will take both of us," Gran said. "Maybe even more. But we'll be there. You just keep us updated about your progress."

"Thanks, guys." I smiled gratefully at them.

Gran waved at the target. "Keep practicing!"

By the time we'd finished, fireflies had come out and lit the garden with their golden gleam. The waxing moon was high in the sky, glowing bright as a beacon.

"You're getting good at this," Tabitha said.

"Thanks." My stomach grumbled. "Although I could definitely use some dinner."

"Why don't you go pick up some fish and chips from Codswollop's?" Gran said. "I'll have the usual."

"Sure thing, Gran."

"I'll come with you," Tabitha said. She looked at Catrina. "Do you want to stay with Gran?"

Catrina nodded enthusiastically, then ran into the house. Gran followed her in, chuckling.

"I don't even want to know what she's up to in there," Tabitha muttered. "It's going to be crafting a potion to give someone pig ears, I'm sure of it."

"She's already mastered the tail, so why not add a set of ears?" I asked.

Tabitha rolled her eyes. "Because then I have one more thing to apologize to the other parents about." She grinned. "But if I'm being honest, I'm glad she can defend herself."

I was, too. It hadn't been any fun to be on the bottom of the social hierarchy at school, that was for sure.

Tabitha and I left the garden and headed into town. There were a few people sitting outside at pub tables, but it was a quieter night. Even the chippy was quiet, but Joe was quick to fill our order.

When we stepped back onto the street with our take-away, the first thing I smelled was smoke. I frowned. "Where's that coming from?"

Tabitha looked around, and I joined her. When I spotted the smoke coming from the B&B where Callan was staying, I gasped.

"Oh, hell, Mrs. Aspen's place is on fire," Tabitha said.

We sprinted for it, reaching the front yard with about half a dozen other people. Smoke billowed out of one of the front windows. Callan stood in front of the window, his hands directed towards the blaze. Massive jets of water sprung from his palms, extinguishing the flames. Next to him, Mrs. Aspen hugged her dog Lucifer as she stared in horror.

It was over almost as soon as we arrived.

Mrs. Aspen rose and went to the window, looking in at the devastation.

I walked up to Callan and asked quietly, "What happened?"

"Kitchen fire. Not sure how it started, but she was cooking dinner."

Mrs. Aspen turned and looked at Callan. "Well, you're out on your arse, young man."

"He just put out your fire," I said, indignant on his behalf.

"But not before it went through the floor to his room above." Mrs. Aspen pointed at the window. "So, like I said, out on your arse."

"Well, that's inconvenient." Callan frowned.

"Inconvenient?" she shrieked. "My house is ruined!"

"My apologies," he said, and he sounded sincere. "Of course, this is terrible. I will help you repair it."

She blinked at him, surprised. "But you didn't do it."

"All the same, I will help. And I'll find another place to stay tonight."

"Everywhere in town is booked," she said.

"Of course it is," he muttered too low for anyone but me to hear. Louder, he said, "I'll be fine. I'll just collect my things."

As I watched him go into the house, Tabitha joined me and said, "Did you hear what I heard?"

"That he needs a place to stay? Yes."

"Are you thinking what I'm thinking?"

"You'd better not be thinking about my place."

She shrugged. "I mean, you could. It would be the nice thing to do."

It was also desperately tempting, which annoyed the hell out of me. And yet, he really didn't have a place to stay.

Callan returned with his bag draped over his shoulder. It looked a bit singed, and I suddenly felt really bad for him. He stopped at the driveway, as if considering his next options. If all the hotels and B&Bs in town were full, that meant he'd have to drive all the way to the next town over.

"Callan," I called out, surprised to hear myself speaking. But was I really that surprised?

No.

Once Tabitha had mentioned the idea, I'd latched on to it.

He approached, and before he could say anything, I blurted, "You can stay in my spare room."

He blinked at me. "Really?"

"Really." I shifted. "*Spare* room, mind you. Not my room."

"Of course." He smiled at me. "I wouldn't dream of it."

Oh, I would.

CHAPTER
TWENTY-ONE

ARIA

THE NEXT MORNING, I awoke to the smell of coffee. After I'd shown Callan to the spare room last night, I'd locked myself in my room. Figuratively speaking, at least. I hadn't been worried about him coming into my room so much as I'd been worried about me sneaking into his.

But I'd reminded myself how much was on the line and how I wanted to beat him. *Needed* to beat him, for so many reasons. Which meant I needed my sleep and for my mind to be laser focused.

Thankfully, those thoughts had kept me in bed until morning. When I stumbled out into the kitchen shortly after dawn, I found Callan standing over the stove.

"What's going on?" I asked, rubbing my eyes.

"I'm making breakfast."

"You're what, now?" I walked over to the stove and saw

that there were pancakes in the pan. A cup of coffee sat invitingly next to it. I picked it up.

"Hey, that's mine."

"Not anymore."

He laughed, and I took a sip. "You didn't have to do all this."

Yes, he did.

I looked over towards Boris's voice and realized that he sat at the dining room table, ready for his pancakes.

"You gave me a place to stay in my hour of need. Of course I needed to."

"Well, thank you. I am a big fan of pancakes."

He shot me a worried grimace. "Really? Because I wouldn't expect much from these."

I laughed. "You're not any good at making pancakes, and yet that's what you chose to make?"

"I'm not any good at making anything. I was hoping it would be a *thought that counts* situation."

"It's definitely that kind of situation."

He flipped the cooked pancakes onto a plate and poured some more batter into the pan. I reached for a pancake and bit into it.

"Well?" He asked.

"Not bad!" I took another bite. "I could definitely eat a few of these."

Hey! You're supposed to share.

"I'm going to bring some to Boris before he loses his furry little mind."

You do not want to see me if that happens.

"No, I do not." I brought Boris a plate of pancakes, along

with the bottle of honey. I set it on the table and turned back to Callan. "Where did you find this stuff, anyway? I didn't really have any food in the house."

"Tabitha had it."

"You went to Tabitha's house?"

He nodded and flipped the pancakes.

Oh, Tabitha was going to have a field day with this. I could just imagine her now... *So what exactly did you do to Callan to make him want to cook you pancakes?* Then she would waggle her eyebrows suggestively.

"Yours are ready." Callan handed me a plate.

"Thank you." I took it to the table and added honey, then ate my breakfast as quickly as I could. "This is amazing, and normally I would savor it, but we really need to get to the garden."

"Agreed." Callan turned off the stove, then picked up a plate piled with pancakes and turned to me. He ate standing up, and I realized that he was already dressed and everything. No cooking in pajama pants for this man. "I would have expected you to be up earlier."

"I can't go until the potion that Gran made has finished brewing." I looked at the clock over the garden door. "Which should be in about twenty minutes." I scarfed down the rest of the pancakes and polished off the coffee. "Thank you again for this."

"Any time."

I raised a brow at him. "Really?"

"Really."

Okay, that was way too close to flirting, and we were

competitors. I reminded myself that I had to win this thing, and that meant no flirting with the competition.

"I'm going to get dressed and head to Gran's. Do you know what you're doing for your greenhouse?"

"Yes. But I'll head to the shop with you."

"Need an ingredient?"

"No, but I've got time and want to see you in action."

"Spying on the competition, eh?"

He shrugged and smiled. "You helped me, so I want to help you."

"But you already helped me by building the extra greenhouse over the one that the plants are eating."

"Maybe I'm just trying to get in your good graces in case I need another favor. After all, once the full moon comes, you're going to be very powerful."

"Okay, I buy that. And I could probably use some help. How are you with a blowgun?"

He quirked a brow. "Blowgun?"

"I'll explain on the way." I turned and went into the bedroom to get dressed.

By the time we made it to Gran's shop, it was only a few minutes before the potion was meant to be finished. Gran was already in the shop and standing in front of the cauldron. She had a row of darts lined up.

"Almost ready!" she said as I walked in the door, Callan behind me. She smiled when she saw him. "You have backup?"

I nodded as I stopped next to her. "I'll take all the help I can get. And thank you again for this, Gran."

"As if you need to thank me." She kissed my cheek. "I'd do anything for you, my love."

"Thanks, Gran."

Ten minutes later, we were headed to the garden. Each of us carried a blowgun and a bag of poisoned darts.

"You're sure you don't mind helping with this?" I asked as I unlocked the gate. He had practiced a bit in the back garden while Gran had dipped the darts in the finished potion, and he was surprisingly good. It would be helpful to have him on my side, but this was a competition. He had limited time to solve his own problems, and I couldn't quite figure out why he was so cool with helping me.

"It's all selfishly motivated, I assure you."

"Good." I hurried towards my greenhouse, nerves chilling my skin as we got nearer. How much worse would it be by the time we got there? Would I even have the time—or the capability—to fix the damage?

Nope. I couldn't borrow problems. I had enough to deal with, and I needed to focus on the present.

The sight of the greenhouse made me wince, though. Callan's glass shield was still holding, but probably only because the plants were determined to eat the iron of the original greenhouse. They didn't have any interest in simple glass.

As for the original greenhouse...

Nearly half of it was missing.

I pulled open the door, which was fortunately farther away from the plants and therefore still standing, and walked inside. Immediately, several of the flowers turned their heads to look at us. They had no eyes, of course, but there was still the distinct feeling of being watched.

They had grown huge, fueled by the iron they had eaten, and there were hundreds of flowers on dozens of thick stems. The tangled mass of greenery wrapped around the iron, the blossoms chomping through metal and glass. It reminded me of the hydra of Greek myth, and I prayed it wouldn't be able to regenerate its blooms as we tranquilized it.

Slowly, so as not to startle the plant, I loaded a dart into the hollow pipe and raised it to my lips. Gran had said I would have to hit the plant multiple times and in multiple places in order to tranquilize the whole thing, so I couldn't waste my darts. Callan did the same, loading up his blowgun.

As the plant studied us, we shot our first darts at it. Callan and I each hit a different portion of the stems, and they lost their strength, dropping to the ground and lying still as rope.

The rest of the stems and blooms seemed to have realized that something was happening, and they abandoned their metallic meal and shot towards us. I dove behind a collection of large terracotta pots that had been piled up near the door. The clay shattered as one of the stems slammed into it.

With fumbling hands, I loaded the blowgun and blew my dart at the attacking plant. The dart landed true, and the stem flopped to the ground. Panting, I peeked around the pile of pots. More stems were surging towards me, but they couldn't reach. Their roots bound them to the ground, thank fates.

Callan had crept closer and managed to land two darts

into different parts of the plant. I ran out from my hiding place and found a new one closer to the plants that were still struggling to reach us, pulling at their roots to get every centimeter of traction they could.

I crouched at the base of a tropical tree with huge green leaves and loaded up my blowgun. From above, a chattering noise sounded. I looked up and spotted a monkey hanging from a branch above me. As my eyes met his, he reached out and grabbed my blowgun, moving so fast that I couldn't stop him.

"Hey!" I shouted. "That's mine!" I had *so* not planned for this.

The little wanker climbed higher into the tree, chattering away as he inspected the gun. I'd already loaded a dart into it, and he seemed particularly interested in it. He raised it to his mouth and blew.

The dart shot free, hurtling straight towards me. I lunged to the side, feeling a sharp flare of pain on the outside of my left thigh.

I looked down to see that my jeans were ripped and a thin line of blood marked my skin.

Shit.

The tranq dart had got me. My leg was already going to sleep. I glared up at the monkey. "Give that back."

He chattered gleefully, then hurled the empty blowgun at me, clearly already bored. It landed with a light thud on a pile of fallen leaves, and I dragged myself over to it. The leg that had been hit was half asleep, but at least the tranquilizer didn't seem to have spread any further. This wasn't ideal, but at least I could still move.

"Are you okay?" Callan called from his spot hiding behind another tree.

"Never better." I looked up at the tree above me, spotting the monkey still watching me. "But watch out for monkeys."

"Noted." He turned and fired a dart at the plant, landing another hit.

I needed to get down to business and join him. Despite my injury, I was able to land six more darts. The plant was almost entirely unconscious now, and we finished the job within a few minutes.

Once the coast was clear, we stood and stared at the sleeping plant, panting. I put some weight on my leg, pleased to see that the potion had worn off. Thank fates it had been formulated for plants, not humans, or my leg definitely wouldn't work.

"We did it," I said, a little too surprised for my liking. "Thanks."

He nodded. "Are you going to touch it?"

"Yes, but you can get out of here. Go fix up your place."

"I'm fine, I—"

I shot him a glare that was equal parts confused and annoyed. He needed to be working on his own greenhouse, and I had no idea why he was still here with me.

"You're right," he said. "I'll get out of here. Got lots of work to do." He turned and left.

"Thank you again!" I called after him.

Once he was gone, I turned to face the plant. It looked so peaceful in sleep, the petals curled over to cover most of the fangs. At a glance, one would have no idea that this plant would eat your face off.

I approached it, senses on high alert. When I got near enough to touch it, I reached out a hand and laid it gently on the smooth green stem.

Immediately, I felt the plant's hunger—but not for water. For iron.

I'd been right about that, but my iron pill plan would never work—the plant was making that clear enough. Though it was eating the iron in the surrounding greenhouse by using its fangs, the plant was still hungry. Endlessly ravenous, in fact. I could feel that the roots were reaching out, straining deep into the soil to find what they needed and yet failing to find it.

The iron that they needed had to come from the soil, that was clear enough. But how? There had been no mention of it in the care and feeding book that I'd read, and I doubted that someone had been tossing iron supplement pills onto the soil in whatever jungle Mr. Sparrow had found this plant in.

I needed to know more about where it had come from so that I could give it iron the way it needed.

I left the greenhouse, texting my progress to Tabitha as I went. Mr. Sparrow kept an office in the middle of the garden, and I went immediately to it. He was there, sitting in a garden chair while reading a romance novel.

He looked up, a keen expression on his face. "Aria! What can I help you with?"

"I was hoping you could tell me more about where you got the Wizard's Butterwort from."

"It's giving you trouble, isn't it?"

"That's one word for it."

"I'm not surprised. It's been looking a little peaky for

weeks. Starting to wilt between rains, snapping all the time at anything."

"Well, it's been eating the iron of the greenhouse and I need to find out why. I was hoping you'd have information about its environment in its native habitat."

He grimaced. "Eating the greenhouse? I don't see why. I have perfectly mimicked the environment it came from."

"You didn't expect that to happen?" I asked, wondering how much he'd planned these things.

"I expected you to need to bring the Wizard's Butterwort back to health, but I didn't anticipate this." He blew out a breath. "The stakes are quite high, now."

"You're telling me." I leaned forward. "And maybe you can also tell me everything you remember about the plant and what you saw when you collected it."

"Well, I went to the rainforest to gather a sample. I'd expected to have to hike far into the jungle once I got off the train, but I got lucky. There was some growing very close to the station and warehouse where they'd kept the spare train parts."

"A warehouse in the jungle?" I asked.

He nodded. "That's what I think it was. It was an old building from the nineteenth century, abandoned long before I arrived. There was old rusting junk everywhere around it." He tutted disapprovingly. "People can be so thoughtless and messy sometimes."

I leaned back in my chair, my mind racing. "So you said this plant was growing near the warehouse and the train station."

"Precisely."

"And there were rusted metal bits on the ground."

"Half buried, too. Like they'd wanted to clean the place up and thought they could hide it underground, but the work got to be too much so they quit."

"The iron must have leeched into the soil over the years as the parts degraded in the humid environment, and the Wizard's Butterwort developed a taste for it."

Excitement lit Mr. Sparrow's eyes. "I think you're on to something, dear!"

I was pretty sure I was. The plant had done fine for the first few months it had been here, no doubt still enjoying the iron it had absorbed into its roots. But once that was used up, it had gone looking for more.

"Thank you, Mr. Sparrow." I rose. "I've got to get back to the greenhouse."

"Good luck, dear!"

As I hurried through the garden, my mind raced. I needed to mimic exactly what the environment had been like in the jungle if I wanted the plant to recover.

I had an idea, but I would need help. I called Tabitha, hoping she would be able to come earlier than expected.

CHAPTER
TWENTY-TWO

ARIA

IT TOOK us two backbreaking hours, but Tabitha and I managed to load up three tons of rusted metal into the back of a borrowed lorry. The old shipyard where we'd found the stuff was a twenty-minute drive from the garden, and time was starting to run short.

"I sure hope you're right about this," Tabitha said as we pulled to a stop at the gate to the Garden of Enchantment.

"I think I am. We even got historic iron. That shipyard was abandoned in the nineteenth century. We can't get any closer than that."

"Actually, it would be great to get closer—like, from a geographical standpoint. We're still a ways from your greenhouse, right? And we've got all this metal in the back."

"Good point. Maybe Mr. Sparrow has some roads around

the outside of the garden that will allow us to drive closer. The paths through it are way too pretty to drive on."

"Let's go ask."

We were about to climb out of the vehicle when I spotted Mr. Sparrow approaching the gate. He grinned as he saw us and came around to the window.

I rolled it down.

"I thought I heard someone approaching," he said, craning his neck to look into the back of the lorry. "Looks like you've got a plan."

"We have, but is there a road around the garden so we could drive this stuff a bit closer?"

He pointed to an area to the right. "You can go over there. I've built a little path for lorries like this. You won't get all the way there, but you'll get close."

"Thank you."

He nodded. "You'd better hurry, though. Sunset is only a few hours away."

I looked up at the sky, realizing the sun was lower than I'd thought. Bugger. It was going to be close.

"You'd better call your gran," Tabitha said. "She'll need to get started repairing the greenhouse."

"Yeah, good idea." I called Gran to update her, and she promised to leave immediately.

Tabitha and I drove as close to the greenhouse as we could, then climbed out and began dragging the huge metal pieces through the garden. Tabitha could have used her magic, but she was planning to save it to help Gran rebuild the greenhouse. Anything we could do by hand, we would.

I was panting and sweaty by the time I'd dragged the first

load to the greenhouse entrance, and we still had at least twenty more to go.

I needed a better plan.

Could I get the plants in the garden to help me the way that Gertrude had done with her tea set?

It was worth a try.

There were several large trees along the path that might be able to help.

I walked to one of them and pressed a hand to its trunk. Now that I knew I was speaking to the tree and not just myself, it was easier to do. It was funny how belief made so many things possible.

"It would be amazing if you trees could help me move some metal down this path towards the greenhouse. I'd be in your debt."

At first, I thought nothing had happened. Then the trees around me began to shiver slightly. Had they understood me? I knew that trees could communicate through underground networks of fungal threads called mycorrhizae, so maybe the tree that I'd spoken to had talked to the others.

There was only one way to find out.

I hurried to the truck and told Tabitha my plan. We rolled some of the metal out of the truck bed and moved it to the path by the trees. One of the pines reached down with a bough and shoved the metal further down the path. Another tree picked up the work from there.

Tabitha and I had to assist them, rolling some of the big old pipes along the ground to make sure that they reached trees that were slightly farther apart, but within twenty minutes, we had all the iron at the entry to the greenhouse.

Gran arrived a moment later, accompanied by Margot from the bakery.

"I told you I wanted you to win," she said. "I'm here to help your gran."

"Thank you, Margot. I'm going to owe you one."

"No, dear. We'll all owe you one if you can win this thing."

I wasn't sure about that, but now wasn't the time to argue with her.

Fortunately, the plants were still asleep, which allowed Margot and Gran to start magically rebuilding the greenhouse. Tabitha helped me distribute the iron around the bases of the Wizard's Butterwort, burying some of it so that we mimicked the plant's original environment.

The vines and blossoms had begun to stir as we finished.

"We need rain," I said. "To get some of the iron to leech into the soil. And I need to ask the plants to not attack the new greenhouse."

Margot and Gran had done a fabulous job. Even Catrina had helped once she'd arrived from school an hour ago.

"We need to hurry," Tabitha said. "Sun is almost down."

"Can you make rain?"

She cracked her fingers in front of her. "Yep."

It began to pour inside the greenhouse as Gran, Catrina, and Margot finished fixing the last of the structure. The plants were shifting more energetically now, as if they were really starting to wake up.

I darted towards one, not wanting to lose my moment. If they were sleepy, they were less likely to attack.

I rested my hand on one of the green stems and tried to

feed my thoughts into the plant. *Please don't eat the greenhouse. There is now iron in the soil for you.*

I couldn't tell if it worked, but when a few of the blooms raised their heads, they didn't immediately bite me. That had to be a victory.

Slowly, I removed my hand and backed up. The plant didn't attack. It didn't go for the greenhouse, either. Once every blossom was awake, we stood and stared at them.

"I think they're all better," Catrina said.

"I think so, too." Now that they were fully awake and had had a moment to acclimatize themselves, I could check. I approached slowly, raising a hand. "I'm going to touch you again to see if you are happy with your new environment."

The Wizard's Butterwort waited patiently while I pressed a hand to one of the stems. Immediately, I could feel that it was content. I grinned widely. "The iron worked!"

CALLAN

EXHAUSTED, I stared at the trees in my greenhouse.

When I'd left Aria earlier today and headed towards my own problems, I'd had no idea how I was going to fix the climate issue. The trees were the cause, but I couldn't just chop them down. The roots would still be there, and I was certain Mr. Sparrow would disapprove if I destroyed his trees.

So I'd decided to move them, taking the troublesome

trees at the edges and putting them closer to the center of the greenhouse, away from the underground barriers. It had taken all day, and every ounce of my magic, but I still wasn't one hundred percent sure that I'd got every one that was causing an issue. Aria wasn't here to read the trees for me, and I had no way of assessing the roots myself.

But time was pretty much up, and the cold inside the greenhouse was starting to get to me. I was numb all over, and my body was exhausted from the strain of pouring all my magic into the trees to lift them out of the dirt and nestle them safely back in the frozen ground.

I staggered towards the exit of the greenhouse, muscles aching as I let myself out into the far warmer summer garden.

The first thing I noticed was that the ice was thawing. The plants that had died were still shriveled and brown, but the problem was gone.

Hopefully, it would be enough.

As the sun approached the horizon, I walked towards the clearing where we'd met Mr. Sparrow on the other two occasions we'd been given our tasks.

The other competitors were standing there, though Lilac and Evan looked dejected. I could only guess that meant their greenhouses were still in trouble. Aria looked happy, though, her smile so broad that I could see it from all the way across the clearing. Her gran, Tabitha, and Catrina were with her, along with the café owner, Margot.

The others had helpers as well, though I didn't know their names. I actually had no idea what they'd been trying to fix at their greenhouses, either.

When Mr. Sparrow saw me, he clapped his hands with delight. "You've made it!"

"I have." I smiled. "And I think—hope—I've succeeded."

"You have, dear boy. I can feel the health of the plants from here."

I could feel nothing, which was another sign I probably wasn't the one who should win this place. If I had to bet, Aria would learn how to feel the plants from a distance, too, and she'd do it in no time.

"I'm pleased to announce that four of you have successfully completed the challenge. Callan has addressed the issue with the climate control in the arctic greenhouse. Aria had fixed the hungry Wizard's Butterwort that were determined to devour her jungle greenhouse. Serena has taken care of the uncontrolled growth of the Phoenix Starfire, and Terry addressed the mutation of Windroot that threatened the entire crop. Evan and Lilac—I very much appreciate your participation, but I am afraid you are finished with the competition."

"It was fun, thank you," Lilac said.

Evan nodded. "I feel the same."

Mr. Sparrow rubbed his hands together. "On to the final challenge! Each of you will be required to build an enclosure for a magical creature. It will need to provide everything they need, from food to mental stimulation so that their lives are rich. It is up to you which animal you choose, but points will be awarded for difficulty of task and execution. You may have help with this task as well, but there will be only one winner. I'll see you back here in three days' time, right at sunset. Best of luck to you!"

CHAPTER
TWENTY-THREE

ARIA

AFTER MR. SPARROW finished telling us what the next competition would be, I left the Garden of Enchantment with Gran, Tabitha, and Catrina. Fireflies lit our way out of the garden, and the nearly full moon shone brightly overhead.

Callan caught up with us near the gate. "Mind if I join you?"

"Sure thing," I said.

Catrina stuck right by his side, immediately peppering him with questions. They walked in front of us along the path, Callan seeming to be as patient as a saint with her.

Tabitha nodded towards them. "That's a bit of a surprise."

"Oh?"

"She doesn't take quickly to new people. Especially men."

"Who can blame her?"

Tabitha laughed. "Seriously, though. I think he's a good guy."

"Yeah, I think you might be right." But now wasn't the time to think about that. Now was the time to focus on winning the competition.

When we reached our cottages, Callan turned to me. "Are you going in for the night?"

I shook my head. "I want to do a little work first, but you go ahead."

"Work, at this hour?"

"I've got a competition to win, don't I?"

"Fair enough." He grinned. "I supposed we're not cooperating in this one, are we?"

"Not a chance in hell. I'm going to kick your butt, and the best way to do that is to take you by surprise." I nodded towards the house. "The door is unlocked, though." I couldn't believe how casual I was being about the fact that he would be spending a second night at my place. I was starting to treat him like a housemate.

"Thank you." He looked towards my gran, Tabitha, and Catrina. "I'll see you tomorrow. Thank you for the company on the walk back."

"Bye!" Catrina waved.

Gran leaned towards me and whispered, "I like that one."

I rolled my eyes, then looked at Tabitha. "Can we go to your house for a bit? I'd love to brainstorm ideas."

"For sure." She grinned widely. "I've even got ice cream."

"Perfect." I looked at my gran. "Will you come? I could use your thoughts on this."

"I'd be honored, my dear."

We headed towards Tabitha's cottage, which was a larger version of mine. It was decorated in a similar style, down to the tables and couches. Tabitha saw me looking and shrugged. "What can I say? I got a deal."

"I like them."

The cottage was messier, with Catrina's school papers spread over the table and an intricate miniature castle set up in front of the fireplace. Catrina caught me looking and grinned widely. "It comes to life at the full moon. The fires in the hearths will light, and any dolls that are inside will move on their own."

"Wow. At the full moon?"

"Yep."

It wouldn't be the only one coming alive at the full moon, if I could get my magic to work. But I didn't tell them that. I'd be keeping that one to myself for a while. The idea that I might be able to fix my magic was still tender and new. Best to hold on to it.

"Catrina, clear the table," Tabitha said. "Ladies, have a seat, and I'll bring the brainstorming fuel."

Catrina made quick work of sweeping the paper off the table and into her schoolbag, and Gran and I sat. A moment later, Tabitha appeared with a bottle of rosé and a tub of chocolate chunk ice cream. Catrina brought over the bowls and glasses, and Tabitha served everyone generous portions.

"I think I should have double ice cream since I can't have wine," Catrina said.

"You drive a hard bargain, kid. But I like how you think." Tabitha dug the spoon back into the tub. "I'm willing to compromise and give you an extra scoop, but no more."

"Deal." Catrina stuck out her bowl, and Tabitha added the ice cream.

I smiled. I was so glad to be home with the people I loved most.

"So, what are you thinking for your magical creature?" Tabitha asked.

"That's a tough one," I said. "It's going to need to add value to the garden but also be difficult to acquire. I'm sure that will get me extra points, and I want them."

"Difficult to acquire, but easy to maintain," Gran said.

I nodded. "Good point. Whatever I bring in, I need to be able to take care of it with little fuss once I win the garden."

"I like how you think." Catrina pointed her ice cream spoon at me. "Positivity is key."

"What about nuzzlebugs?" Tabitha asked. "The children at Catrina's school love them. They would visit the garden if you had those."

"Hmm. Not a bad idea." Nuzzlebugs were a type of fluffy little creature that loved to snuggle with anyone warm. They were particularly tolerant of children and were often used in therapy.

"Too easy," Catrina said. "I love them as much as the next kid, but there's not much challenge there, is there? Jenny Anderson even has one."

"Good point. I don't want one if Jenny Anderson has one." I nodded approvingly at her. "But I like where Tabitha is going with the idea that we could get a creature that brings value to the community. Plants like people—most of them do, at least—and it would be good to have people visiting the garden more."

"What about glimmerfish?" Gran asked. "People could put their feet in the water and enjoy the fish."

It was a good idea. Glimmerfish were beautiful glowing fish that made the water vibrate slightly. When one submerged a hand or foot, the feeling was lovely and very calming. Except...

"I'm not sure if there is a pond big enough in the garden, and if there isn't, I'd have to make one. And that would be like having an aquarium."

"Oh, those are a pain," Gran said. "Floris talks about hers all the time and how she'd like to just release Nemo back to the sea, but he's so attached to her that she can't."

I wasn't familiar with Floris or Nemo, but it was a perfect example of my problem with glimmerfish.

I mulled over my options. "I think it would be ideal to find an animal that is native to Cornwall or Devon so that it would easy to integrate them into the garden. I don't think I have the skills to build a whole new greenhouse to keep a creature that requires a special environment."

"Dreamweavers?" Tabitha suggested. "If you could get some of those, it would be amazing."

"Dreamweavers." I grinned. "That's a fantastic idea."

The butterfly-like creatures were beautiful—but that wasn't their main appeal. When they fluttered around a person or animal, they emitted a sparkling mist that affected the mind. It was a dreamy, wonderful sensation to be near them, as relaxing as a massage or a second glass of wine. And if a person fell asleep beneath them, they were sure to have wonderful dreams.

"The town would love to have dreamweavers nearby," I said. "We could even put hammocks in the garden to allow people to sleep near them."

Gran clapped her hands. "Oh, I've always loved dreamweavers! Not nearly as destructive as regular butterflies."

Tabitha and I laughed at the memory. Catrina was too invested in her ice cream to ask for clarification.

"How are you going to get them, though?" Tabitha asked. "I know I was the one to make the suggestion, but now that I think of it, aren't they difficult to find?"

"Yes. And they're clever enough that I don't want to just yank them away from their home and stick them in a new garden. They wouldn't like that." Unlike nuzzlebugs, which were adorable but simpleminded enough to like living anywhere with food and someone to pet them, a dreamweaver would have distinct preferences. If they didn't like their new home, they would leave, and rightfully so.

"So what will you do?" Catrina asked.

"I'll have to find a population and ask them to move. That'll be the challenge that wins me the competition. I'll just have to create a glorious habitat for them, one they can't turn down."

"And you'll have to find just the right colony," Gran said. "One that isn't very happy where it is."

I nodded. "I've got an idea for that. It'll require research, but I think we can find something."

Tabitha raised her wine glass, which was nearly empty. "To dreamweavers!"

I clinked my glass with hers. "To dreamweavers!"

Once we'd finished our wine, I headed to the library. It would be closed at this hour, but I could use the secret key and borrow a few books about dreamweavers. I needed to know everything I could about them, and there was no time to spare.

It didn't take long to let myself in and collect the books, though I did take a few minutes to pet Maurice. Once he'd finally fallen asleep in front of the fire, I returned home.

The light in the windows indicated that Callan was still up, and I wondered if I should have spent more time in the library. It would be easier to just not see him.

"Don't be a wimp," I muttered.

Talking to yourself?

I looked down to see Boris coming out of the bushes. "Do you just hang out there, waiting to ambush people?"

No, but maybe I should.

"You should not." I let myself into the house, and he trundled past, headed towards the kitchen.

Callan looked up from his spot on the couch. He'd built a cozy fire and had a book open on his lap. The scene was so homey—and he was so handsome—that I wanted to curl up next to him and read right alongside.

"Good night?" he asked.

I nodded. "You?"

He shrugged and held up the book. "I think I've found an idea for my habitat."

"Oh?"

"I'm not telling. It's a competition, remember?"

"Right, of course. A competition in which I'll wipe the cauldron with you." I went to one of the chairs across from the sofa and sat down. As much as I wanted to curl up next to him, I wasn't an idiot. I knew exactly where that would lead us, and I had no time to spare. More than that, I couldn't afford to lose focus. I was so close.

"I'm going to do some reading, so no distracting me," I said.

"Consider it done."

I set the books on the table beside me and chose one, then began reading about dreamweavers. Every few minutes, I found it impossible not to look up at Callan. His mere presence created an energy in the air that made my heart race slightly faster.

Twice, I saw him looking at me at the same time.

Finally, he spoke. "Are you ready for tomorrow?"

"You mean the full moon?" I'd been thinking about it all day.

"Yes."

"As ready as I'll ever be. But I haven't told my gran or Tabitha. What if it's a bust?"

"It won't be a bust. But I don't blame you for keeping it quiet."

"Thanks." I closed the book. There was no way I was going to get any work done while I was sitting in the same room as him. "I'm headed to bed."

I stood and gathered up the books. I was nearly to the bedroom door when he called my name, and I turned. "Yes?"

"I'd like to go with you tomorrow night."

I stared at him for a moment. "Really? There won't be anything for you to do."

"Still, I'd like to be there. If you'll let me."

"Um..." I had no idea what to make of the offer. "I'll think about it."

CHAPTER
TWENTY-FOUR

ARIA

THE NEXT MORNING, I awoke to an empty house. The sun hadn't risen yet, but it was clear that Callan had already gone. He had to have headed to the garden.

What was he planning for his habitat?

It would be incredible, of course.

I'd just have to make sure mine was better.

I didn't like the thought, so I shoved it away. There was no need to borrow trouble. Quickly, I threw on some clothes and headed to the kitchen. Half a pot of coffee was still warm, and I smiled gratefully. There was even a muffin next to it, and I had no idea where he'd got it from.

That's mine. Boris trundled towards me, crumbs on his whiskers.

"No, it's not. I can see that you already ate yours."

No, I didn't.

"Liar." I took a big bite of the muffin.

He stared at me, aghast.

I poured myself a takeaway coffee in the mug Gran had left for me and said, "I'll be at the garden today if you need me."

What I needed was that muffin.

"Head into town and go see Gran. She might hook you up."

He tapped his head with a little paw. *I like where your mind's at.*

I grinned and left the house, walking quickly towards the Garden of Enchantment. The sun was beginning to rise as I reached the gates. They were still locked, and I wondered if Callan had come here or gone somewhere else to start his plans. It was possible he'd locked the gates behind him because it was so early. That was probably it.

I headed into the garden and took a tour, covering every inch of the place as I looked for somewhere inviting to put the dreamweavers. I'd have to add more plants to suit them, but I wanted to start with a foundation that they liked. That meant finding water, to start.

When I spotted the little creek at the far west side of the garden, I knew I'd found my spot. Even better, there weren't many plants already here, just some native bushes and flowers. I didn't want to modify anything that Mr. Sparrow had worked hard to construct. And anyway, we were meant to create a place for the animals we were bringing, not use something that was already finished.

Once I had the spot chosen, I headed towards town to borrow Gran's car and an old wagon that we had in the back garden. As expected, I found Boris in her kitchen, sleeping off a food coma at the window seat.

Gran looked between the badger and me, then raised her hands in defeat. "I know what you're going to say—that I spoil him. And I can't argue."

I laughed. "It's fine. I don't think I need to keep an eye on his sugar intake."

Not true. I'm a right terror on too much of the good stuff. Boris's sleepy voice made me laugh.

"What can I do for you, dear?"

"I was hoping to borrow your car and the wagon. Along with some tools. And maybe a few plants. I won't clear you out, though."

"Anything. Just help yourself."

"Thanks, Gran." I leaned down and gave her a kiss, then headed out back.

It didn't take me long to collect the gardening tools I needed. I loaded them into the boot of Gran's little car, then returned to the garden and unearthed a few plants that I would move to the Garden of Enchantment. Dreamweavers liked variety and rareness in their habitat, and Gran had quite a few nice specimens. I made sure not to take too much of any one thing. Once the car was full, I headed back into the house and found Boris still asleep on the bench seat.

"Wake up, sleepyhead. It's time to get to work."

He blinked groggily up at me, then sat upright, his fluffy little belly looking extra plush after all the treats he'd eaten. *Work? You must be joking.*

"You're a familiar, aren't you?"

Yes. And that just means I grace you with my presence. Not that I work. He shuddered.

"Well, you're working today. Now come on." I picked him up, and he thrashed in my arms.

Put me down! Kidnapping!

"Nope, you're going to earn your keep. And I promise I'll pay you well with bacon sandwiches."

He stilled, giving me a considering look. *Bacon sandwiches?*

"Yep. Two if you work hard. Three if you work *extra* hard."

But I could just get bacon sandwiches from your gran.

"She's not home tonight. She's got bridge with the girls, so she'll be out until late. I'm your only chance at bacon sandwiches."

Fine, let's get to work. You need my help, anyway.

"That's true, I do." I carried him to the car and put him on the front seat.

I drove us to the Garden of Enchantment and parked outside the gate. Boris was helping me load the plants into the wagon when Serena appeared. She carried masses of glittery white fabric in her arms, but she took the time to stop and look appraisingly at what we were doing.

"What are you building?" she asked.

"It's a secret."

She laughed. "Hardly. I could figure it out if I just came over to look."

"Then you'll have to do that." I stopped piling plants into the wagon and straightened to give her a smile. "We're on a deadline, so if that will be all, I'll be going."

"I don't know why you bother. You're not going to win."

Boris stilled, then turned to glare at her. His lips pulled back from his little fangs.

"Be nice, Boris."

No.

"Yes." I gave him a hard look.

"You're talking to him?" Serena asked, surprise on her face. "Why did *you* get a familiar?"

"I don't know. He chose me." I knew the shock in her voice was because familiars only chose the strongest witches, and that definitely wasn't me. "Anyway, later."

I didn't bother to wait for a response. I just picked up the handle to the wagon and left, pulling it along. "Come on, Boris."

He grumbled, but I heard him trundle after me. *You should have let me take care of her.*

"I really don't want to know what you mean by *take care of*, but I'm going to tell you right now that whatever it is, it's against the rules."

Or what?

"Bacon sandwiches."

Oh. Right. You are holding my beloved hostage.

"Now you get it."

We arrived at the spot I'd chosen and got to work, planting everything we'd brought from Gran's house. Boris was extremely good at digging the holes, and we made record time. Once it was all in the ground, we returned to my house and made several trips to collect every plant that would thrive in the Garden. Fortunately, that was most of them. It was a sad sight to see my house losing its green, but it would be worth it.

Anyway, winning was about making sacrifices, right?

By the time we were done, we were both exhausted. Boris flopped against a rock, resting his back against the gray surface. *It looks good. I would live here if I were a dreamweaver.*

"That's what I'm hoping." I planned to have the garden finished before I approached a colony and asked them to move. It needed to be appealing to them in case they wanted to follow me back. I would add cushions and hammocks for people so that they could spend time around the dreamweavers, but that could happen tomorrow.

It would be sunset soon, and I needed to get ready.

"I'd say you earned your bacon sandwich. Come on." I headed towards the car, and Boris followed at a quick pace.

When we reached my house, I realized that there was a distinct flaw in my plan.

I hadn't got any bacon.

But I couldn't let Boris down. He'd worked so hard, digging dozens of holes for me to put the plants in. In the kitchen, I fished around in the cabinet and found a package of chocolate biscuits, which I handed to him. "Here's your starter course. I'm going to go get bacon."

Fortunately, when I headed over to Tabitha's house to see if she had any, I got lucky.

"Come on in." She gestured me into the cottage. "I'll get it from the fridge."

"Thank you so much." I stepped into the house, spotting Catrina over by the fireplace with her castle. She was so absorbed that I didn't bother her, and instead followed Tabitha towards the kitchen.

"How did it go today at the garden?" Tabitha asked as she pulled the bacon from the fridge.

"Good. I think we're getting it set up nicely."

"Need any help?"

"Maybe, but not yet. Though I'm pretty sure I've found a colony of dreamweavers I'm going to approach tomorrow."

"Oh?" Tabitha handed over the bacon.

I nodded. "I read up on all the colonies last night. There are some that live in the woods near an abandoned mining village in Cornwall about forty miles from here. I think they might be missing human company by now."

"Ah, good thought." Tabitha grinned. "They really like people, don't they?"

"That's what the books said. They want to give good dreams as much as we want to have them, and once the people left the mining village and no longer visited their forest, they probably got lonely. At least, that's what I'm hoping."

"I like where your head is going with this. Let me know if you want company tomorrow."

"I will, thanks. Still deciding if I should go alone so as not to frighten them. Or maybe they would like more people, if we're working on the assumption that they're lonely. I have no idea."

"Well, I'm there if you need me."

"Thanks." I raised the bacon. "And thanks for this. I owe Boris some bacon sandwiches for his hard work."

"Oh, you've got to deliver on that promise. I would hate to see what he did if you let him down."

"Nothing good, I can assure you."

She laughed, and I returned to the house, where Boris was polishing off the last of the chocolate biscuits.

"Main course, coming right up." I went to the stove and cooked up as much bacon as the pan would hold, then did a second batch.

Callan walked in as Boris was finishing his third sandwich. He wore gardening clothes and looked like he'd spent a sweaty day doing manual labor.

I was super into it, of course.

"Is it breakfast for dinner?" Callan asked.

"No, just bacon sandwiches for Boris, who was a very big help today."

Callan raised a brow at Boris. "So you can be bribed?"

Of course I can be bribed. Boris looked at me. *Tell him, in case he wants to bribe me.*

I rolled my eyes. "He says that of course he can be bribed, and he's open to any offers. But don't think about bribing him before the competition is over. He's my little digger, and I'm not sharing."

Children, children. There's enough of Boris to go around. He burped and patted his stomach.

"What did he say just then?" Callan asked.

"You don't want to know." I handed him a plate with a bacon sandwich. "But here's your gourmet dinner, if you're hungry."

"Thank you, I'm famished."

His words made me want to ask him what work had

made him famished. What creature was he bringing to the garden? Of course, it would be spectacular, but more spectacular than dreamweavers?

I banished the thought.

"It's nearly sunset," he said, looking out the window. "Clear night, too."

I nodded, nerves racing through me. It was a good thing that it was a clear night, which meant the moonlight would have a better chance of working—if that's how this was supposed to go. I still didn't quite understand the details. Part of me wished it were cloudy, though. Because then, if it didn't work, I could blame the clouds instead of myself.

Aria

BEFORE RETURNING to the Garden of Enchantment, I took a quick shower and changed my clothes. I was itchy as hell from all the dirt that had got stuck to me, and whatever was about to happen seemed like it would be a big deal. It felt strange to go there dressed in my dirty gardening overalls.

Also, if this whole process killed me, I wanted to be wearing clean underwear.

I chose a simple green dress that I'd always liked to wear on summer days, and I pulled my hair back with some flowering vines from the pot that thrived in my bathroom.

When I returned to the living room, Callan stilled. "You look beautiful."

"Thanks." I smiled. "Let's get out of here. My nerves are killing me."

"It'll be great." He held open the door for me, and we walked in silence towards the Garden of Enchantment.

There was something comforting about the silence. When he reached out to take my hand, I gripped his tightly. He was a lifeline, though I felt like I shouldn't need one.

Fortunately, the garden gate was locked when we arrived. Hopefully, the place would be empty. The last thing I wanted was for Serena to show up with her snide comments.

"Do you know where you want to go?" Callan asked as he unlocked the gate.

"Towards the back. I found the perfect place today."

He opened the gate for me. When I walked through, that familiar shiver of awe passed over me. This place really was special, and if my magic were going to unlock, it would happen here.

I started towards the path that led to the rear of the garden. He joined me, and we walked side by side as the lightning bugs fluttered all around us. The light of the full moon glowed brightly on the flowers that bordered the path, bringing the garden alive with color despite the fact that it was night. They must be some sort of night-blooming flower to be so bright.

Finally, we reached the part of the garden that I'd chosen. There were more than a dozen varieties of flowering trees, along with wisteria and lilac hanging heavily from beautiful wooden arbors. It bloomed year round in Mr. Sparrow's garden, and the scent of the flowers filled the air. Beneath the trees were flowers and bushes of more varieties than I could count.

"This looks perfect," Callan said. "I've never seen so many types of plants in one place."

"Fingers crossed." I stopped at the edge of the clearing, unsure of how to progress. "Do you have any idea what I should do?"

"Afraid I don't. I think this one is all you. Follow your gut."

I nodded and released his hand, then stepped into the clearing. The moonlight was drawing me forward. It gleamed on the grass, making it look like a soft velvet blanket beneath an inky darkness. All around, the magic of the forest flowed through me. I could feel the life thrumming inside the plants that scented the air.

When I reached the middle of the clearing, I lay on the grass. Overhead, the fireflies fluttered in an intricate, swirling dance. As the moonlight caressed my skin, I felt the ground beneath me hum with life. The grass felt like it was giving me its energy. Vines and leaves unfurled from the forest around me, reaching out to brush over me.

Magic sparked between the plants and the moonlight, and inside my soul, something unlocked. I drew in a deep breath, filled with such joy that I felt almost weightless.

The plants lifted me into the air, their vines supporting my body as I floated through the forest. Tree limbs and flowers reached out to gently touch me. Every bit of contact made my soul feel lighter, my magic freer.

As I flew, petals and leaves floated toward me, spinning and twirling around me in a kaleidoscope of color. I could sense every plant in the garden, like my soul had made a connection with theirs.

When the vines finally put me back on the ground in the middle of the clearing and retreated, I felt like my entire being had come alive. Spring flowers had bloomed in the clearing despite the fact that it was summer--ruby red tulips and brilliant yellow daffodils and white hyacinth. Their perfume was glorious.

I stood and laughed, full of such joy that I couldn't contain it. When I lowered my head, I saw Callan still standing at the edge of the clearing.

The air between us became electric. It lit up my soul, and I walked towards him, unable to help myself. There was so much power and joy coursing through my veins that I wanted to share it with someone.

I stopped in front of him.

"That was incredible," he said, the faintest hint of awe in his voice. "*You're* incredible."

I reached up and kissed him.

CHAPTER
TWENTY-FIVE

CALLAN

ARIA PRESSED her lips to mine, so soft and sweet that it made my head spin. A low groan tore from my lips as I pulled her close.

She draped her arms around my neck as her soft moan ghosted over my mouth. I cupped the back of her head and traced my tongue over her lips. They parted easily, and I dipped my tongue inside to taste.

Desire shot through me, hard and fast. It gripped me in its fist and made me want to touch every inch of her, taste every inch.

"Callan." She sank her fingers into my hair and pulled me closer, her mouth ravenous on mine. "I want you. Now."

It was all I needed to hear. I picked her up so that her legs wrapped around my waist, then knelt and laid her on the ground. Flowers bloomed around her head, small pink blossoms that smelled divine. She smiled broadly and reached up for me.

I sank down onto her, the length of her body hot and soft against mine. I'd never felt anything so incredible in my life, and I couldn't help the soft groan that escaped me as I settled between her thighs. She rose up to press against me, closing her eyes in an expression of bliss.

I wanted her to wear that expression forever. Heart pounding, I leaned down and pressed my lips to her neck, tasting the sweetness of her skin. I pressed kisses to her chest as she gripped my head, wrapping her legs around me and moving in a rhythm that made pleasure grip me dangerously tightly.

"Take off your clothes," she murmured, reaching for my shirt to pull at it.

I rose over her and yanked the shirt over my head. The appreciation in her eyes made me grateful for all the hours in the gym.

"Now the trousers." She pointed to them.

I unbuckled them quickly, shucking them off along with my underwear and boots. When I was fully naked in the moonlight, she stared up at me, a smile stretching across her lips. She rose to her knees and pulled her dress over her head.

Beneath, she wore pale blue underwear and a matching bra. The sight of her took my breath away.

"Aria." My voice was a low groan. "You're going to kill me."

She pulled off her bra and reached for me.

I went to my knees like a sinner in church, reaching for

her. Her skin was soft as silk beneath my palms, and I ran my hands up and down her sides before pulling her close.

She kissed me with a passion that made my head spin, then pushed me to my back. She pressed her fingertips to her underwear, and they disappeared.

A brilliant smile swept across her face. "I can't believe I did that with my magic."

"You did." My voice was hoarse. I was happy for her—I truly was—but I was also riveted by the sight of the curls at the apex of her thighs.

She climbed on top of me, pressing her lips to my throat as she whispered, "I don't trust myself to magic some birth control without practice, though."

"I can." It wasn't a spell I used often, but any mage worth his salt knew how to stop himself from getting a woman pregnant.

"Good." She sank down onto my length, her heat making me shudder. She threw back her head, the moonlight cascading over her pale skin. "You feel amazing."

"You *look* amazing." I gripped her hips and helped her find a rhythm. "And you feel even better."

She laughed, pure joy in the sound, and found her pleasure in my body. I followed her, the orgasm spreading through me like golden light.

When it was over, she curled up against my side. "That was incredible."

"It was more than that."

She smiled and looked up at me. She was so beautiful that it defied words. But then her expression changed. A frown crossed her face, and she sat up.

"We shouldn't have done that." She grabbed her dress and pulled it over her head, then shoved her underwear in the pocket. "We're competing against each other."

"It's fine. This doesn't have to affect that."

"Sure." She laughed as if I were crazy. "I need to stay focused. I'll see you later." She was gone before I could say a word.

~

Aria

THE NEXT MORNING, I woke with a headache and the feeling that I had started down a path from which I couldn't turn away.

I'd slept with Callan.

The entire night had been amazing. Not just the part with Callan, which had been a major mistake that would lead towards eventual heartbreak, but my magic. Unlocking it had been incredible. I could feel it deep in my soul that an unheard-of level of magic was now open within me, and that my gift for plants had expanded.

I really felt like I might be able to win this thing. I loved the Garden of Enchantment, and more than that, I wanted to prove myself after decades of being considered a failure.

Aren't you getting up? The sun has nearly risen.

I groaned and leaned up on my elbows, finding Boris sitting on top of my dresser. At least he wasn't inside it. "I'm coming. Why are you up so early?"

I want to meet the dreamweavers. Now that I've helped build their garden, I feel invested.

"All right." I smiled, glad to see he was starting to feel like part of it. "Just let me dress."

He trundled off to the kitchen while I pulled on some clothes. I'd washed the scent of Callan off me last night.

The house was empty except for Boris when I reached the kitchen. The door to Callan's room was open, and he was clearly gone.

Good. Hopefully, he was working on his project.

Are we bringing anyone else? Boris asked.

"Tabitha." I needed the company. Boris was great, but I was sure he wouldn't understand what had just happened between Callan and me.

Boris grinned. *I like Tabitha.*

"Good. I think she likes you."

Boris grinned more widely, but showing that many fangs just made him look a bit threatening.

I turned towards the kitchen and started the coffee, then sent a text message to Tabitha asking her to come along. By the time the coffee was ready and I'd found some granola bars in the cabinet, Tabitha was at my door.

She beamed when she saw me. "You look happy!"

"More than happy."

"You had sex." She rubbed her hands together. "I knew it. Tell me everything."

"In the car."

"Right, of course." She hiked a thumb over her shoulder, indicating the small SUV in front of my house. "I brought Beula, so we don't have to borrow your Gran's."

"Perfect." I handed her a granola bar. "Let's hit the road."

Boris followed us to the car and climbed into the back seat. Tabitha got behind the wheel and turned the car on while I buckled myself in and pulled up the directions on my phone. Once I'd found them, I handed the device to her.

"Great, now that we have that out of the way, tell me all about it," she said as she pulled away from the house.

"Well, there's—"

"Hang on," she said, stopping the car. "What happened to your magic? I can really feel it."

"So, that's another story."

"Go on."

I told her everything, from Gertrude to the garden and all the way up to the amazing night with Callan. When I was done, she blew out a breath. "That's a lot."

"I know."

"The part about your magic is phenomenal, though I'm not surprised. I knew it was only a matter of time before you figured it out."

"Thanks."

"What about Callan?"

"What about him?"

"Are you going to do it again?"

"No way. I can't afford to be distracted, and he's just going to leave when this is over."

"I think it's wise to focus on the competition." Her tone was measured. "But he might not leave. You should ask him what his plans are."

I heaved a sigh. "Maybe I will, but only when this is over. Though I think it's a long shot. You've seen the news about him—he's not the kind of guy to want to settle down in a little village with one woman."

"Maybe the news is wrong. And you're not just any woman."

It was too much to hope for, but I couldn't help the flicker inside my chest. "Maybe. But there's no way I'm bringing it up before the competition is finished. That kind of distraction is the last thing I need."

"Fair enough." She looked down at the bright screen of the phone that showed the directions. "We're nearly there. But where *is* there, exactly?"

"The abandoned mining village. The sources that talked about the dreamweavers gave directions that start from the village itself."

"At least the sun will be up if we're going towards a scary, abandoned village."

"It might not be scary."

"Come on, an abandoned mining village? Definitely scary."

"We'll see."

We arrived a few minutes later, and it was possible that Tabitha had a point. As expected, the old stone buildings were run down, with many of them missing roofs and glass in the windows. But it was the air of abandonment that really unnerved me.

"See?" Tabitha pointed. "Creepy."

"Thankfully, we're not going there." I turned to the back seat and spotted a sleeping Boris. "Time to wake up, buddy. We've got some dreamweavers to find."

He grumbled and sat up, then rose on his back legs to press his hands against the window as he looked out. *Creepy.*

"Join the club." I climbed out of the car. The cool morning breeze whipped my hair back from my face. I'd memorized the directions last night, and I searched for the copse of trees that was meant to be on the west side of town. When I spotted it, I pointed. "There it is."

Boris trundled off, and we followed. The wet grass quickly soaked my shoes, but I didn't care. With my magic finally unlocked inside me, I could feel the power surging into me from the grass. It made me feel almost giddy, and like I could fly if I wanted to.

Probably best to save any attempts at aerial acrobatics for later, though.

"You really are glowing," Tabitha said. "It's amazing."

"Thanks." I grinned at her, then frowned down at my bare hands. "Do you mean, like, literally glowing?"

"No, you're not a walking nightlight. You just look happy and confident. It's a good look."

"Thanks. It's a good feeling."

We reached the edge of the trees, and I felt the pull of the forest. The plants inside seemed to sing to me. If I focused, I could feel them all. It was still a slightly jumbled sensation of different magical signatures floating on the air, but with time, I might be able to determine what was around me without even looking.

That was crazy, though, right?

But it really felt possible.

"Where to now?" Tabitha asked.

"According to what I read, there was once a path through the trees, though it could be grown over."

Boris snuffled on the ground, searching for any sign of a path. After a moment, he sat on his butt. *Got nothing.*

"Let's just go in and look around," Tabitha said. "The directions didn't say it was a long walk, did they?"

"No." I started into the forest, enjoying the feeling of the plants all around me. Their power vibrated on the air, and if I attempted to draw it into myself, I could.

"Are you trying out your magic?" Tabitha asked as we walked.

"Yeah. The plants are giving me power. It's amazing— like a friendly fizzing feeling inside my body."

"Nice." She nodded. "That's a bit what it feels like when I draw the ether into me, then I use it for my magic."

"I'm so glad to finally be normal."

"You're not normal," Tabitha said. "You're better than normal."

I grinned and gave her a side hug before stepping over a low-lying bush. We'd been walking for about fifteen minutes when I caught sight of something glittery and bright out of the corner of my eye. I turned, spotting a creature that looked like an overly large iridescent lavender butterfly.

"There." I pointed. "We've found them."

"Let's approach slowly," Tabitha said. "They might be shy after so many years of not being around people."

"Good point." I looked down at Boris, whose little face looked excited. "Best behavior, mister."

Obviously. I'm no animal.

"Of course not."

We walked slowly towards the fluttering dreamweaver, who hovered high over our heads, checking us out. A few joined the first, and a pale, sparkling mist began to drift down from them. As soon as it hit me, serenity flowed through me. Every muscle in my body relaxed, and I looked at Tabitha. Her eyes were half closed, and a small smile pulled at her lips. Boris had flopped over onto his back and was already blissfully dozing.

Fat lot of help he was.

"Hello," I said, trying to keep my thoughts on the job at hand. "I'm Aria. I've come from the village of Charming Cove. We have a beautiful botanical garden there and many people who would enjoy your company. I was hoping you might come back with us."

The dreamweaver fluttered closer, as if interested in what I had to say. It was impossible to tell if they were able to understand me, but I got the feeling that they were getting the gist.

In the distance, a soft snuffling sounded. I looked to the right, searching the underbrush for whatever creature was nearby. A tiny pink snout peeked out from the bushes, and I gasped.

Was that a baby pig?

"Tabitha," I whispered, pointing.

"I see it."

The little pig had trotted out of the bushes. It was about the size of a house cat and so cute, I thought I might die. It had soft, pale pink skin and the sweetest eyes I'd ever seen. Magic sparked around it, little glimmers that vibrated on the air.

"It's a pinkling," Tabitha said, excitement in her voice. "I've never seen one, but always wanted to."

"Me, too." I knelt and held my hand out for the pinkling. They were a rare type of magical pig that was excellent at hunting for mushrooms—a bit like the truffle-hunting pigs of France, but better. They were never, ever turned into bacon.

As the little creature trotted towards us, the dreamweaver fluttered down to hover protectively around it.

"I think they're friends," Tabitha said.

The pinkling stopped in front of me and sniffed at my hand, then rubbed its face against my fingers like a cat. I gave him a scratch, a giddy sensation rushing through me.

"I wonder if the previous tenants of the magical village had one for a pet, and it stayed here when they left?" Tabitha asked. "I didn't think they were native to this area."

"I don't think they are." The sound of more snuffling caught my ear, and I looked up to see four more pinklings coming out of the same underbrush.

They trotted up to us, giving little piggy kisses with their noses. It felt like the brush of butterfly wings. Overhead, more dreamweavers had appeared. They fluttered around the pinklings and us, a glittering mist coming off their wings. As it fell onto the pinklings, the little pigs made happy, squeaking sounds. When it fell on me, I wanted to join them.

"This place is amazing," Tabitha breathed.

"I know. It's incredible." I looked up at the dreamweavers. "The pinklings are your friends, aren't they?"

The dreamweavers fluttered their wings even more quickly, which I took to mean *yes*.

"Do you think they would be willing to leave the pinklings?" Tabitha asked.

"Doubtful, though maybe. I'd feel guilty separating them, for sure. We need a better way to communicate with them." I nudged Boris with my hand. He was snoring away, and only grumbled. I gave him a little shake, and he woke up with a glare.

What?

"I need your help. Can you try to communicate with the pinklings or dreamweavers?"

Pinklings? He sat up and looked around, and then his face lit up. *Pinklings!*

"Yes. Can you ask them if they will come to the Garden of Enchantment if I build a habitat for the pinklings? Tell them there are lots of people who would love to spend time with them."

I can try. He looked between the pinklings and the dreamweavers, then relayed my message. I could understand what he said, but if the creatures responded, I couldn't tell.

After a moment, he looked at me. *They say that they'll come, but they need the perfect habitat for their pinklings friends. After the humans left, the pinklings appeared. The dreamweavers bonded with the pinklings in the way they would bond with humans, and they don't want to be separated. But they would enjoy an environment with more people, too.*

"Amazing." Excitement lit me up. "What exactly do the pinklings want in their environment?"

Boris relayed the message, and after a few moments of listening, he turned to me. *They want these bushes that are all around here. The pinklings eat them. And also lots of flowers, which we already have.*

I looked at the vegetation, recognizing the kern bush. It had flowers that looked like horns.

"Does the Garden of Enchantment have those?" Tabitha asked.

"No. And I don't think we should take them from here. They would view it as us destroying their home."

"So we need to get them from somewhere else."

I nodded. "I have an idea where we can find some, but we'll have to hurry." I turned to Boris. "Please tell them that I will plant a lot of kern bushes, and that we will be back to pick them up tomorrow if they are still willing to come."

Boris relayed the message, then turned to me with a wide grin. *All done. I think you're going to win this thing, and it will all come down to me.*

I grinned at him but didn't correct him. He was right. His help had been invaluable. "Thank you, Boris." I looked between the pinklings and the dreamweavers. "We need to go get those kern bushes, but we'll see you tomorrow."

As we left the creatures behind, Tabitha asked, "Where are you going to find kern bushes? I've never even seen them before."

"They're a type of ancient Cornish plant. The word *kern* is Cornish for *horn*, which I think refers to the flowers." I pulled my phone from my pocket. "I met a botanist at the Lizard who has an incredible greenhouse. I'm hoping she has some."

"If she doesn't?"

"I don't even want to think about that." We stepped out

of the forest, and I called my gran, asking her to contact Matilda and get the number of the botanist.

Within minutes, she had the info for me, and I called the greenhouse. I could feel Tabby's anxious gaze on me as I talked to the botanist's granddaughter and made arrangements to come pick up the plants. I was grateful she had them to sell, since she'd mentioned that most of her stock was already spoken for. I hung up and looked at Tabitha. "You're going to have to drive like a bat out of hell."

She nodded. "I can do that."

CHAPTER
TWENTY-SIX

ARIA

DRIVING to and from the Lizard took all day, but we made it back to the Garden of Enchantment by early evening. The car was loaded down with so many kern bushes that we could barely fit in alongside them. Boris had to sit on my lap, and he started out very annoyed, grumbling and shifting for the entire first hour. Eventually, though, he decided he liked a cuddle.

I didn't hate it, either, to be honest. He smelled surprisingly good, and his fur was softer than I'd expected.

Tabitha pulled up outside of the garden and parked the car.

"Wake up, pal." I jostled Boris, who grunted and tried to roll over. "Nope, no more sleeping. Get those diggers ready."

You're the worst.

I pushed open the car door, and he scrambled out,

rubbing his eyes as he looked around. I followed him, going to the boot to open it and unloading the kern bushes. I'd left my wagon at the front gate, and Tabitha went to collect it.

Tabitha, Boris, and I loaded up the bushes and dragged them into the garden, then got to work planting. Boris dug the holes, while Tabitha and I put the plants in and covered them with lose soil. Every time I touched the leaves, a little zip of magic passed between the plants and me. It felt amazing.

"I think they're starting to look better," Tabitha said. "When you touch them, I mean. Their leaves get perkier."

"Maybe they were just wilted from the car ride and like being in the soil."

"Come on, you're a plant witch who just came into her magic. Give yourself a little credit."

I smiled at her. "Maybe you're right."

"I know I'm right."

We spent the next two hours getting the rest of the bushes in place. I was more conscious of my magic after what Tabitha had said, making a point to give each plant a little zap of power as I put it in. And I was pretty sure she was right—they did look healthier.

Hopefully, the dreamweavers and pinklings would like their new habitat. All that was left was to get the hammocks and giant cushions that I'd ordered and arrange them. They should be arriving tomorrow morning, and I'd have a chance to put them in place before I went to pick up the new residents.

Tabitha brushed off her hands and proudly surveyed out work. "I'd say we're done for the night."

"Agreed." I draped an arm around her shoulders. "I couldn't have done it without you."

What about me?

"I definitely couldn't have done it without *you*. No one digs a hole like you, Boris."

He preened. *I like a person who can appreciate my brilliance.*

"Let's go get some sleep." It was already late, and exhaustion was pulling at me. Nerves, too, considering the fact that Callan was likely to be back in my house right now.

Tabitha drove us home, dropping us at my front door before heading to hers. The lights were on in the living room, and I could see Callan through the window. He was walking into the kitchen, shirtless.

Of course he was shirtless.

I couldn't get a break.

I drew in a deep breath and opened the door, coming face to pecs with the glorious expanse that was his chest. Apparently, he'd come to the door while I'd hesitated, and I'd nearly barreled into him.

"Hey." His voice was soft—almost uncertain, as if he wondered whether I was still mad at him.

Was I? Not really. "Hi."

"I was just getting a beer. Do you want one?"

"Sure." I debated telling him to put on a shirt but decided that would give away too much of what I was thinking.

He went to the fridge and pulled out two bottles, then opened them and handed one to me. "Long day?"

I nodded. I really needed to get to bed, especially since I now had my magic. I'd used a lot of it, and the best way to recoup my ability to draw more magic from plants was to sleep. It was like a muscle that needed rest. Which meant I needed to get into bed soon—alone.

I took a sip of the beer. "How's your habitat coming along?"

"Good. Just a bit to do tomorrow, then I'm done." He sipped his beer, and the moment of silence allowed me to realize how much sexual tension there was. It heated the air and made my breath come short. My skin was so warm that I wanted to rub the cold beer bottle against my forehead.

I was losing my damned mind.

CALLAN

I STARED AT ARIA, the cold beer sweating in my hand. I tried to focus on it instead of her, but all I could think of was how incredible last night had been.

"How is your habitat coming along?" I asked, wanting anything to distract me from those thoughts. "Care to give me a hint?"

"I don't know." She leaned against the counter and sipped her beer, her gaze on mine. "Are you sure you won't steal my idea?"

"I don't have time to implement it, and I probably don't have the skills."

She laughed. "You're Callan Hawthorne, most powerful mage in the country. Of course you have the skills."

"When it comes to gardens, I don't think anyone can

beat you. Especially after last night. How's that working for you, by the way?" I hadn't had a chance to see how her new magic was coming along. As much as I wanted to hear about her plans for the garden, that was more important to me.

"Really well, actually." She smiled. "My gift for plants has definitely improved. I'm excited to see what else I can do."

"Like the regular stuff?" I waved a hand towards the furniture. "Telekinesis and manifesting?"

"Yeah. And I want to practice. Desperately. But I want to save my power."

"You used a lot of it today?"

"Enough. How about you?"

"I'm building an enclosure for moonlight mares, which definitely took some work."

"Hey! You shouldn't tell me what you're up to. We're competing. It should be secret."

"The competition is almost over, so neither of us has a chance of changing our plans. And I know you're not going to use the information against me."

"True." She nodded reluctantly, then whistled low. "Moonlight mares, though, huh? Those are impressive. Beautiful, for sure."

"More impressive than what you've got?"

"It'll be a toss-up. I was going for dreamweavers, but I've got a surprise that will come along with them."

I felt my brows rise. "A surprise, huh?"

"Pinklings."

"I don't stand a chance against pinklings and dreamweavers." I tilted my head back and looked at the ceiling, trying to look disappointed but not surprised in the least that she was blowing me out of the water with her habitat.

"Do you have any idea what the others are doing?" she asked.

I shook my head. "I haven't seen them, and I've been careful not to explore too widely in the garden in case I stumble on them and get accused of sabotage."

"You would never."

"They don't know that." But her faith warmed me. And standing here talking to her was the best part of my day. I'd have said it was the best part of my year, but that had occurred last night. Just the memory of it was enough to send heat through my veins. "I should probably get to bed."

"Me, too." She drained her beer, then stepped froward to put it on the counter.

I'd started moving at the same time, and we came chest to chest in a split second. Our gazes caught, and I couldn't help but fall into the depths of hers. The golden sparkles snared me, and I breathed in her scent, feeling desire rush through every inch of my body.

Her cheeks flushed, and her lips parted. The sight made something clench inside me, and it took all I had not to reach out and pull her closer. My world had narrowed until she was the only thing in it, and I wanted to drown in her.

"Callan." Her voice was a low rasp, her gaze riveted to my lips. "I think this is a bad idea."

"Of course." I stepped back, dragging myself away from her. She was right. Tomorrow was a big day. "I'm headed to bed." I spun on my heel and went into my room, shutting the door behind me.

CHAPTER
TWENTY-SEVEN

ARIA

I AWOKE the next day feeling like a kid on Christmas morning. Actually, I hadn't been nearly this excited as a kid. But today was the big day, and I was hopeful. I would finish getting the hammocks and cushions in place in the garden, then I'd go get the dreamweavers and pinklings.

I had a hard time imagining anything better than that combination. Callan's moonlight mares were very cool, but unless he had a dozen of them, I had a good shot at beating him. And if I could beat the great Callan Hawthorne, then I could probably take down Serena and Terry as well.

What's with the cocky grin? Boris asked from my lingerie drawer.

I threw a pillow at him. "Get out of there!"

Fine, fine. He grumbled and climbed out, and I hoped there were clean underwear on the drying rack. But he had a point. I really shouldn't be getting cocky. It was too soon for that, and it might compromise my performance.

I looked down at my hands and wiggled my fingers, ready to use some magic today. It really was starting to feel more natural, and I was excited to see what I could do. Even though I'd had trouble falling asleep—thoughts of Callan were to blame, obviously—I'd got enough good sleep that my ability to draw power from plants had regenerated. I was ready to go.

I climbed out of bed and made quick work of dressing and grabbing a coffee for the walk. Callan was nowhere to be seen, thank goodness. It made everything easier.

My first stop was town to pick up the hammocks. I'd ordered them by phone at the local shop, and they were just as lovely as I'd hoped. Once I had them loaded into gran's car, along with some large cushions, I drove over to the garden.

As I climbed out of the car, I noticed that the garden gates were partially swung open. That was weird. If another competitor had got here before me, they would have propped them neatly.

What was the deal?

Probably nothing. I was getting paranoid.

As quickly as I could, I loaded the hammocks and large cushions into the wagon and towed it down the path. I was about halfway there when I began to hear the sound of snuffling and chewing.

Weird. I didn't think anyone had built an enclosure for animals near the path towards my section of the garden.

A few moments later, a goat ran across the path.

Greenery hung from its mouth as it chomped away, and my stomach pitched.

I dropped the handle to the cart and sprinted towards my little plot. As I neared, the sound of the goats got louder. When I arrived, I stumbled to a halt and gaped.

No.

There were goats everywhere. *Everywhere.*

White goats, brown goats, black goats. There were dozens of them, and they chewed at the plants I'd so painstakingly planted. Everywhere I looked was devastation. Bushes had been torn out of the ground and trampled, flowers had been bitten off right at the bloom, and even the stream was filled with rocks and mud. The water was overflowing the banks and spreading through the grass.

Shock rippled through me as I watched the goats mill around, eating and kicking and spitting.

Did goats even spit?

These ones did.

They were ravenous and destructive and just plain awful —and they'd destroyed everything I'd worked on.

Anger and despair rose in me, and I raised my hands. I didn't have a plan, but I did have magic. It welled inside me, fueled by my sadness and rage. I released it, screaming, "Go!" at the top of my lungs.

The goats stopped dead in their tracks, staring at me with their creepy goat eyes. Then my magic hit them, a wave of power that bowled them off their feet. They tumbled to their sides, making their weird goat noises as they fell.

Stunned, I watched them stagger upright. I hadn't hurt

them, thank goodness. As much as I hated what they'd done, I didn't want to kill a bunch of idiot goats.

But I didn't want them here.

"Go!" I screamed again.

That shook them into action. They turned and ran, racing from the garden as fast as they could.

When they were gone, I stared at the garden in despair. It was quiet all around, as if the goats had scared away the woodland creatures with their horrible behavior.

Where had they come from?

I'd never seen goats in Charming Cove. It didn't matter, though. What mattered was trying to fix the damage that had been done. I walked through the garden, inspecting the wreckage.

Many of the plants had been torn up and nibbled at, but not all of them were destroyed. All of them *were* out of the ground, however. I'd need to get Boris out here ASAP to help me put them back in. I'd be able to use my new magic, but I was still getting the hang of it. I needed all the help I could get.

The stream would have to be cleaned, too. Piles of dirt and rocks were damming it up, and it was the first really compelling evidence that all of this damage hadn't been done by goats.

But who would want to sabotage me?

Any of the competitors.

Any except Callan, that was.

Would I even have time to fix all this?

My shoulders sagged. I wouldn't know until I started, and I was going to need help.

With shaking hands, I pulled the phone from my pocket and dialed Tabitha. She picked up, clearly out of breath, and asked, "What's up?"

"Trouble. I need your help."

"Of course. I'm at your gran's with Catrina. Do you need them, too?"

I looked at the wreckage, my heart sinking. "Definitely. And can you pick up Boris from my house?"

"Sure thing. We'll be right there."

I took one moment to let the worry and sadness rush through me. When it threatened to drag me down, I drew in a ragged breath and shoved it away.

"That's enough of that. This is my origin story, damn it." I wasn't a superhero in a movie, but right now, I felt like one. I still didn't know who the villain was, but I wouldn't let them defeat me.

I got to work, putting plants back in their holes as quickly as I could. Every time I touched one, the leaves and flowers perked up, but it wasn't enough. They still looked like hell, even with a little help.

I started experimenting with my magic, giving each a tiny jolt as I put it back in the ground. Leaves and flowers grew back, but it was a real drain on my power after a while.

Finally, the others arrived. Their cries of shock alerted me to their presence, and I turned.

"Don't bother asking me who did it," I said. "Technically, it was goats. But I don't know who released them here."

"I'll find out." Catrina cracked her knuckles. "Then they won't know what hit them."

"Thanks, kid." Her words warmed me, and also frightened me on behalf of whoever had done the damage. From the look on the little girl's face, they would be getting more than a tail.

Gran brushed her hands together. "It's a lot of work, but we'll get it done."

"We have three hours before we need to go pick up the dreamweavers and pinklings," I said.

"Let's get to it," Gran said. "We need to know if some of the plants need to be replaced entirely. I might have them in my garden."

"You can't empty out your garden for this, Gran."

"I can do whatever I want with my garden." She pointed to a row of kern bushes that had been torn out and stamped on. "Now get those back in the ground. Your pinklings are looking forward to them."

"Right." I smiled at her, grateful for her presence and good attitude.

Magic flowed around the garden as the five of us—Boris included—used sweat and witchcraft to repair the damage. We were about halfway done when I heard the approach of footsteps and heaving breath.

I rose and turned, spotting Terry. His eyes were wild as he said, "There are goats in the village! They're destroying everyone's gardens."

Shit.

He spun on his heel and ran off, clearly panicked. I didn't blame him. If the goats had come from here—which they must have—then we were partially to blame. *I* was to blame. I was the one who had banished them instead of capturing them. They'd gone on a rampage elsewhere, possibly through Terry's part of the garden as well, then headed into town to get started on their destruction.

"Were there a lot of goats?" Tabitha asked, worry in her voice.

"At least thirty. Maybe forty. I was too startled to count." I pinched the bridge of my nose and closed my eyes. I couldn't believe this was happening. "I have to go catch them."

"You have to finish fixing your garden!" Catrina said.

"I know, and I will. But I should have stopped them when they were here. I can't be responsible for them ruining everyone else's gardens as well. It's the middle of summer, and you know how much people love their gardens." Everyone's vegetables and fruits were coming in. Hours, days, weeks of labor would be lost. In good conscience, I couldn't let that happen. And there was no way I'd be qualified to win a gardening competition if I stood by and let goats destroy the townspeople's gardens, especially when I'd been the one to drive the goats towards them.

Gran nodded approvingly at me. "You go catch those goats. We'll do what we can here, then we'll go pick up the dreamweavers and pinklings. With any luck, you'll get back in time to put the finishing touches on the garden before we return."

"Thank you, Gran." It was the best—and only—idea that we had.

"Do you think they'll come with us if you aren't there?" Tabitha asked.

I nodded. "They know you, too, so they'll come." I looked

at Boris. "Do you agree? You were the one who could speak to them."

They liked Tabitha, so it will be fine. Anyway, I'm coming with you to catch those goats. Something a lot like a thirst for vengeance glinted in Boris's dark eyes.

I'd have to rein him in, but he would be good to have at my side. "Thank you, Boris." I looked at Tabitha. "He says they'll come with you. Good luck. And thank you again."

"Just hurry," Tabitha said. "We'll see you later."

I nodded. "Yeah. And thank you, guys. From the bottom of my heart, truly."

"Duh." Catrina asked. "What's family for?"

"I couldn't have said it better myself." Warmth replaced some of the disappointment in my heart at I turned and hurried down the path towards the entrance. Boris followed alongside, running as fast as his little legs would carry him.

When we passed the area where the path veered off towards Callan's part of the garden, I saw him. He was hurrying towards me, worry on his face.

"I heard something about goats in town," he said.

"Yeah, my fault. I'm off to catch them."

"Your fault?"

"No time to explain. I'll see you when I get back." I hurried past him, but he moved to catch up.

"I'm coming to help."

"Are you sure? Have you finished with your part of the garden?"

"Pretty much."

"Great. And thank you."

I FOLLOWED Aria through the garden, Boris trailing behind.

"Why do you feel responsible for these goats?" I asked as we exited the garden and I followed her to her car.

"They were destroying my habitat, and I banished them, but I didn't actually think about where they might go. I was so worried that I focused only on myself." Disgust echoed in her voice.

"Hey, take it easy on yourself. Anyone would be worried."

"Right, but not everyone would just banish them and go about their business."

"I probably would."

She gave a little huff of a laugh and shot me a sidelong look. "Then we're both jerks."

"Perfect for each other." As the words flowed from my lips, I realized how true they were. She really was perfect for me. I wanted to spend every day with her, listening to her laugh.

She said nothing, and I regretted the words in the silence. Maybe she didn't care for me the way I cared for her.

Of course she didn't. I'd taken away the place that allowed her to see her grandad's spirit. And she was amazing.

There was no more time for thinking, though. We'd arrived in town, and the chaos was immediately obvious. People ran through the streets, brandishing gardening tools and their magic, trying to drive the goats away from their front gardens and vegetables patches.

Aria stopped the car and climbed out, shock on her face. "Holy broomsticks, this is worse than I expected."

I looked where her gaze was directed, catching sight of a group of elderly witches fighting off a small group of goats who were trying to get to their prized peonies. There was even a sign over the little garden, *Prized Peonies of Charming Cove*. Shrieks sounded as the women threw blasts of magic at the goats, driving them back. But the creatures were determined and kept charging. One of the women, a lady with a lavender bouffant and red lipstick, picked up a rock and hurled it at the nearest goat. It bonked onto his head, and she crowed with victory. "I've got you, you furry bastard."

The goat didn't seem to be hurt, but he did hesitate before resuming his approach. Another witch took the opportunity to loop a rope around its neck, and two other women joined her. They pulled the stubborn goat to a fence and tied it off so it couldn't reach their flowers.

Two more of the women managed to freeze a goat with their magic, and a third bound its legs with rope.

"I think they've got it under control," Aria said. "But the school garden is under attack. Look."

I spotted what she was talking about. Near the edge of town was a community garden that had a large sign proclaiming it to be part of a local school project. The children and their parents were trying to fight the goats off, but there were just too many.

Boris looked up at Aria and did some of the chattering

and squeaking that I associated with him speaking to her, then scampered towards the goats.

"He says he's going to go reason with them," Aria translated.

We followed, racing down the street after the badger. I spotted Terry running towards a goat on the roof of a building nearby. The creature was using the height to eat the blooms off a fruit tree.

When we reached the goats at the vegetable patch, Boris had already turned around and was running back towards us, eyes wide as he shook his head. He skidded to a stop in front of us, panting as he chattered to Aria.

She shot me a glance. "He says they can't be reasoned with."

We were now close enough to see their eyes, and Boris was right. They looked manic, far wilder than goats usually looked.

"They've been enchanted," I said.

Worry flashed on Aria's face. "They didn't look this crazy when they were at my garden. I wonder if my magic did this to them?"

"Doubtful. You'd have to intentionally put this kind of spell on them."

"Maybe, but we don't know what I'm fully capable of."

"Don't blame yourself for this until we know if it's actually your fault. Save your energy for catching them."

"Right. Of course."

"I'm headed towards that group over there." I pointed to a group of a dozen goats who had cornered some school children trying to protect their tomato plants. Their parents were dragging the kids out of the way, but there were still more kids than adults.

There were quite a few witches and mages in the group that was trying to repel the goats, but the adults were more distracted by trying to control and protect their children.

"I've got this group." She started towards a group of eight goats that were devouring rows of green beans. She knelt and pressed her hands to the ground, and I left her to it.

I reached the goats who were bearing down on the children and raised my hands, letting my magic flow through me. I envisioned a large metal cage building itself around the goats and used my magic to manifest my desires. As the power poured from my fingertips, the metal bars appeared one by one, the cage constructing itself from nothing but magic and willpower. It surrounded eight of the goats, and I had to catch the other four by hand and shove them in. The bastards really were unnaturally strong, and it was no surprise that the townspeople hadn't managed to stop all of them yet.

When they were locked up, I turned to see Aria finishing off a corral built of thorns that she'd conjured from the ground.

Boris stood in front of them, and I could tell that the little creature was trying to talk to the goats. I went to them, wondering how many more of these creatures could still be loose in town.

CHAPTER
TWENTY-EIGHT

Aria

I STARED at the thorny corral, pleased with myself. The goats had already chomped on plenty of the kids' plants, but I'd stopped them from ruining all of them.

Callan appeared at my side. "Nice work."

"Thanks. You, too." Between us, we'd caught all the goats at the school garden. I turned to Boris, who was still talking to the goats.

He turned to me a moment later, his expression serious. *They don't know what enchanted them, but it's also hard to get them to speak straight. They're out of their minds.*

I translated for Callan.

He nodded, worry on his face. "Not ideal."

A shout sounded from behind him, and I peered around his broad shoulder to see one of the children pointing at the large metal cage Callan had built. The goats were beginning to chew at the metal bars, just like my plants had done. I didn't think there was a connection, but I really needed a break from metal-eating magical beasts. They were even managing to break through the steel.

"They'll be out soon." My mind raced. "We need to break the spell that's on them."

"Normally, I could do it, but it will take too much time," Callan said. "They'll destroy the town before I can figure out what's wrong and how to neutralize it."

"That's a specialty of yours?" I asked.

He nodded.

"Cool. But I was thinking of something else. Gran sells a potion that will break spells. We need to go get it." I should have thought of it sooner, but I hadn't realized how crazy these goats would be. The potion was so valuable that it was kept in a safe, so it wasn't something I would normally use. "Let's go."

I ran towards Gran's shop, pulling my phone from my pocket as I went. I dialed Gran as quickly as I could, grateful that she picked up on the second ring. "Aria? Is everything all right?"

"I need the spellbreaker potion—as much of it as we've got."

Gran gave a low curse. "It's locked up. I'll have to come get it out for you."

"Are you still at the garden?"

"I'm in the car with Tabitha, but we're just nearing town on our way to get the dreamweavers. I'll have her drop me off."

"Perfect. I'll see you there."

As we neared the shop, I caught sight of the florist fending off two rabid goats with a broom and blasts of pink magic. Across the street, a goat had got stuck in one of the decorative flower pots along the coast path, but didn't seem to mind because it was busy chomping on the flowers in adjacent pots.

"It's chaos," I muttered as we arrived at the shop.

Tabitha's car pulled up a moment later, and Gran hopped out. Catrina waved from the window as her mother drove off, calling, "We'll bring back the dreamweavers!"

"This is madness," Gran said as she unlocked the shop. "Pure madness." She pushed open the door and led the way to the back of the store, where there was a secret safe. It was actually a small room, and it revealed itself when Gran waved her hand in front of the false bookshelf. Another burst of very specific magic, and the door swung open.

"The potion is a concentrate, mind you," Gran said as she hurried in. "You'll have to dilute it to use it."

"We can do that," I said, following her into the room.

She stopped in front of the shelf she sought, then pointed to the bottles. "These are the ones you want. Looks like we have about a dozen."

I grabbed as many as I could carry, nodding for Callan to do the same. Gran grabbed a few, and we returned to the main part of the shop. As we walked by the back window, Gran stopped and stared out at her garden. "That bastard."

I looked out, catching sight of a goat jumping off the tall stone wall that protected the garden. The creature landed in the middle, unharmed. It began to chop on the yellow roses, and Gran hissed. Grandad had planted the roses decades ago.

"Go fend them off, Gran," I said. "We've got this. We'll bring you a potion bomb when we're done."

"See that you do." She set the jars on the nearby counter and strode out to the garden, her magic already flashing around her.

"I don't envy that goat," Callan said.

"Me, neither." I stopped at the main work table and laid out the bottles, then retrieved the ones my grandmother had left on the shelf.

I'll help. Boris climbed up onto the table, rubbing his little hands together.

"Be careful." I worked as quickly as I could, gathering jugs of water and the thin glass orbs with screw tops that acted as potion bombs. They were essentially Christmas baubles with lids, and once they'd been filled with a potion, they could be thrown.

"We'll do an assembly line." I pushed a pile of metal caps towards Boris and gave the jugs of water to Callan. "Fill the bottles halfway."

He did as I asked, working swiftly. I added the potion, then handed the bottle off to Boris, who capped it. Magic flowed through the air as we worked, speeding up our movements. Within minutes, we had nearly fifty potion bombs and were running out of concentrate.

"That's going to have to do." I grabbed a dozen bags and filled them up. I gave half to Callan and saved the rest to hand out to the other townspeople. "We'll pass these around. Now, let's go."

I want a bag.

"You're too small to carry it, but I'll hand you potion bombs."

As long as you're quick about it.

"Oh, I will be."

We delivered a potion bomb to Gran, who stayed behind to take care of the goat that she'd driven into the corner, and then we raced back out into the chaos of the street. Goats that had been captured were eating their way free of their bonds, using their magically gifted strength and appetite to break free of iron, rope, and wood.

I handed a potion bomb to Boris and took one for myself, then hurled it at the nearest goat. The orb flew through the air in a perfect arc and crashed onto the back of the shaggy brown creature. The thin glass shattered, and the potion splattered all over the goat's fur. The creature gave an annoyed bleat, then shook its head. The crazed look in its eyes faded, and it sat down, clearly exhausted. Within moments, it was asleep.

"Thank fates, it works." I handed out bags of potion bombs to the nearest townspeople as Boris and Callan threw their bombs at other goats.

As word of the solution spread, along with the potion bombs, we began to get the situation under control. Soon, there were more sleeping goats than rampaging ones.

When it was over, I surveyed the wreckage. All over town, the flowers had been destroyed. Vegetable patches had been torn up, and grass had been trampled. Exhausted goats lay everywhere, snoring loudly as they slept off their feasts.

I looked at Callan, my heart sinking. "This is a mess."

"We'll fix it." Worry flashed on his face. "How much work is left at your habitat?"

Too much. We were only a couple hours away from the dreamweavers and pinklings arriving, and I was so far from finished that I was going to be in major trouble.

But I couldn't leave a mess like this. There were disappointed people everywhere, many of them with sad expressions as they tried to repair the damage that had been done.

"My habitat is fine," I said. "I've got to help with cleanup here."

"I'll help you."

"Thanks." I went to the nearest person, who I recognized as Margot. She was trying to fix the row of flowers that bordered the path along the sea. For as long as I remembered, she'd been in charge of this part of the community landscaping.

"Let me help you." I knelt next to her and pressed my hand to the soil, feeding some of my magic into the ground to help the plants grow.

Margot looked up at me, horrified. "What are you doing here?"

"Helping. It's partially my fault, anyway."

"I don't believe that for a minute. The part about it being your fault, I mean."

"Well, it is."

"I don't care. You need to get back to the Garden of Enchantment and finish your habitat."

"You know about that?"

"Everyone in town knows about it. And we all want you to win, so scram."

"But I need to stay here and help clean up."

"There will be time for that later." She glared at me, then made a shooing motion. "Go."

"Uh—"

"I mean it!" She stood and propped her hands on her hips, glowering. "You are meant to win that competition, Aria. Now get to it."

I stood, surprise and gratitude racing through me. "Okay."

She nodded, satisfied. "And don't try to stop and help anyone else along the way. They won't let you."

I gave her a smile and left. Callan and Boris followed. Margot was right, though. When I hesitated near the Prized Peony patch, the women waved me along, insisting that I needed to get to the Garden of Enchantment.

I wasn't going to look a gift horse in the mouth. If there was still damage when I returned to town, I would fix it all.

For now, I needed to get back and salvage what was left. We reached the car, and I drove as quickly as I could, making it to the garden gates with only an hour to spare before the dreamweavers' expected arrival time. It was almost the end of the competition—only a few hours until sunset—so we were cutting it close already.

I didn't know how far my family had got with repairing my part of the garden, but I hoped they'd made a good dent.

When Callan, Boris, and I entered the garden, we nearly ran into Serena. She stared at us, delight on her face. "Have you both been in town this whole time?"

"Yes."

320

She laughed. "Then you are so screwed. You'll never finish in time."

"Callan is already finished, and I have time."

"Finished?" She arched a brow and looked at him. "There are no animals in his enclosure."

I looked at him, shocked. "What? You said you were done."

He shrugged. "The town was more important. And I *am* pretty much done. I just need to pick up the animals."

"Well, then, get to it." I gestured towards the exit.

"I'd rather come help you."

"But then you wouldn't finish your habitat."

"I'm aware. But you were meant to win this place, Aria."

I smiled at him, unable to help the surge of warmth at his words. "Thank you. But I can do this myself." I could feel Serena watching us, but I wouldn't be proving myself to her or any other bully who had called me a magical loser as a kid. I was proving myself to *myself*. And I really believed I could do it. "I want to do this alone. But I'll see you when it's all over."

"You've got this."

The confidence in his smile made me feel like I was floating. I gave him one last smile, then turned and headed to my part of the garden.

Serena, who had gone off down the path before me, caught my eye. "Did you sabotage me?" I called after her. "Were the goats your doing?"

"No." She turned to me, horrified. "I don't like you, but I would never do that."

I believed her, and it didn't matter, anyway. I needed to focus on fixing my habitat.

But when I reached it, my heart dropped.

Oh, no. Boris flopped to his butt beside me, clearly despairing.

There was one last goat, and the little bastard stood amongst my plants, working on undoing the repairs that my family had so painstakingly made. From the look of it, they hadn't managed to finish, or maybe the goat was just particularly hungry.

Didn't matter. There was still a massive amount of damage.

I shouldn't have turned down Callan's help.

No. I can do this.

Movement across the clearing caught my eye, and I craned my neck to see between the trees. A man walked away from me, a shovel in his hand.

It was Terry.

He was wearing the same shirt and cap I'd seen him in earlier.

That jerk had been the one to sabotage me!

It was him. Boris growled.

Anger flared, but I shoved it down. "We'll deal with him later. Right now, we need every second to repair the garden and get rid of that goat."

Then I'll go deal with Terry.

"I need your help here."

Boris looked around. *Fine. You're right.*

The only blessing was that I had one last potion bomb in the bag still over my shoulder. I withdrew it and walked towards the goat, hurling it at the creature with a half-hearted throw. It was good enough to land on its back, and the goat was fast asleep in no time.

Boris trundled up next to me. *I know this looks like a big mess, but you've got this, Aria. I believe in you.*

"Thank you." I ruffled his head, grateful to have him on my side. "Let's get to work."

He grinned and scampered towards the nearest bushes, and began to work on digging holes. I followed behind him, planting the bushes as fast as I could. I fed my power into the plants as I worked, reviving them into a profusion of beautiful blooms.

Time passed quickly—way too quickly. We were only partway done when I heard the chattering voice of Catrina approaching.

No way.

I looked up, horrified to see Tabitha and Catrina leading the dreamweavers and pinklings towards the garden. Gran followed along, and I assumed she'd caught up to them after taking care of the goat in her garden.

I stared around at the partially finished wreckage of the habitat. There were still a couple of hours left until the end of the competition, but if the dreamweavers refused to stay, I'd be out of luck.

My skin chilled as I watched them approach, panic making my legs weak. The group stopped at the edge of the garden, and the dreamweavers fluttered their wings in a way that looked anxious. The pinklings stopped as well, staring out at the disaster.

They're disappointed. Boris frowned up at me. *I can tell.*

Panic flared. "Tell them I'm going to fix it. Ask them to please give me one more hour."

He looked around at the chaos, clearly skeptical, but he turned to the dreamweavers and relayed the message.

They want to leave. They don't like liars.

I felt tears prick my eyes. "Tell them I didn't lie. Explain the goats." Suddenly, I was grateful for the goat that I'd found here. At least I had visible proof. I pointed to his sleeping body. "We even have one right here."

I'll try. Boris turned to them, and I waited, breathless. I didn't know if I could actually do what I promised, but I was going to have to find a way. Not just to win the competition, but because I'd asked these two special species to leave their home and come here.

They'll give you an hour, but no more. And if you fail, all dreamweavers will know what you've done.

I winced, then looked at them. "I promise I won't fail you. Thank you for coming."

I could feel my family's gaze on me as I turned and looked at the wreckage. There was absolutely no way to physically fix this in an hour—not even with my family's help. Not even if we used our magic.

I'd been using my new magic, but I was going to have to amp it up about a thousand notches.

Trembling, I knelt and laid my hand on the grass. I was exhausted from fighting the goats and trying to fix the garden all day, but I had to keep going. Boris snuggled up to me, his warm body pressed against my leg. His presence helped steady me, and I leaned into him as I poured my power into the ground, envisioning the roots growing. I was attempting more than I ever had before—more than I ever thought possible.

And it worked—for a while. The plants that had already been planted were flowering even more than before, but I was growing too tired.

I had to keep going.

I poured more and more magic into the garden, envisioning the final product. The power flowed from me as bushes and flowers that had been torn from the ground moved back into position and bloomed brighter and fuller than before.

And yet, it wasn't enough. There was still so much left to be done, and my strength was flagging. No matter how hard I tried, I couldn't stop myself from sagging to the ground in exhaustion.

The grass welcomed me like a comfortable bed.

This is it.

Despair struck. When a witch became this weak, she *had* to rest and recover. We drew our magic from a source like the ether or plants, but we had to have the strength to draw it. Rest gave us that strength.

But I didn't have time for that. By the time I was well enough and my strength had replenished, the dreamweavers would be gone.

No.

I couldn't let this be the end. There had to be more.

CHAPTER
TWENTY-NINE

ARIA

I LAY IN THE GRASS, exhausted, and could hear the worried whispers of Tabitha and my gran. From the sound of them, they were approaching. Probably to pick me up and take me home to bed.

The mere idea made frustration swell.

I wasn't going to lose this because I needed a *nap*. Sure, I'd run myself down in a way that an experienced witch would never do, but I hadn't had a choice. The dreamweavers were counting on me.

I closed my eyes and breathed deeply, trying to draw more power from the plants around me. I was too weak for it to work, but something else seemed to be happening.

The grass underneath me was vibrating slightly. Energy flowed into me, a bit differently than before. Strength returned to my limbs, allowing me to draw more magic from the garden around me. I opened my eyes and sat up.

Gran and Tabitha stood over me, concern on their faces.

"Give me a moment," I said, my voice slightly distant as I ran my hands through the grass. It moved towards me, the little stalks reaching out to touch my skin.

I gave them a bit of my magic, which was nearly all gone, feeling a connection with them that I'd never felt with any other plant. They grew slightly longer, and in return, more energy flowed into me.

Were we creating a cycle?

Excitement flooded me.

I'd never heard of this, but maybe it was a plant witch thing?

As I gave them my magic, they gave me energy. Not just magic, but the energy to draw *more* magic. I'd been so focused on fixing the broken plants that I hadn't realized the connection I'd had to the grass. I still didn't fully understand what was happening—it was so complicated that maybe I never would. But my connection with the garden allowed me to replenish my energy and keep drawing magic.

"You look a bit better," Tabitha said. "Some color has returned to your cheeks."

"I'm feeling better." I looked at Boris. "Will you ask them to be patient a little longer? I'm almost done."

He nodded and turned to relay the message. I laid back in the grass, letting it touch as much of my body as it could. Energy flowed into me. In return, I gave the grass a bit of my magic. It created a cycle of health, and I used it to draw more magic from the garden and repair the damage that the goats had done.

I felt both calm and elated at once. All around me, the garden was repairing itself, blooming wildly, fragrant and bright. I knew I wouldn't be able to perform this level of magic outside of a garden environment, but for right now, that was perfect. I had everything I needed right here.

When it was done, I felt it—almost like the final puzzle piece was fitting into place. Slowly, my muscles aching from the work, I stood and looked at the dreamweavers and pinklings.

The dreamweavers were no longer hovering anxiously at the edge of the habitat. Instead, they'd floated inside. The pinklings snuffled happily at the kern bushes I'd planted throughout the space, and the dreamweavers began to flutter their wings, their glittery magic floating to the ground. When some fell on me, a feeling of calm washed away all my worries.

"This is incredible, dear." My gran squeezed my shoulder. "What you've done is truly amazing."

"I've got to say she's right," Tabitha said. "That was incredible, Aria. You just kept *going*."

I smiled at them. "Thanks. It felt good."

I looked at my work, thrilled to have finished before the end of the competition. Catrina was busy playing with the pinklings, giggling as they snuffled at her. Whether or not I won the competition, the new residents would be happy here, and the townspeople would enjoy visiting.

"There's only one thing left to do." I brushed my hands

off. "We need to put the hammocks back up and see if any of the cushions are salvageable."

Fortunately, most of them were. Within twenty minutes, we were done with the habitat. And it was a good thing, too, since it was only ten minutes until sunset.

"Let's go to the clearing," I said, then looked at Boris. "Will you tell the dreamweavers that we'll be gone for a little while, but we'll return? And ask if there's anything else they need?"

Boris nodded, then relayed the message. They didn't need anything else, so we went to the clearing. Serena and Terry were already there, though Callan wasn't.

I glared at Terry, and Boris growled.

"Just wait," I murmured to my familiar. "It will work itself out." And if it didn't, I'd take care of it. But I had a feeling that Mr. Sparrow knew what was going on in his garden.

Mr. Sparrow and Callan arrived at the same time, and Mr. Sparrow clapped his hands and grinned widely. "You're all here! Excellent. I'm looking forward to seeing the results of your labors." He spun in a circle, looking at all of us. "I'm sure you have some very impressive things to show me."

"I certainly do," Serena said.

"Excellent." Mr. Sparrow cleared his throat, then looked at Terry. "Although I am afraid that one contestant is disqualified for cheating."

Satisfaction surged through me. As I'd expected, Mr. Sparrow was aware of what had happened. Whether he'd learned of it in time to potentially stop the damage, I might never know. But at least Terry was out. I didn't want to look at him anymore.

Terry stepped forward. "But I—"

Mr. Sparrow flicked a hand, and a sturdy-looking leaf whipped through the air and plastered itself to Terry's mouth, cutting off his words. When Mr. Sparrow spoke, his voice was cold. "You may see yourself out. We'll take care of your glimmerfish, do not fret."

Glimmerfish. That's what Terry had chosen. He'd no doubt used the pond already on the property, then panicked when he'd seen how much work we were putting in and known he couldn't compete.

Had the goats hurt Callan's or Serena's habitats as well?

"Now, let's go see these habitats of yours!" Mr. Sparrow clapped his hands. "Guests are welcome to come along, too."

I hadn't even noticed the large group of people standing at the edge of the clearing. Serena's family, along with Mrs. Aspen. She must have come to support Callan, which was surprising, given that she was about as friendly as her dog, Lucifer. But he'd said he'd help repair her kitchen after the fire, and maybe he had. There were quite a few other towns-people as well, all excited to witness the grand finale of the (locally) famous competition. Gran, Tabitha, and Catrina went to join the other guests, and we trailed after Mr. Sparrow.

It had grown dark as he'd talked, and the fireflies came out to light our way. With a wave of his hands and a small flare of magic, Mr. Sparrow conjured floating lanterns, and their glow helped illuminate the path. The crowd was big enough that Callan wasn't able to come walk beside me, though I couldn't tell if he actually tried to.

We visited Serena's habitat first. It was a beautiful clearing surrounded by large oak trees with thick gnarled roots that poked out of the ground. Velvety grass filled the center, along with large, flat rocks. The stream that fed my part of the garden also ran through this clearing, and a trio of piskie cats sat at the bank.

I gasped at the sight of the beautiful creatures. They had the sleek black fur and brilliant green eyes that I'd heard of, as well as an extra-long tail. They were about twice the size of housecats, and magic sparked around them.

"They're friendly," Serena said. She pointed to the largest oak tree at the edge of the clearing. "Their den is in there. They'll stay in the garden for the most part, though they might roam occasionally."

Mr. Sparrow clapped, clearly delighted. I joined him, equally impressed. Worry tugged at me, though. This was an *excellent* addition to the garden and would definitely compete with mine.

"Let's head on to Callan's habitat," Mr. Sparrow said.

The large crowd followed him down the path, the lanterns floating along to guide our way.

When we reached his habitat, I gasped. It was beautiful, of course. We were right at the edge of the garden where it butted up to a small expanse of moorland. Small, twisted trees dotted the space. Even from here, I could feel how ancient they were. I hadn't seen these in the garden during my tours, and they had to have come from elsewhere. It would have been a challenge to get them here, for sure. Bluebells filled the space between the trees, creating a carpet of navy beneath the floating lanterns.

Amongst the trees sat a large wooden crate. The door was open, and I moved forward to confirm that the two moonshadow mares were still inside.

They were.

Their coats glowed a golden white, but I couldn't see much detail besides that. They were still too shy to come out.

Mr. Sparrow tutted. "It is a lovely habitat, and the moonshadow mares would make an excellent addition to the garden. *If* they come out of their crate, that is."

Callan nodded. "I understand. I misjudged the time it would take to get them used to the space. They're timid animals, and they needed longer to adjust."

He hadn't misjudged anything. He'd sacrificed to save the town.

"I'm afraid we'll have to disqualify you since we don't yet know if the moonshadow mares will like the habitat you built," Mr. Sparrow said. "But it is a beautiful space."

Damn it.

"Wait!" Catrina's voice called out through the crowd. "They're coming out!"

We watched, delighted, as the mares walked hesitantly from their crates. They were beautiful, gleaming with a pearlescent sheen under the moonlight. They walked through their new home, sniffing and chomping at the grass.

"How delightful!" Mr. Sparrow clapped. "A lovely addition to the garden, and I revoke your disqualification. Now let's move on to our final habitat—Aria's."

Worry shivered through me. This was it. As we followed

Mr. Sparrow along the path, my heart raced. Would the dreamweavers and pinklings still be there? Would the guests like them? Would Mr. Sparrow?

When we reached my habitat, the sight of it took my breath away. I hadn't had a chance to really look at it closely after repairing it. I'd been too exhausted as we'd focused on frantically getting the hammocks up and the cushions out.

It was gorgeous. The plants were in perfect health, with full, heavy blossoms in all colors of the rainbow. The dreamweavers fluttered through the trees above the pinklings, scattering their magical dust over everything.

"Well, my goodness." Mr. Sparrow blew out a breath. "Dreamweavers. I never thought I'd see them here. And pinklings!" The delight in his voice was clear.

I stepped forward. "In the spirit of full transparency, I was only trying to get the dreamweavers. But this colony insisted on traveling with the pinklings."

"How lucky for us." Mr. Sparrow approached one of the tiny pink pigs and held out his hand. The little creature snuffled at him, then tipped his head down for a pet. When Mr. Sparrow rose, he turned to us all. "It is clear that the winner is Aria. Not only is her habitat the most impressive, but she had to overcome incredible odds once Terry sabotaged her." He held up his hands in apology. "I would have stopped him had I noticed him doing it, but I did not realize until I saw him returning with the shovel. It was then that I learned, and by then, it was too late."

"But Aria fixed it!" Catrina crowed.

Tabitha shushed her.

"Indeed, she did." A wide smile spread across Mr. Sparrow's face. "Well done, Aria. I can think of no better person to take care of the garden when I retire."

The crowd clapped, and I was glad to see that even Serena was applauding. I didn't like her, but it would be nice if it were a little easier to be around her. We'd be living near each other, after all. And she was also a customer of the Garden of Enchantment, which was about to be my business.

Callan caught my eye from his spot across the crowd, a wide grin on his face as he mouthed, *Well done.*

I smiled back at him, excited to talk to him when this was all over. With the competition out of the way, we could talk about the future. Would there be one? The idea was enough to terrify and exhilarate me all at the same time.

"Aria, dear?" Mr. Sparrow's voice caught my attention, and I turned to face him.

"Yes?"

He approached and gripped my shoulders. "You really did exceptionally well. Congratulations."

"Thank you."

"Will you come tomorrow so that I can give you the keys?"

Elation filled me. "Really? But you'll stay on longer, right? I can't imagine this place without you."

"Of course." He winked conspiratorially at me. "I had a feeling you'd be the one to win this."

"Well, that makes one of us." A joyous laugh escaped me. *I'd won.*

CHAPTER
THIRTY

ARIA

THAT NIGHT, the town threw me a massive party at The Sea Shanty. Callan was nowhere to be found, though. He'd been missing after I'd said goodbye to Mr. Sparrow, and I hadn't seen him since.

When I'd stopped at my house to change my clothes for the party, all of his things were gone.

He'd left.

It was just as I'd feared. Now that the competition was over, he had returned to his jet-setting life of travel and supermodels. Deep down, I'd known it could never work out between us, but I'd thought he would at least say goodbye. The depth of my sadness made one thing clear, though.

I care about him.

I cared about him *a lot*. Tears pricked my eyes, and I

dashed them away. The Sea Shanty was not the place to be crying.

"Are you all right?" Tabitha asked, a frown in her voice.

I looked up. She held two beers in her hands, just like on the first night we'd come here when I'd arrived in town. I smiled broadly, trying to look fine.

"Okay, now you look mad." She examined me up and down. "What's wrong? You just won. You should be happy."

"I am." The entire town had already congratulated me, and that had been great. "I absolutely am. It's just..."

"It's the fact that Callan is nowhere to be seen."

"Right." He'd just *left*.

"Maybe he had to go do something," she said.

"Then why didn't he tell me?"

"I don't know. He's an internationally famous billionaire. They're weird."

"He's not a billionaire," I mumbled.

"Semantics. I'm sure he's got a reason."

Maybe he did. But it was hard to imagine what it might be.

"Come on, drink up," Tabitha said. "Tomorrow, we'll fix that. Tonight, you'll celebrate. You only get to save the town once, you know." She tapped her lip, her expression thoughtful. "Twice, actually. It was your idea to dose the goats with the potion. *And* you won the garden and saved your shop, which in turn saves the town."

"I'd say that's an exaggeration."

"It isn't. Now drink."

I did as she said, taking several large sips of the delicious ale she'd brought me. The party was outside on the ocean-front lawn, and the band played on the little wooden stage to the side. People danced and cheered, and a horde of sleepy goats were curled up on the grass about forty feet away. Someone had built a pen around them, thank goodness.

Gran approached, a martini in hand as she smiled at me. "You did it, my dear. I knew you could."

"Thanks, Gran." I hugged her. "I couldn't have done it without you."

"Sure, you could."

"I disagree, but we'll never know, will we?"

"Well, it doesn't matter. We're family, which means we're a package deal." She gestured to me, Tabitha, Catrina, and herself. "When the garden gets you, it gets us, too."

"Hear, hear!" Tabitha raised her glass. "To family and teamwork. You'd better believe we'll be there to help you when you take control."

"I'm going to be the piskie cat wrangler," Catrina declared.

I laughed. "I'm not sure if cats can be wrangled, but if anyone can do it, you can."

"Exactly." She grinned widely. "I think we should dance."

"Me, too." I downed the last of my beer, then grabbed her hand and ran out to join the crowd dancing in front of the band. Tabitha and my gran followed. As we danced underneath the stars, I was pretty sure that I was in heaven. Almost.

The next morning, I awoke with a much more manageable hangover than last time. The party had lasted until the wee hours of the morning, and it had been one of the best nights of my life.

Except that Callan hadn't been there. And I still hadn't heard from him.

It doesn't matter.

That was a damned lie, but I kept saying it as I dragged myself from the bed and took a shower. When I arrived in the kitchen, still dressed in my robe, I found Boris trying to make pancakes.

It was a disaster.

There was batter everywhere, and I was pretty sure I smelled singed fur.

"You have got to be kidding me," I groaned.

He turned from his spot standing on the counter next to the stove, then grinned at me. *The spatula is harder to hold than I expected it to be.*

I looked at the batter splattered all around him. "I'm shocked."

He glared. *You'll be nice if you want a pancake.*

"Are there any that are cooked?"

Not yet, but there will be.

"I don't have the energy for this." I left him to it and started the coffee, hoping that I could use my new magic to quickly clean up his mess when he finished.

Once the coffee finished brewing, I poured myself a cup.

Your breakfast is served.

I turned to see Boris carefully balancing a single pancake on a spatula that he held with both paws. It hit the floor before it made it to the plate at his feet, and his face fell.

"Five second rule." I swooped down and grabbed the

pancake. The five second rule was absolute nonsense, but Boris looked so upset that I couldn't bear it. I bit into the pancake and smiled. "It's good."

It was terrible. Badgers weren't good at measuring, if I had to guess. But it was edible, so I ate it. "Thank you. That was delicious."

He smiled. *Good.*

"And thank you again for your help with the garden. I couldn't have done it without you."

Bacon sandwiches for life?

"Within reason." If I promised him as many as he wanted, I'd never leave the stove, and he wouldn't be able to move within a month.

Excellent. He rubbed his paws together. *When do we go to the garden?*

"I'll dress, and we can go." I was excited to walk into it as the future owner.

When we left the house, I found a massive bouquet of wildflowers on my front doorstep. Beneath them sat a box. I smiled as I picked them up. "What in the world?"

Oooh, nice. Who are those from?

"Let me find the card." But I couldn't find the usual little card that came with bouquets. "There's nothing."

Open the box. Maybe that will tell you.

I did as Boris instructed, finding a beautiful pair of secateurs. They would be perfect for trimming plants, and they were engraved with *Plant Whisperer*.

I stared down at them. They were from Callan. He was the only one to ever call me the Plant Whisperer.

Well? Who are they from.

"Callan."

Why did he leave them at the door?

"Because he's gone. He must have had them delivered." But it was such a thoughtful gift that I was convinced it was a parting present. This had to be what he did with the super-models, too. Should I count myself lucky that I merited such a nice goodbye gift?

No. Definitely not.

I tossed the secateurs back in the box and set everything on the table by the door. "Come on, we're leaving."

Boris followed, silent as we walked. I didn't want to talk about it, so I was grateful.

Ten minutes later, I walked into the garden as the new owner. And it felt good. The gate was already unlocked, and I found Mr. Sparrow in the little building that acted as his office.

"Tea?" he asked when I entered.

"Yes, please." I took a seat in one of the chairs.

As we drank our tea, Mr. Sparrow taught me all about the garden. The next day, there were more lessons. And more lessons the day after that. There was a lot to know to run a garden this size, and I wanted to do the best that I could.

Every night, I wondered about Callan, though. Why had he left like that? I hadn't expected him to stay forever, but such an abrupt departure was inexplicable. Thinking about him hurt like hell and didn't seem to be getting any better, either.

It wasn't until the seventh night that I found him waiting for me at the garden exit. It was dark out since I'd stayed late to visit his mares, but there was enough moonlight to see him clearly.

"Callan." I stopped dead in my tracks, my gaze eating him up. He was as ridiculously handsome and fit as ever, with his shoulders filling out his jumper in a most magnificent fashion and his hair blown back by the wind.

"Aria." His blue gaze met mine, solemn and calm.

"Where have you been?" Anger bubbled inside me. "You just left!"

"I left the note."

"There was no note."

He frowned. "It should have been with the flowers. It said I would be back when I had finished something important."

"And you couldn't tell me in person?"

"It was *really* important. Trust me, you'll agree."

My heartbeat thundered. "What do you mean?"

"Will you come with me?"

I wanted to. Fates knew I wanted to. But what if he hurt me again?

I'd risk it.

"Sure." My heart thundered as I followed him to his car. We climbed in, and his scent washed over me, evergreen and spice. "Where are we going?"

"You'll see."

He drove in silence through the town, and I couldn't bring myself to break it. I didn't know what to say. It was almost intoxicating to be this close to him, however, and I had no idea what was about to happen. I was glad to have the explanation, though I hated how long he'd been away.

When Callan turned onto a familiar road, I stiffened. "Where are we going?"

"I think you know."

"My grandad's tower." I'd made a point not to visit since returning home because it would be too painful. And once I'd started to like Callan, I'd known that it would just make me angry with him, and I hadn't wanted that. Especially given the role I'd played back then.

When the headlights cut across the tower in front of us, I gasped. The café was gone. The entire building and all the tables and pavilion—*gone*.

"How?" I whispered.

He shrugged. "Like anything. It just took time."

It had taken more than time. It had taken magic and money to get rid of the café as if it had never existed. I held my breath as he pulled the car to a stop near the tower.

"I spoke to someone who knows about this kind of spirit visitation," he said. "They visited once I'd removed everything and said that your grandad's spirit will return if the place is quiet for long enough. I wasn't sure if it would work, so I needed it to be a surprise in case I failed."

"He can come back?" I asked, hope filling me.

"Yes, as long as it's returned to its previous state."

"It has been." I stared through the windscreen, shocked by how familiar it still was.

"Not entirely." He opened his car door. "Come and see."

I climbed out of the car, my legs trembling. As I followed him to the castle, I realized that the grass was still missing from where the café had been. He gestured to it. "I could have had it fixed before I brought you here, but I thought you might want to have a hand in returning this place to its former glory."

My gaze flicked to him, surprised joy flashing though me. "You were right."

He smiled. I couldn't bear it. I ran and leapt into his arms, pressing a kiss to his lips. "Thank you, Callan."

He held me to him, smiling down at me. "I should have done it as soon as I got back to town."

"We were a little busy."

"True. And it gave me a grand gesture to make once I screwed up."

I kissed him again. "It's the grandest, most wonderful gesture."

"I love you, Aria. I've never said it to anyone before. You don't have to say it back, but I had to say it to you. I love you. And I want to be with you always."

Happy tears tightened in my throat. "I love you, too. How could I not?"

He swung me around, kissing me as fireflies danced overhead.

"Does this mean you're staying?" I asked.

"It does. I can work from anywhere."

I laughed and kissed him again. When he finally set me down and looked towards the patch of dirt that still needed grass, I smiled.

"I think I have some work to do." I stepped away from him and knelt on the ground, pressing my hand to the dirt.

It was easy to bring the grass back—an effortless joy that made me feel more connected to the tower than I ever had. And with time, my grandad's spirit would return.

I could feel it in my gut.

When I was done, I stood and went to Callan. He wrapped an arm around my waist and looked towards the tower. "Will you show me the best bits again?"

"I'd be delighted to."

Together, we walked off towards the future.

THANK YOU FOR READING!

I hope you enjoyed reading this book as much as I enjoyed writing it. Reviews are *so* helpful to authors. I really appreciate all reviews, both positive and negative. If you want to leave one, you can do so at Amazon or GoodReads.

ACKNOWLEDGMENTS

Thank you, Ben, for everything. There would be no books without you.

Thank you to Jena O'Connor and Ash Fitzsimmons for your excellent editing. Thank you to Susie for your eagle eye with errors. The book is immensely better because of you!

ABOUT LINSEY

Before becoming a writer, Linsey Hall was a nautical archaeologist who studied shipwrecks from Hawaii and the Yukon to the UK and the Mediterranean. She credits fantasy and historical romances with her love of history and her career as an archaeologist. After a decade of tromping around the globe in search of old bits of stuff that people left lying about, she settled down and started penning her own romance novels. Her Dragon's Gift series draws upon her love of history and the paranormal elements that she can't help but include.

COPYRIGHT

www.LinseyHall.com
https://www.facebook.com/LinseyHallAuthor

Milton Keynes UK
Ingram Content Group UK Ltd.
UKHW010705260923
429409UK00004B/308